"This isn't what you wanted, is it?" Jin-mei asked Yang beneath her breath.

"There is no one else I would rather be wedded to," he replied without hesitation.

Jin-mei whipped around to face him, causing the pearls in her ears to swing dramatically. "You're trying to be clever with your words. You could very well mean that you have no desire to be married at all, to anyone."

It was hard not to smile. "I think you and I will suit each other quite well, Jin-mei."

Jin-mei. The sound of her name slid smoothly over his tongue, as if he'd been calling her that for years. Such a pretty name, like the clear chime of bells.

"It's a compliment," he added, seeing her perplexed expression.

It was the best arrangement Yang had ever made. He had the magistrate's protection, his silence and his daughter... Surely it couldn't be this easy?

Author Note

When I first imagined the world of *The Sword Dancer*, I envisioned a wild land filled with heroes and bandits with the lines between them completely blurred.

For those who have read *The Sword Dancer*, I hope you enjoy seeing what happens to Li Feng and Thief-catcher Han. Like all great romances, the rooftop marriage proposal was a beginning rather than an end, and their adventure continues here.

For history buffs: the places and people in this book are part real and part imagined. Fujian province was the seat of several rebellions. Rogue warlords were a plague upon imperial power in the late part of the dynasty. And when you read about the rebel figures that emerged throughout Chinese history, many of them made their wealth through the salt trade.

The Linyin Stone Forest is an actual place. The pictures of it are dramatic and awe-inspiring. According to travel sites, it wasn't explored until centuries later during the Qing Dynasty due to the dense growth that obscured it from view.

Perhaps I'll be able to visit one day, and imagine the colorful bandits who made those hidden caverns their hideout.

Jeannie Lin can be found online via Twitter, Facebook or her website. To be notified when her next book comes out, sign up at jeannielin.com.

Jeannie Lin

A Dance with Danger

Recycling programs
for this product may
not exist in your area.

ISBN-13: 978-0-373-29834-1

A Dance with Danger

Copyright © 2015 by Jeannie Lin

Printed in U.S.A.

www.Harlequin.com

USA TODAY bestselling author **Jeannie Lin** started writing her first book while working as a high school science teacher in south central Los Angeles. Her stories are inspired by a mix of historical research and wuxia adventure tales. Jeannie's groundbreaking historical romances set in Tang Dynasty China have received multiple awards, including a Golden Heart Award for her debut novel, *Butterfly Swords*.

Books by Jeannie Lin

Harlequin Historical

Rebels and Lovers

The Sword Dancer
A Dance with Danger

Linked by Character

Butterfly Swords
The Dragon and the Pearl

Stand-Alone Book

My Fair Concubine

Harlequin Historical *Undone!* ebooks

The Taming of Mei Lin
The Lady's Scandalous Night
Capturing the Silken Thief
An Illicit Temptation

HQN Books

The Lotus Palace
The Jade Temptress

Visit the Author Profile page at Harlequin.com.

Thank you to my husband for putting up with the papers that litter our living room and the all-nighters I had to pull to finish this book. I blame the twins for the mess, but hubby knows it's all me.

Chapter One

Tang Dynasty China—AD 848

'*The mountains are high and the Emperor is far away.*'

Bao Yang had always been fond of that particular proverb. It certainly held true in Fujian province where rugged mountains enclosed them to the north, west and south. To the east was the ocean fed by a lattice of streams and rivers. This was a land set apart from the heart of the empire, away from the eyes and ears of imperial authority. This was a land where a person with determination and a little cleverness could carve his own destiny, regardless of his birth.

Even a man with a price on his head.

Yang should have been afraid to return to the city where not long ago he'd tried to have a powerful warlord assassinated, but he had connections. He knew who would turn a blind eye and who could be bribed.

It wasn't that there was no law in Fujian. Imperially appointed bureaucrats still oversaw the administration of the cities, but it was the merchants who dominated the rivers and ports. The surrounding mountains were inhabited by bandits and smugglers. Wealth and commerce were the forces that truly ruled this province.

He was approaching the city of Minzhou now by river, where there was very likely a warrant out for his arrest for attempted murder. Or at least for someone who looked like him. To his knowledge, his name was still unknown—for now, although he didn't know for how much longer. His connections had bought him some valuable time.

The fisherman at the crossing was willing to take him down the river for a few copper coins. Yang hid beneath the wide brim of his hat as the tiny boat drifted into the city, joining the fleet of merchant vessels and ferries that fed the bustling markets.

As the fishing boat crossed beneath one of the main bridges, Yang kept his gaze directed forward. There was a guardsman in the lookout tower, but his bow remained slack in his hands as he scanned the water. The arrows rested soundly in their quiver.

'The city guards have been wary of strangers lately,' the fisherman said as he dragged a long pole along the river bottom, propelling them forward. 'It's best that you find your friend quickly and seek shelter before curfew so you aren't hassled by the night watch.'

'Is the city unsafe?'

'There was some unrest a while back. Bandits, I hear.'

'Thank you, Uncle.'

Three months had passed since he'd broken out of Minzhou's prison house along with his co-conspirators. It was dangerous to return now, but not as much as one might think. Any thief-catchers searching for him would expect him to be in hiding. It was the regions to the north where there was price on his head. The regions that General Wang Shizhen had taken over with his army.

The fisherman steered clear of the busier docks to set Yang ashore at the edge of the market. From there, he moved quickly to a more secluded part of the city, slipping into a public park. A small stream ran through it, branching off from the main river. The walkways appeared empty and the broad canopy of the banyan trees provided cover.

Moving quickly, Yang set about tracking down his associate. He'd built up a wide network of associates over the years of which this particular official was the most powerful. If there was ever a time Yang needed to rely on calling in favours, it was now. He'd been working in the shadows before, seeding disruption and rebellion, but now this was war.

Yang needed the city magistrate's allegiance which was going to require some craftiness on his part. Magistrate Tan was, after all, the same man who was responsible for throwing him into prison in the first place.

Jin-mei dabbed at her forehead with a handkerchief and adjusted the angle of her parasol to block the sun. As they neared the height of summer, there were fewer people enjoying the park in the midday heat, but her daily stroll along the river was one of the few opportunities she had to escape the house.

She had set out with her amah, but the old nursemaid only made it ten steps into the park before she sank down on to one of the benches in a viewing pavilion.

'Don't go too far!' Amah warned, waving her on.

The woman had been considered elderly when Jin-mei was only a child. Now that Jin-mei was nineteen, Amah was ancient and could be forgiven for not wanting to exert herself. The dear old servant had also become less strict with age.

Jin-mei was wearing the lightest robe she owned, a finely woven silk in a peach-blossom pattern, but still the late summer heat was getting to her. She wiped at her face again, this time using the edge of her sleeve. When she lowered her arm, she could see a man crossing the bridge over to her side of the river. Given the man was a stranger and she was alone, Jin-mei slowed her step so they would have no reason to encounter one another.

Unfortunately, he'd seen her as well. He halted at the centre of the bridge before striding towards her with purpose. She should have ducked beneath the shadow of her parasol to avoid his gaze, but she found herself caught in it. Now that he was close enough, she understood why.

Her heart pounded. She knew him.

Most of her father's visitors were grey-haired and uninteresting, but the young Bao Yang had seemed so dashing and full of mystery. He had a gleam in his eye and a half-smile that had always made her stomach flutter. That had been four years ago.

She'd only seen him from behind a screen while listening in on conversations she wasn't supposed to be hearing. There was the one time when she'd attempted to stumble 'accidentally' into the hallway. She had fallen in hopes that Mister Bao might catch her and, well, become immediately smitten with her. Instead, her father had sternly told her to go to her room while the handsome young gentleman had watched her pick herself off the floor.

How odd to see him after all these years! She remembered that arch in the shape of his left eyebrow which gave him an inquisitive look. His nose was slightly off centre and she'd always wondered if it had been broken or was it naturally so. All of these little flaws, yet when put together, they created a face that was inexplicably intriguing. She had been convinced he was the handsomest man she'd ever seen.

Jin-mei wasn't nearly as foolish now, but seeing Yang again brought back a little ache in her chest. That gleam in his eye was still there, even though they were supposed to be only strangers in passing.

'What are you doing here?' she asked when they were finally close enough to engage in conversation.

He gave her a startled look at being addressed so directly. Only then did she realise how impetuous she had sounded. 'I apologise. It's just that I—'

Yang laughed and the easy sound of it banished her moment of discomfort. 'It is I who should apologise. I must have startled you. I am here to seek the magistrate.'

He didn't recognise her. Some demon inside of her awoke at the opportunity. Here was a chance for her to make an impression on him. A more favourable one than she had at fifteen, picking herself off the floor in a tangle of silk.

'I know where the magistrate can be found,' she said.

'Then I am fortunate fate has brought us together.'

'Are you flirting with me?' she asked incredulously. She realised only after the words had left her mouth that such directness would be considered rude. 'Sir,' she added after a pause.

His smile didn't waver. 'Miss,' he began, a counterpoint to her delayed honorific, 'are you always so outspoken?'

'It's just that I know you. Well, I don't know you,' she amended, 'but I feel as if I do.'

'I feel as if I know you as well,' he replied smoothly. He glanced at something over his shoulder, before returning his attention to her. 'Will you accompany me?'

He flashed her a crooked smile and then they were

walking side by side along the river, shielded by the shade of her parasol.

Bao Yang *was* flirting. No man had ever treated her with such charm. Her mother had been slender and tall and long-limbed, as graceful as a willow in the breeze. Unfortunately, Jin-mei took after her father's side. Father was short with rounded features, moon-faced and on the plump side.

She was no great beauty to take hold of men's hearts upon a glance. Jin-mei hadn't expected any man to ever flirt with her. In her dreams, she had always impressed potential suitors with intelligent conversation and astute sensibilities.

'What is a proper young miss doing walking alone in this park?' he asked. 'There might be questionable men about with evil intentions.'

'What men are these? I see no one but yourself.' She attempted a coy look, glancing at him from the corner of her eye. An uncomfortable silence descended as Bao Yang regarded her thoughtfully. She was no good at this at all. Her original plan would have to suffice. 'Minzhou is probably the safest city in the province. There are guards on every street, patrolling day and night.'

'Every street,' he echoed contemplatively.

They had almost reached the final bridge that marked the boundary of the park. Once they crossed over it, they would be in the main market area. Jin-mei tried to think of some way to prolong their time together.

'How was your journey?' she asked. 'You seem to have come from far away.'

'Not far at all.' Yang glanced once more behind him and then to other side of the river. 'I live in a small village, only two days from here.'

'Small village?' she asked with a raised eyebrow.

He nodded. 'Héjin Crossing, near the foothills.'

She absolutely knew that for a lie. Bao Yang lived far to the north-west in Taining County, the same place her family had lived before Father was transferred to Minzhou prefecture. She started to question him about it, but his step had quickened. He continued along the water towards the base of the bridge rather than over it.

'How curious,' he remarked under his breath. 'Is that a dragon carved into the stone?'

'Where?' She drew closer, but saw nothing of the sort in the foundation.

He turned to her and took her wrist gently. The gesture sent her pulse racing.

'Let us get out of the sun where we can speak more privately,' he suggested, setting his hand lightly against the small of her back.

As courtship went, his ploy wasn't particularly clever, but Bao Yang's touch was subtly insistent without being demanding. There was a quiet urgency in his voice that both puzzled and intrigued her. In her confusion, they were already to the bridge before she found her voice.

'I am not that sort of woman.'

'I don't think you're that sort of woman.' He was serious now, no longer flirting. Bao Yang removed his hold on her to step into the shadows. 'But there are city guards nearby. If you cry out now, I'm dead. You hold my life in your hands.'

How had he compelled her down there? It was nothing more than a few looks, some polite conversation, a series of light and gentle touches that just breached the boundaries of etiquette, but went no further.

Yang was standing apart from her now, well out of arm's length. She could flee and he wouldn't be able to catch her. For a moment, she did consider fleeing. This man before her was someone who was hiding secrets. Someone very different from the gentleman she thought she'd known all those years ago.

Yet he met her eyes with a look that pierced her, pleading with her silently, as if she were the one with all the power. Jin-mei didn't know why, but she found herself stepping after him beneath the bridge.

'Thank you,' he said quietly.

Once again, his hands barely closed around her shoulders. Her heart pounded, and she held her breath, waiting. It was as if she were moving of her own will and his touch no more than a suggestion.

Lowering her parasol, she looked up at him. 'Why are you hiding?'

He lifted a hand to quiet her, head tilted to listen for sounds from above. She had never been so close to a man who wasn't family. The front of his robe brushed against hers. Even with the dim light beneath the bridge, she could make out the hard line of his jaw. The air was cooler in the shade of the bridge and the two of them were closed off as if cocooned in their own private sanctuary.

'I shouldn't do this,' he began, sending her pulse racing with just the mere suggestion of the forbidden, 'but I must ask a favour of you.'

'Yes.'

She'd spoken too quickly. Yang smiled at her, his eyebrow lifting in wonder. 'You're quite fearless, aren't you?'

Jin-mei could hardly breathe with him so close, looking at her as though—looking at her in a way no one ever had.

'I'm not.' Not usually. There was something about his manner that made her reckless. She ran her tongue over her lips nervously. 'I wasn't entirely truthful before. I do know exactly who you are.'

His charming expression faltered. 'I'd certainly remember if we'd met.'

'It was years ago, Mister Bao.'

He appeared startled at her use of his name, but before he could reply a loud voice boomed in from the world outside.

'What are you two doing?'

Jin-mei jumped, but Yang steadied her with his hands over her shoulders. Though she was breathing hard, he appeared speculative. He kept his gaze on her, meeting her eyes while he addressed the guardsman behind him. 'My lady companion was feeling faint in the heat.'

'Get out from there immediately.'

The silence was cut by the sound of a sword being drawn and then another and then another.

What was happening? She didn't know when the trembling started, but now it wouldn't stop. In a panic, she grabbed on to his arm. An unreadable look flickered across Yang's face. Calmly, he let go of her and stepped out from beneath the bridge. She ducked out just behind him to see them surrounded by what looked like the entire city garrison. A familiar figure in a dark green robe stood among them, his jaw clenched in fury. Her stomach plummeted and her palms started to sweat.

'Magistrate Tan,' Yang greeted, surprisingly composed among so many armed men.

Jin-mei bowed her head, her cheeks burning. 'Father.'

At that, Yang turned slowly around to look at her, a deep frown creasing his brow. Having men draw swords on him didn't shake him, but apparently what she had said struck him speechless.

Chapter Two

An hour later, Yang was relocated to a private room at a local drinking house while the armed guards were sent away, tasked with returning the magistrate's daughter home. For the moment he was left alone and he tried to use the opportunity to prepare some sort of explanation for being caught in a compromising position with Tan Li Kuo's daughter.

Jin-mei, Tan had called her. The name was fitting. Clear like the ring of a morning bell. Audacious and impulsive Jin-mei, with her elegant phoenix eyes and her delightfully inelegant way of saying whatever was on her mind. Was it any wonder Yang had been thoroughly charmed?

She wasn't innocent as much as she was without guile. Even the flush in her cheeks and the colour of her lips had been real, not painted on with rouge or gloss. Fresh-faced and quick-tongued. For someone accustomed to trickery, Jin-mei's openness had bemused and bewitched him.

Maybe he had forgotten himself just a little in the park. He had a weakness for fascinating characters. Not just lovely, adventurous women, but for people in general. He'd been accused at one time of collecting people. Of keeping them handy for whenever they suited his purposes.

Yang straightened as Magistrate Tan entered the room. The other man closed the door behind him before seating himself across the table.

'I didn't know the young lady was your daughter.'

The steely-eyed look Tan shot him told Yang their long-time association was hanging by a thread. He wondered how many of the five punishments the magistrate considered exacting upon him at that moment.

Instead of slicing into him, Tan opted to pour the wine, though with a grave silence that was far from friendly. Tan Li Kuo was short in stature, with a sagging middle and a round moon-faced appearance that gave the impression of youth and ineptitude. As far as Yang could tell, Tan usually played down to that image.

Tan wasn't playing any games at the present time. Yang swallowed and ran his hands over his knees as he searched for a way to salvage the situation. 'About what happened—'

Ignoring him, Tan reached for his wine. Taken aback, Yang raised his cup as well and drank. At least they were trying to remain civil. The civility lasted only for a heartbeat.

'What exactly were you doing with my daughter?' Tan demanded sharply.

'I was actually on my way to see you.'

The magistrate raised his eyebrows at that.

'But there were guards about and I needed to remain hidden.'

'So you lured Jin-mei into a dark and secluded area?'

Yang winced. 'It was just the madness of the moment. Nothing happened, I assure you.'

Tan's expression darkened at his feeble explanation.

The truth was simple. Yang was a fugitive and Jin-mei had seen him. Coaxing her into hiding was preferable to either dragging her forcibly beneath the bridge so she couldn't alert the guards, or fleeing for his life through the city. He doubted he would be able to convince the magistrate of that logic.

'In any case, you shouldn't be here.' Tan kept his tone even. 'I've kept your identity hidden, as promised. You should have disappeared into the mountains by now.'

Like a common bandit. Despite their alliance, the magistrate had never thought well of him. Tan was still an administrator at heart while Yang, for all his wealth and status, was an outlaw. More so now that he'd tried to murder a man with his own hands.

'Wang Shizhen saw my face,' he explained. 'It won't be long before he comes after me.'

'You wanted him to see you,' Tan replied calmly.

They had collaborated to assassinate the fearsome general at a private gathering. Though Magistrate Tan was a man of the law, he knew the best way to get rid of a tyrant was a quick sword through the weeds.

'He was right in front of me. I had to do something.'

Tan stabbed a finger towards him in accusation. 'You acted on emotion. That banquet was the only chance we'd had to do this cleanly and now that chance is gone.'

Yang took another drink, feeling the burn of it down his throat. General Wang Shizhen had wrested control of the northern part of the province where he ruled through intimidation. He and Tan had been plotting for a long time how to stop the warlord, but Yang hadn't told the magistrate the real reason he wanted General Wang dead. A reason that went much deeper than personal gain or political rivalry.

That bastard had owed him blood. It wasn't a moment's impulse that had Yang sinking the knife into the general. It was a matter of family honour and a promise he'd made to himself as well as a cold and wandering spirit long ago.

'Was it worth it?' Tan asked quietly.

Yang regarded his accomplice. The magistrate was older and in many ways shrewder. He kept his secrets close and rarely revealed his intentions. Tan also preferred to remain safe in the shadows.

'I wanted to look him in the eye,' Yang confessed. 'I wanted Wang Shizhen to know he was going to die and why.'

He had succeeded in sinking his knife into the warlord's chest, but the satisfaction was only momentary. General Wang had survived the attack and would exact vengeance.

'A mistake, my friend,' Tan said with a sigh. 'After months of careful planning.'

'We'll create another opportunity. Wang Shizhen has other enemies. We'll find them.'

Magistrate Tan regarded him wordlessly, taking full measure of him with a keen eye. As the silence continued, an uneasy feeling gathered along Yang's spine. The magistrate had already made things clear—this show of emotion was a weakness. Yang forced his hands to unclench.

'I came back because I need your help. Wang has issued orders for my capture, but he won't stop at that.'

'I don't see what I can do for you.'

Yang swallowed his pride. 'I need your protection. Not for myself, but for my family.'

What family he had left. The war had begun. There was a time when General Wang had thought Yang was completely under his thumb, but now the truth was out.

'We knew what the consequences were if we failed,' Tan replied. 'Your best option now is to flee. Get as far away from the general's stronghold as possible.'

The magistrate was very careful with words. It didn't escape Yang's notice that Tan hadn't yet answered his request. Tan Li Kuo had co-ordinated the attack through coded messages from hidden meeting places. No one aside from Yang knew of his involvement.

'Are we no longer friends then?' he asked warily.

The question itself was a falsehood. They'd never been friends. Tan was the most powerful ally he had, but he could also be a formidable enemy.

Tan held his gaze for a long time. Too many people mistook the lack of sharpness in his rounded features as a sign of dullness, but they couldn't be more wrong. The magistrate used those assumptions to his advantage, often taking on a cheerful, careless manner, yet he made no effort to portray such an image now. A deep line formed between his eyes.

'I am very disappointed,' he remarked finally.

'As am I. It was the difference of a finger's length. Life and death.' Yang downed the rest of the wine and set his cup on to the table in agitation.

Tan hadn't touched his drink the entire time. 'Not about Wang Shizhen. You speak passionately of your family, Mister Bao. Yet what of my family? There's still the question of my daughter.'

'Your daughter?'

The moment after the question left his lips, Yang regretted it. Apparently that matter wasn't closed. 'I sincerely apologise for any impolite behaviour on my part.'

'Impolite is a rather mild way of putting it.' The magistrate's frown deepened. 'There were too many eyes at the park today to keep the incident quiet.'

Yang cursed himself for being so blind. He had misread the official's growing displeasure as apprehension over the failed assassination plot. But Tan Li Kuo was a father who had just found his daughter in a scandalous position. Family honour would always come first.

'She is my only daughter. To have her shamed so publicly is unacceptable. There is only one acceptable resolution. A gentleman such as yourself must see it as well.'

Tan couldn't possibly be suggesting…

'But there's a price on my head,' Yang protested.

'To the north,' the magistrate replied coolly. 'Wang Shizhen holds no authority here.'

Yang hadn't realised how dangerous his situation was until that moment. He needed Tan's protection to keep his family safe, but worse than that, he himself was completely at Tan's mercy.

He had publicly insulted the magistrate's daughter and there was only one way for Tan to save face. All in all, it wasn't the worst of solutions. It would tie the two of them closer together, and Yang needed a powerful ally. And having the lovely Jin-mei as his wife was hardly punishment. Maybe fortune was still smiling on him.

'If the magistrate would allow this unworthy servant to make amends…' Yang took a deep breath, letting the turn of events sink in '…may I ask permission to marry your daughter?'

Jin-mei stabbed the needle into the handkerchief and set it aside. 'Must we spend all day embroidering?' She pressed her hands to her lower back and attempted to stretch. 'We've been here for hours. My back hurts. My eyes hurt. Even my fingertips hurt.'

Lady Yi, her father's wife, let out a pleasant little laugh while her needle continued to fly in and out of the silk. They were in Lady's Yi's sitting room. Though they had started at the same time, a hummingbird with green-tipped wings had emerged on her stepmother's handkerchief along with a vibrant red peony for the little creature to hover over. Jin-mei had only completed one crane in what was supposed to be a pair soaring through the clouds.

'We can't stop now. The wedding is only three days away,' Lady Yi chided gently.

'Yes, the wedding.' Why did her chest draw tight whenever anyone mentioned the wedding? Her pulse quickened with what could be either excitement or fear. She was pretty certain it was fear. Jin-mei took a breath to try to calm herself.

The day after their meeting in the park, Bao Yang had brought gifts and sat with her and Father for tea. After that an astrologer was immediately consulted to choose an auspicious date for their union. Between the stars and the moon and their birth dates, a good date just *happened* to be occurring only a week later. How convenient.

She picked up her embroidery and continued working on the wings of her crane. Though she wasn't as clever and quick as Lady Yi with the needle, she was competent. She was also meticulous. She hated nothing more than making mistakes and having to pick out the stitches.

The handkerchief was a square of blue silk decorated with a pair of cranes to symbolise love and union. It was meant to be added to the dowry that would be sent to Bao Yang to show off her skill with the needle and thus desirability as a wife.

'All of this rush is completely unnecessary,' Jin-mei complained. 'We were only alone for a moment. It wasn't as if he had any time to debauch me.'

'Jin-mei!' her stepmother scolded lightly.

'It's true.'

Though he'd stood so close, almost holding her in his arms. She'd thought of those moments a hundred times over the past days, seeing Bao Yang's crooked smile and how the light from above had cast his face in dark shadows. If they hadn't been interrupted, he might have kissed her.

That last part was her own imagination. She had a more vivid imagination for events than she did embroidery designs. Yang seemed to be the sort of man who would know how to kiss. Her heart was beating faster again. This time she was pretty certain it was excitement.

'Father never seemed so rigid about etiquette in the past,' Jin-mei pointed out, starting on the second of the cranes.

'You're his daughter. His treasure.'

Her heart warmed a bit. She was her father's daughter and always had been. Mother had been his first wife, but she took sick and passed away when Jin-mei was still young. For years after that, it had been only the two of them while Father was working for the census bureau and making a name for himself. Lady Yi had given birth to two sons much later, but Jin-mei remained his only daughter.

'You remind him of your mother,' Lady Yi said gently. 'The love of his life.'

Jin-mei looked down, embarrassed. 'Don't talk like that, Lady Yi.'

'It's true. He's never forgotten her. I don't mind,' she assured with a little smile 'Your father is a good husband. I couldn't wish for a better one.'

Her stepmother was so good-natured. Jin-mei had always believed he'd chosen Lady Yi to bring balance to their household. Jin-mei had inherited her father's intense and driven nature, but where could ambition possibly lead in a woman?

Apparently to the pursuit of a husband. Jin-mei had been intent on wooing Yang with her intelligence, hadn't she? She had dreamed of him since the first time she'd seen him in their parlour when she was fourteen and hopeless to let him know she existed. Years later, nothing had gone according to plan, but he had indeed finally noticed her and they were now betrothed. Yet she couldn't be rid of this sick feeling in her stomach.

'Lady Yi, I don't know how to explain this, but I'm worried.'

Her eyebrows lifted. 'Worried?'

It was obvious Yang had been coerced into proposing marriage. 'What if he doesn't want me?'

Lady Yi set her needle into the cloth. 'I understand.'

'You do?'

Her stepmother moved to the trunk in the corner. She tossed a sly look over her shoulder before lifting the lid.

'This is my wedding gift to you.' Lady Yi returned with something wrapped in red silk and placed it in Jin-mei's lap. The object was round and had some heft to it.

'Shall I open this now?'

'Well, certainly before the wedding.' Lady Yi sat back on her stool to watch expectantly.

Jin-mei unwrapped the silk to reveal a bronze mirror. 'How beautiful!'

There was a gleam in Lady Yi's eye. 'Look at the other side.'

The back of the mirror was elaborately engraved. She read the inscription aloud. 'In front of the flowers and under the moon.'

The design in between the characters wasn't like anything she'd ever seen. She bent to take a closer look. 'Oh, heaven!'

Now she understood the reason behind Lady Yi's sly smile. There were engravings of four different couples on the back; men and women joined together with arms and legs intertwined. Her cheeks heated as she stared at the figures, but she couldn't drag her eyes away.

'With your mother gone, it is my responsibility to instruct you on such matters.'

Jin-mei was still examining the explicit images. She had thought herself confused when all she knew of coupling was from poems that alluded to the clouds and the rain. Now she gaped at the mirror, turning it sideways and then back. 'How is this...possible?'

'Everything manages to find its place,' Lady Yi said wisely. 'Men and women are made to fit together.'

And they seemed to fit in interesting ways at that. Bronze arms and legs writhed over the back of the mirror. In three days, she was to share her marital bed with Yang doing *that*. Her throat went dry.

A knock on the door made her jump. Hastily, she dragged her embroidery over her lap just as her father entered.

'Husband.' Lady Yi stood to greet him. 'We are nearly finished putting Jin-mei's dowry together. She is very excited about the wedding.'

Father nodded and laid a hand over Lady Yi's shoulder. Her stepmother always appeared so delicate next to Father's heavier build. 'May I speak to my daughter privately?'

This was worse than the time Father had caught her sneaking out to the Spring Lantern Festival. With her face burning, she glanced down at her lap. The mirror wasn't entirely covered. An image of a man lying on his back with the woman straddled on top of him peeked out from the corner of the silk. Her stepmother's delaying tactics as she turned to make a comment to her husband gave Jin-mei enough time to pull the handkerchief over the amorous couple.

Lady Yi then exited the room, and Father pulled the stool beside her before sitting down. 'How is my daughter?'

'Well.' Her voice was pitched a note too high. 'How was Father's trip?'

Father grunted. 'A disaster, but everything is taken care of now.' With a deep breath, he met her eyes. 'I left so quickly after the betrothal, I never asked you whether you had any objections to this marriage.'

'What objections would I have?' she asked. 'Mister Bao is a long-time friend of Father's. He seems a gentleman.'

She'd looked away while saying it. Her father would undoubtedly notice. All of a sudden, she wondered if he could read the events of that fateful afternoon on her face: how she'd tried to flirt instead of walking away, Bao Yang disappearing beneath the bridge with her following like an eager young duckling. Then there was the near kiss—even if that had only been in her own imagination.

'My only objection is having to leave you,' she said, as a dutiful daughter should.

'Dear girl, you can't stay with this old man for ever.'

A tiny ache grew in Jin-mei's chest. She would miss him. As excited as she was at the prospect of being wed to someone she found to her liking, this was the end of her childhood. She would leave home to become part of a new family she knew so little about.

'Bao Yang said something to me that I've been wondering about. He told me if he was discovered, his life would be in danger.'

Her father frowned. 'When did he say such a thing?'

'In the park. That was why he went to hide beneath the bridge.'

Yang had made it sound as if she had the power of life and death over him. The situation was so startling and exciting that before she knew what was happening, she was beneath the bridge and practically in his arms.

'Mister Bao isn't in any danger,' Father assured. 'He must have been teasing you.'

It hadn't seemed as though he was teasing, but she would have to trust her father on this. Yang was a guest in their villa outside the city while awaiting the wedding date. Certainly there was no danger for him there.

Father kissed her forehead. 'Now I must go to the tribunal, but we'll have dinner together this evening. Not too many more meals before my daughter is a married woman, hmm?'

She ducked her head shyly. 'Yes, Father.'

He pinched her cheek, something he hadn't done for years. She usually hated the gesture, but today she didn't mind so much. She listened for the door to close before setting the bronze mirror aside.

'Is everything all right?' Lady Yi asked when she returned to her stool.

'Yes, of course,' Jin-mei said, picking up her embroidery.

They set about once again working on their designs, but Jin-mei couldn't escape the nagging feeling at the back of her mind.

When she was very young, Father had explained to her that magistrates were trained to read faces in order to discern whether a subject was telling the truth or lying.

The discipline was called reading the five signs. The easiest trick was to watch the eyes: look for a twitch to the left or right, rapid blinking, the inability to focus. Father's skill had made it very hard for her to misbehave during her childhood.

Perhaps because of such training, her father's gaze was difficult to decipher. Jin-mei had learned instead to watch his mouth. After she'd asked about Yang's remark, Father's mouth had tightened for half a count before twitching into a grin. For that one breath, he had been calculating what to say to her, carefully constructing his response. If she were a magistrate, she would have insisted her father was hiding something.

Chapter Three

Fate was a funny thing. Five days ago, he had been hiding from the city guards. Today Yang was getting married to the magistrate's daughter. Such was fate. If it wasn't such an important occasion, he would have laughed aloud when he arrived by sedan chair at Magistrate Tan's residence.

It was late in the evening, during the hour of the Dog, which had been deemed auspicious for them by the fortune-teller. More importantly, the sky was dark and the streets relatively empty due to the curfew.

The wedding was to be a quiet one with the festivities to take place far outside of Minzhou at the magistrate's villa. Though the city's constables didn't have his name or face to attach to the earlier attack on the warlord, neither he nor Tan wanted to risk too much attention. It was enough that any rumours of impropriety surrounding Lady Tan would be immediately banished by news of her marriage.

The porters carried an empty sedan chair alongside him for his intended bride while lantern bearers illuminated the way. Attendants bearing wedding gifts lined up at the head of the procession.

Tan Li Kuo had negotiated a long list of demands on behalf of his daughter. There would be a proper bridal procession to the guest villa where Yang was staying. The bridal suite had been laid out there as well as preparations for a respectably sized banquet. His dear daughter would receive the lavish wedding she deserved.

Who would have thought the crafty official would turn out to be so sentimental?

Two red lanterns hung on either side of the gate. Tan emerged just as Yang stepped down from the sedan. The magistrate's expression was so serious, exaggerated by the shadows of the flickering light.

Yang bowed formally. As he straightened, doubt crept in. The magistrate's black eyes fixed on to him; judging Yang as if he were kneeling before the tribunal.

'Honourable sir,' Yang began, returning the magistrate's hard gaze without flinching. 'I have come on this auspicious day to take your daughter as my most precious bride.'

Perhaps the cold stare meant that Tan had reconsidered this hasty marriage, but that was nonsense. The entire procession wedding procession was gathered in the street.

Tan regarded him with the iron look for another heartbeat, then his stern expression cracked into a grin. 'Why so formal?' He chuckled, patting Yang heartily on the back. 'We're soon to be family.'

The show of cheerfulness was more in line with Tan's usual demeanour, but something felt out of place about the whole situation. Perhaps that was inevitable given the nature of the arrangement. He and Tan might have been long-time allies, but they were far from friends.

Yang let out a breath as the magistrate escorted him into the courtyard. The entire house was lit gaily with lanterns. All the servants were dressed in their best, their faces bright as they looked upon his ceremonial red robe. A romantic melody played on the *pipa*.

In the parlour, they shared tea and sweet cakes while speaking of inconsequential things. Tan's wife was present, a charming and cultured woman with eyes that smiled. The bride herself was nowhere to be seen.

'I think I know why you're looking around so eagerly,' taunted the magistrate.

'You old goat!' Lady Yi swatted her husband's arm. Then she said to him, more politely. 'I'll bring Jin-mei out to join us.'

Yang grinned. This was just like a real wedding.

Well, of course it was a real wedding. Jin-mei was to be his wife. He had no particular objections to being married, though it would be difficult to raise a family under the current circumstances. Yang was still a fugitive and one of the most powerful men in the province wanted him dead.

Navigating this situation would take every connection and asset he had at his fingertips. But Yang was nothing if not resourceful. He prided himself on it.

Jin-mei emerged wearing a green-silk robe accented with gold embroidery. Their gazes met and he suddenly forgot all of the schemes and ploys that had brought him to this moment.

He hadn't had much opportunity to look closely at her before now. Her lips were painted red and her cheeks flushed. The elaborate wedding costume overwhelmed her, making her appear small, but there was a womanly shape to her bosom and a generous curve to her hips. Her look was nervous as she regarded him, but far from timid. Maybe Tan was right. Yang was eager to know her better, this pretty girl who was to be his wife.

He could do worse. Much, much worse.

He gave Jin-mei a smile because she looked as though she might need some reassurance. When she returned it, he felt a hitch in his chest. He'd had lovers and companions in the past, but never anyone who had belonged to him. Never anyone he was bound to care for and protect. Yang found that he was the one looking away, averting his eyes, willing his heartbeat to steady.

When he turned, he saw Tan watching him carefully. Magistrate Tan was a shrewd, calculating man—the most dangerous man he'd ever encountered, aside from General Wang. Aside from himself. Now was not the time to show weakness.

Jin-mei approached in small steps that were mismatched with the bold way she'd first approached him. Her spine was fixed and straight and she looked as if she'd forgotten how to breathe. He was no better when he stood rigidly to bow to her. They were like a pair of wooden marionettes on strings.

It was all the ritual and formality. Once they were alone, they would know how to be with one another, he assured himself. There had been no fear in her when he'd lured her beneath the bridge, after all.

The next time they would be alone would be in their wedding bed. As they performed the rest of the ceremony before the Tan family altar, Yang occupied himself by mentally pulling the pins from Jin-mei's hair and kissing away the vermilion that painted her lips until she was once again that wild and fearless creature he'd met by the river.

It was their wedding night. He was allowed such erotic thoughts.

Jin-mei met his gaze with a question in her eyes, a question he looked forward to answering later. She still looked so anxious, but there were too many people about for him to reach out to her and reassure her with just a touch against her wrist or a hand on her back.

Ours may be an arranged marriage, he wanted to tell her. *But it is the best arrangement I have ever made.*

Whether or not that was true was left to be seen, but it was true enough in that moment. Magistrate Tan could have just as easily had him castrated as punishment for ruining Jin-mei's reputation. Despite the failed assassination plot and the warrants out for him, fortune had smiled upon Yang once again. He had the luck of dragons.

With the tea ceremony complete, they had more formalities to look forward to. The long parade back to the villa, the wedding banquet, a lot of greetings and well-wishers.

Jin-mei struggled with her robe as she climbed on to the empty sedan chair, and Yang reached out to steady her.

'Your fingers are like ice.' He squeezed her hand in both of his before letting go to seat himself in the adjoining sedan. 'You're not afraid of me, are you?'

It was meant as a jest, but Jin-mei did appear pale as the procession started towards the gates. A line of attendants trailed behind them along with Jin-mei's family transported in several litters. The setting was far from private, with both of them hefted over the shoulders of the carriers, but at least they could finally speak.

'This isn't what you wanted, is it?' Jin-mei asked beneath her breath.

Attendants flanked either side of the sedan chairs carrying poles with lanterns attached. A hazy glow formed around the entourage, but it left half of Jin-mei's face in shadow and impossible for him to read. She stared directly ahead, as if afraid of his answer. There was a proud tilt to her chin.

'There is no one else I would rather be wedded to,' he replied without hesitation.

Jin-mei whipped around to face him, causing the pearls in her ears to swing dramatically. 'You're trying to be clever with your words. You could very well mean that you have no desire to be married at all, to anyone.'

It was hard not to smile. 'I think you and I will suit each other quite well, Jin-mei.'

Jin-mei. The sound of her name slid smoothly over his tongue, as if he'd been calling her that for years. It warmed him to be able to use it. *Jin-mei.*

'It's a compliment,' he said, seeing her perplexed expression.

Running a hand nervously over her throat, she turned her attention back to the road. They were at the gates now where carriages and horses awaited to take the procession out to the magistrate's villa.

There was only brief conversation on the short carriage ride to the villa.

'Do you spend much time away from home?' she asked.

'Our trade routes take me all over the province.'

'It must be quite dangerous to travel on the open road.'

'Not if one is prepared,' he assured her.

Jin-mei looked out into the night. 'I think I would worry about you all the time.'

Once again, a heavy, sinking feeling weighed down his chest. Jin-mei had a claim to him when no one else had in a long time.

'What...?' Yang paused with the question lingering on his tongue. 'What has your father told you about my family?'

'He told me you've made your fortune on the transport of salt and grain.'

Perhaps now wasn't a good time to reveal his secrets, but he was beginning to wonder if Jin-mei already suspected what sort of shady underworld activities he was also involved in. Magistrate Tan certainly knew enough to destroy him, but he seemed content to remain quiet. With this wedding, their futures were now intertwined.

The best arrangement Yang had ever made. He had the magistrate's protection, his silence, his daughter… Surely it couldn't be this easy?

'When will we go back north to your home—I mean, to our home?' Jin-mei blushed a little as she fidgeted in the sedan chair.

He found it irresistibly charming, which made the next part more difficult. 'I've arranged with your father for you to remain here after the wedding.'

She frowned at him. 'I won't be coming to live with you?'

'Of course you will, Wife.' He used the endearment to assuage her doubts, but the word felt awkward on his lips. 'There's some business I must attend to. Afterwards, I'll return and we'll travel north together.'

She nodded, but didn't look entirely satisfied. He had been accountable to no one but himself for a long time, which made it easy to engage in questionable activities without being exposed. That would all change now with Jin-mei at his side. She had a keen eye. She was clever. And from what little he knew of her, she didn't seem to bite her tongue very often.

Maybe there would be no more reason to hide by the time he returned. Wang Shizhen would be lying cold in his grave and Yang could leave his days of plotting behind. Or the outcome could be the exact opposite with

him being the one left dead. Yang had been fully prepared to accept failure—until now.

'I won't be away long,' he promised, which was a
lie. The slight curl in Jin-mei's lip told him it wasn't a
good lie either.

They arrived at the guest villa which had been decorated with red banners. Once again, they were swept
up in the festivities. They lit incense and bowed to an
altar set up for his ancestors this time. Then they drank
honeyed wine from two cups joined by a red ribbon before Jin-mei was ushered away by her female attendants.
Meanwhile Yang was surrounded by wedding guests intent on pouring more wine down his throat.

The next hour was a blur. Though the guests were all
strangers to him, apparently Magistrate Tan had many
friends. The official was the happiest man at the banquet,
refilling Yang's cup time and time again and drinking
to his health, his happiness and many grandchildren.

Repeatedly, Yang tried to escape to the bridal chamber between the ribald taunting and innuendo that was
required of any wedding. Each time he was dragged back
and plied with more wine until he was in a state that he
rarely allowed himself to be in. Yang was drunk.

'Get him to his wife while he can still perform his
husbandly duties!'

Yang had no idea who said that, but he raised his
cup in thanks and drank. A firm hand clamped over his
shoulder, startling him. It was Tan, now his father-in-
law, who regarded him with an intense look. The magistrate's face was flushed red from the wine, but his gaze
was still sharp.

The grip tightened on Yang's shoulder. 'Jin-mei is my
daughter,' Tan said, serious once more. 'My treasure.'

'I'll take care of her,' Yang vowed.

The magistrate nodded, unsmiling.

A swarm of young men grabbed hold of Yang then, laughing as they escorted him down the hallway to the wedding chamber. Tossing him inside, they shut the door behind him before retreating.

He expected to see his bride there waiting, but the room was empty. The bed was a magnificent one, fashioned out of dark wood with a large canopy overhead. The servants had taken the care to drape the bed in red silk and scatter flower petals and seeds upon it. For fertility.

'Jin-mei?' he called softly.

He crouched to search beneath the bed, in case she was hiding coyly there. That was when he realised how drunk he must be. He fought a wave of dizziness as he straightened.

Perhaps she was away for some womanly preparation he wasn't aware of. He'd certainly never been married before to know.

There was a flask of wine set up on the table beside the bed. He filled both cups and waited beside the bed, thinking of, among other things, performing his 'duties.' When his bride had still not arrived in the next few minutes, he started getting impatient.

Though the event had been unplanned, it was still his wedding. The banquet had lightened the weight from his shoulders for a few hours, and Jin-mei had looked rather tempting while she scolded him in the sedan chair. She also had looked quite charming the first time he'd seen her that evening; so nervous.

He'd never been with a virgin before. He needed to take things slowly. Kiss her hair, her mouth, her throat. Lead her into desire step by step—where was she? Had she become frightened? Maybe her amah and stepmother were providing some final instruction on matters of yin and yang. Funny, Jin-mei didn't seem the shy sort.

By now, Yang was getting *very* impatient. Watching the door, he picked up the wine cup and took a sip, rolling the wine on his tongue out of habit. The drink had been sweetened with honey and steeped in spices. A faint trace of bitterness only came in right as he was about to swallow.

He spat it out, staring at the wine flask and the remaining cup. Poison?

The fog of drunkenness lifted from his mind as his survival instinct came alive. Opening the front of his robe, he closed his hand around the knife he'd hidden beneath his clothes. With the sort of illegal and insurgent activities he was involved with, it was wise to always be armed. It was always wise to taste anything he wasn't sure of very carefully for poison.

His first thought was to find Jin-mei. Someone had taken her.

Yang was nearly to the door when he stopped himself, his head swimming in circles, but still able to function. He recalled how Tan Li Kuo had refilled his wine cup over and over at the banquet. This was the magistrate's private villa. His servants had set up the chamber and all of the guests were his friends.

That two-headed snake.

The wily magistrate had found a way to both preserve his daughter's reputation and exact revenge on Yang all at once. After all, being widowed was a perfectly honourable state for his daughter to be in.

But if Tan wanted him dead, drugging his wine in the wedding chamber was a clumsy way to go about it. There were no guarantees with poison. The magistrate had to have something else planned as well. Someone tasked with making sure the job was completed.

A scraping sound came from the wall. No, it came from behind the wall. With one hand, he felt along the wooden panels. His other hand gripped his knife. It wasn't hard to find the edge of the hidden door and he swung it open, preparing to strike.

A man dressed in a red wedding robe stared out at him from a small compartment.

'That scheming bastard!' Yang seethed.

His mirror image attempted to step out from the hiding space, but Yang stopped him with a menacing shake of his knife. 'What were you going to do? Strangle me? Stab me?'

'No, of course not!' the man cried, staring at the blade. He had gone pale. 'I was just supposed to run from this room screaming.'

'That's nonsense.'

'It's true. I was paid to do it.'

'And that's it?'

The impostor nodded, shaking.

Yang struggled to clear his head enough to piece the magistrate's plan together. It was possible Tan had been planning his death all along. They were accomplices in a failed assassination plot, after all. He alone could implicate Tan in the conspiracy.

He'd been swindled. If this man wasn't the one hired to cut his throat, then an assassin was certainly nearby, closing in for the kill as they spoke.

Yang grabbed the impostor by the robe to drag him out of the compartment. 'It's time to do what you were hired for, my friend. Start running.'

Chapter Four

There was trouble outside.

Jin-mei sat in the bridal chamber while Lady Yi tried to give her final words of advice, telling her 'not to worry if it's not like what you expect the first time' when Jin-mei had no idea what to expect. Suddenly the hum of noise from the banquet turned into shouting.

She started for the door, but it swung open before she could reach it. Father stood before her with a group of men gathered behind him. She saw one of them holding a club.

'Stay here,' Father told her. 'It's not safe outside.'

'Why? What's happened?'

She might as well have not spoken. Father pulled the door shut, and she heard him giving orders on the other side. *'Search the house. Search the woods.'*

Search the woods for what?

Lady Yi stayed with her, and they huddled together on the bed. The cover had been sprinkled with lotus seeds and flower petals for good luck, but the symbols were meaningless now. What had happened to disrupt her wedding? And where was Bao Yang…?

Every so often, Lady Yi would say, 'Everything will

be all right.' Then a little later she'd repeat it. 'Everything will be all right.'

With each repetition, Jin-mei's heart sank. More time had passed, another empty assurance given and still there was no news. She had started drifting off to sleep on the bed when the doors opened.

Again, it was Father. His face was sunken, defeated. 'Jin-mei—'

'Where's Bao Yang?'

'Jin-mei,' he said again, gently this time. Too gently, and she knew.

She started trembling so hard she had to sit down. 'What happened, Father?'

Lady Yi wrapped her arms around Jin-mei as her father told the entire story. A madman had come to the villa wielding a knife. The guests had seen a man chasing Yang into the woods, but then both of them had disappeared.

'That's impossible.' A wave of dizziness passed over her. She reached out to brace herself against the enclosure over the bed.

'I summoned every constable to search the woods. It's possible they fell into the ravine. The river is high from the plum rains and with the rocks down below—'

Jin-mei couldn't listen to any more. She wanted to go to the river herself that very moment, but that was impossible. It was too dark. There was possibly a madman on the loose.

The next morning, Jin-mei did accompany Head Constable Han and his search party as they scoured the ravine. With her heart in her throat, she searched the rocks below for a sign of Yang's red wedding robe, but there was nothing but the waters of the Min River rushing by.

It was improper for her to be out there in the sun,

among so many strangers, but she was no longer a sheltered young girl to be hidden away. A married woman
was granted more freedom. The thought made her want
to weep.

But Jin-mei didn't weep. Everything had happened all
too suddenly for her to know what to feel. Drained and
exhausted from lack of sleep, she finally turned away
from the search and found herself unable to mourn properly for her husband of only a few hours. All she could
do was think of the few fleeting moments they'd shared
together, and the kiss beneath a bridge she'd only imagined. A kiss that would now never come to be.

For the first seven days, Jin-mei remained shut away,
dressed in pale sackcloth and lighting incense for a husband she had barely known. When she finally ventured
outside, it was only at her father's insistence. She had
replaced her white mourning robe with a sombre grey
one and dutifully set one foot in front of the other as she
accompanied the constable's wife through the city. All
she wanted was to return to bed and wake up in a month
when the wound wasn't so new and raw.

Constable Han's wife was close to Jin-mei in age and
it was said that she had once been a dancer who had travelled throughout the province. Li Feng was long-limbed,
poised and moved with a confidence that Jin-mei envied.
Along with being graceful, the other woman was also
full of energy and life. Even her eyes were animated,
catching the light as she spoke. In contrast, Jin-mei felt
as grey and lifeless as her robe.

Their morning consisted of a visit to the temple to
light incense and pray for the spirits of the deceased.
Afterwards, Li Feng had suggested a walk through the
park, but Jin-mei refused. It was too soon. Not even two

weeks had passed since she had met Bao Yang there. Only two weeks to become a wife and a widow.

'Along the market, then,' Li Feng replied, refusing to let her mope. 'I'll take you to my favourite tea house.'

Jin-mei trudged along, a poor companion in every way. It was her first time out in public since Yang's death and she was at a loss. With Yang gone, she had no new family to go to, no wifely duties, no future.

Her life was no different than it had been before. She had returned to her father's house to live and no one spoke of what had happened that night. It was nothing but a dream. Her hopes and fears before the wedding were nothing but clouds that had been blown away with the breeze.

'How long have you been married to Constable Han?' Jin-mei asked, attempting conversation.

'Not long. Only a little over a month now.'

'A month?' Jin-mei's cheeks flushed with embarrassment. 'I should have sent you a gift.'

She hadn't even known there had been another wedding so recently. A magistrate and his constable were so far apart in status that Jin-mei and Li Feng had little reason to socialise. Even this short outing felt awkward and forced.

'There's no need to apologise. My husband has been so busy with his duties as the new constable, sometimes I wonder if we're married after all.'

Jin-mei attempted a smile at the jest, but once again her thoughts returned to Yang. In one part, it was due to grief, but another part was the strange circumstances of how he'd disappeared.

'I apologise for being so forward, but has Constable Han made any progress on the investigation?'

'Han hasn't said much about it, but don't you worry.

My husband will find out who is responsible. He was relentless as a thief-catcher.'

'It's so hard to believe that no one was found; not my husband or his attacker. If I could at least see him—if we were able to lay his body in the ground—maybe I wouldn't feel so empty, as if things were unfinished.' Jin-mei knew she was being morbid to dwell on it, but she had so few memories of Yang. The details of his disappearance loomed large in her mind. 'There are moments when I forget that my husband is dead and I have to remind myself that he really is gone.'

Li Feng touched her sleeve sympathetically. 'Do you want to cry? I can find a private place for us and you can cry as much as you like. I won't think less of you for it.'

'No, I don't want to cry. I don't know if I even should cry. Everything that happened was so strange, I don't know what to do with myself now.'

'I lost my father unexpectedly when I was very young,' Li Feng confided. 'And then I was separated from my mother for years. There were many days when I felt part of myself was gone and floating in the ghost world with them. I had so few memories of them, but the few I possessed, I held on to them like pearls.'

'You understand then!' Jin-mei's throat tightened. That was how she felt: like half a ghost herself. 'My husband was a long-time associate of my father's, but he never paid any notice to me until right before we were married. But then it was as though he could see me so clearly, when no one else could. The last words he said to me were that we would suit each other quite well.'

For the first time since the tragedy, Jin-mei felt tears gathering. A woman never knew whether her marriage would be one of love, but in that moment Yang's expression as he looked at her was far from cold and far from uninterested. There had been a half-smile upon his lips and a wicked lift to his eyebrow.

Jin-mei had believed then that her husband was indeed capable of loving her and she him. She could sense the possibility heavy in the air between them as they swayed upon the sedan chairs. She could feel it in the way they spoke with one another, phrases chasing and dancing with one another. Yet hours later, she had gone to wait anxiously on her bridal bed for a husband who would never come.

'He sounds like a good man,' Li Feng said gently.

Jin-mei knew it was just something to say, but she appreciated it none the less. It was good to talk about him. 'Bao Yang was always so charming and clever.'

Li Feng halted in the middle of the busy market and shot her an odd look. 'Your husband's name was Bao Yang?'

'Yes. Why?'

'How curious. I once knew someone by that name.' She gave her head a little shake. 'No matter. It's such a common name.'

But it wasn't. Before Jin-mei could answer, a loud crash came from the drinking house across the street. A brawl must have broken out on the second floor.

Li Feng grabbed hold of her arm. Startled by the rough treatment, Jin-mei tried to pull away, but the constable's wife directed her out of the street and into the doorway of one of the shops.

Li Feng glanced over her shoulder as two city guards hurried towards the disturbance. 'Stay here,' she instructed. 'I'll be back.'

At that, Li Feng flew across the street and disappeared into the drinking house, leaving Jin-mei to stare after her in bewilderment. There was nothing to do but do as she was told. Jin-mei watched the stream of market-goers flow by, oblivious to whatever was happening in the tavern.

A man appeared on the far corner and something about him caught her attention. He was tall and lean of build with a slight crookedness to his nose. She only saw his face for a second before he turned away, but her heart leapt in her chest.

It was him. It was Bao Yang.

He glanced about briefly before stepping into the street. Jin-mei rushed after him, but with his longer stride, he pulled ahead of her until he was just another head in the crowd.

'Yang!' Several people turned to stare at her, but she didn't care. She tried to shove through, but it was no use. Yang was gone.

Jin-mei was still searching the marketplace when Li Feng found her. 'I apologise, Lady Tan, but my husband was in there—'

'I need to go home,' Jin-mei interrupted. 'I need to speak to my father.'

The constable's wife seemed to have lost any desire for an outing as well. The magistrate's residence was only a few streets away. Jin-mei attempted a hasty fare-well once they reached the gates, but Li Feng stopped her.

'Your late husband... I apologise if this brings up painful memories, but was he from around here?'

'He was a merchant from the north. Taining County.'

There it was again. The tiniest of frowns flickered over the other woman's face. Li Feng held her breath for a beat too long before responding. 'My condolences on your loss, Lady Tan.'

'Thank you for your kind thoughts.'

They exchanged polite bows and Li Feng hurried away while Jin-mei rushed through the gates into her home.

Their residence was a part of the walled compound of the magistrate's yamen. Every morning, Father would have his tea in their private courtyard before passing through the gate that connected the living quarters to the judicial offices and tribunal. Jin-mei had never gone through the gate before, but she did so now.

The guards patrolling the grounds of the yamen raised their eyebrows, but otherwise gave her no trouble as she started down the corridor towards the main courtyard. There, a series of buildings and offices spread out before her and she was at a loss. Jin-mei knew petitioners lined up for the tribunal and prisoners were kept in cells at the back of the compound, but it was intimidating to see it all at work.

She had to ask a clerk for the location to her father's office, but it was surprisingly empty when she arrived. Her father returned a few moments later, surrounded by guards. Constable Han was beside him, engaged in a heated discussion that fell silent when they saw her.

Jin-mei might never be able to read faces as well as her father, but some mannerisms were easy to interpret. Constable Han bowed hastily and excused himself. Father made an effort to compose himself before approaching.

He ushered her into his office and shut the door. 'Jin-mei, what brings you here?'

'Bao Yang is alive.' Her pulse was still pounding. 'I saw him out on the street, but he moved away so quickly, I couldn't catch him.'

'My dear daughter. I know how saddened you are by his loss.' Her father took hold of her hands and his expression was one of anguish. 'It is my own failing that I haven't been able to find his killer.'

He wasn't listening. 'Yang isn't dead. I saw him,' she repeated fervently. 'Right outside of the drinking house in the centre of the Seven Alleys.'

Father nodded, but it wasn't a nod of agreement. It was an obliging nod, a nod of forbearance. 'Jin-mei, you have always been clear-headed, but this tragedy is one very close to your heart. And with it being so soon after both your wedding and his death... Seven days after a person dies, his spirit returns home.'

'I didn't see a ghost. It was him!' she insisted.

'I believe you saw something your heart wanted to see.' Again that nod and a pained look. 'I know you've been lost these last few days. Lonely.'

He drew her into his arms, something he hadn't done since she was a child. For a moment, she closed her eyes and let her father embrace her. It was reassuring to be held close. Jin-mei had indeed been feeling lost. And she was lonely all of the time now, even in their house among family.

'I've never told anyone this,' he began, stroking her hair gently. 'But after your mother passed, I saw her. I was in the garden one morning, drinking tea, and I could feel her there. Then I turned and there she was, just for a moment. I tried to speak to her and she was gone. Not faded away like smoke, just there in one blink and gone in the next. After that I only saw her in dreams, but we never are able to speak to one another, as much as I want to. Is that how it was for you, Jin-mei?'

She was so caught up in her father's story that she had nearly forgotten about Yang. 'I called out to him but... but he disappeared.'

Had she imagined it? That was what her rational mind

was telling her to accept. She pulled away from her father. 'I saw him very clearly.'

'I know,' he replied with a sad smile. 'It was the same way with your mother.'

Father looked away and her heart went out to him. It was as Lady Yi had said, Mother was the love of his life and she always would be. Slowly he returned to his desk and made an attempt to organise his case records to compose himself.

A moment earlier she had been so certain Yang was alive, but Father had cast doubt over everything she'd seen. If Yang had survived the fall, why hadn't he returned to her? She knew of cases where people hit their heads and forgot all their memories. The fall from the ravine could have caused such an injury, but if her husband was indeed wandering through the city in confusion, certainly he would have been found by one of her father's constables.

'I was thinking for a while that it might be good for you to spend some time away,' Father went on. 'Perhaps a trip to the mountains with Lady Yi.'

'During the mourning period? That would be disrespectful—'

Jin-mei caught herself. Once again, she was talking about Yang as if he were indeed dead.

'After the proper mourning period, of course. In the meantime, take comfort that your husband's spirit is with you. He hasn't forgotten you.'

She nodded and took her leave, feeling confused and numb. Father was obviously very busy and she was barely making sense. She had so many questions to ask, but she didn't know where to start. As Jin-mei made the long walk back to the living quarters, she tried to arrange all the pieces. Father's explanation was indeed the rational one, but some instinct inside her refused to let go.

When she was young, she hadn't listened to whimsical folk tales. Her father had entertained her instead with famous case accounts. The stories always featured clever officials who knew a lie immediately. They never accepted the obvious solution and were unsatisfied when the pieces of a puzzle didn't fit together just right.

Jin-mei was unsatisfied.

Once she was back in the familiar surroundings of their house, she realised what was bothering her. Father had returned to his office with Constable Han. The constable's wife had mentioned that Han was in the drinking house—could that mean her father had been there as well? At the very same time she had seen Yang in the street just outside.

It was possibly all coincidence, but Father was acting strange. Constable Han was acting strange. His wife as well. Perhaps heaven and earth had switched places and Jin-mei was the only one who found any of it odd.

Amah was out in the garden, watching over Jin-mei's two brothers, which meant the old nursemaid was sitting beneath the shade of pavilion as the boys fought over a wooden boat.

She passed them by with a nod to Amah and went to her father's study. The room was cool and dark with the shutters drawn. A sanctuary.

She had never, *never* been in Father's study without his permission. Her hand trembled as she opened the drawer. A seed of an idea had been planted inside her. If she didn't rid herself of this suspicion immediately, it would continue to take root and fester.

There were letters in the drawer. She looked quickly through them, finding nothing of any significance. Beneath the letters lay a thin book with a blue cover. She lifted it and saw a folded paper tucked away at the very bottom of the drawer.

Jin-mei opened up the paper to find that it was a note for five thousand taels of silver. Five thousand? It was an extraordinary amount of money. The red seal at the bottom of the note contained the character for 'Bao.' The Bao family chop, perhaps.

If this was meant to be a wedding gift, it was an extravagant one. Bao Yang came from a line of successful merchants, but she hadn't realised how wealthy he was until now. How wealthy he had been...

Slowly, she folded the bank note and put it back beneath the book. There were officials who were corrupt and took bribes, but she'd always been confident that her father wasn't one of them. He'd never shown any interest in money. When he spoke, it was of honesty, of moral behaviour, of law and order.

She could just ask her father why he had so much of Bao Yang's money. They had always been able to say anything to one another. She'd always trusted him. She knew him.

Yet Jin-mei's instincts told her Father had been hiding something for a while now. Ever since Bao Yang had come back into their lives.

Suddenly the details of her wedding night came back to her, not as a personal memory steeped in emotion, but as fragmented pieces. The pieces had always seemed oddly familiar to her, but she couldn't place exactly why. A wedding banquet. A groom chased into the woods. The story had the mark of a classic tragedy.

Jin-mei went to her father's shelves and began to look through the books. There were volumes of history and poetry, but the books she'd always enjoyed most were the extraordinary case records. Stories of scheming criminals bested by clever officials. Once she could read, she had borrowed the books from her father and read them herself. He'd always found her fascination for these tales amusing.

When she finally found the account, her heart stopped. There was a wedding. And a murder.

Clutching the book to her chest, she went to her room. Once the door was shut, she opened the book once more. A woman and her lover schemed to rob her wealthy neighbour by seducing him into marriage. On their wedding night, with guests all around, the groom was seen running from the bridal chamber, his hair in disarray. Mad.

The similarities were too much of a coincidence. Had the entire night been staged? But why? She wanted to run back to the tribunal to demand an answer from her father, but she already knew what would happen. He would deflect her suspicions. He would weave together colourful lies and she would believe him because she wanted to be convinced.

With shaking hands, Jin-mei collected her wedding money and a few belongings into a satchel. She didn't need to read the case record to remember the rest of the details. The groom had thrown himself into the river while the guests looked on in horror. They knew it was him because of his ceremonial wedding robe. Though the river was searched, his body was never found.

Jin-mei had to know what had happened to Bao Yang. Even more than a sense of justice, her father had impressed upon her the importance of finding the truth.

Calmly, Jin-mei informed her amah that she was going to visit the constable's wife, but instead hired a carriage to take her outside of the city walls to her father's villa. Being wed and then widowed within a day must have emboldened her.

Her thoughts buzzed in her head like a nest of wasps. When she'd told Father she'd seen Yang alive, he hadn't argued with her. Instead, her father had nodded sympathetically. He'd listened without judgement, and even agreed with her that she was not mistaken in what she'd seen. Most particularly, he'd brought up her mother. They rarely spoke of Mother, but Father had done so, confiding in Jin-mei and telling her a story that made her heart ache. He'd cast all her doubts aside and effectively quieted her.

Because as a magistrate, he knew how to detect falsehoods and how to create them. Father was a master of lies.

The villa was no longer draped in red and lit with lanterns. It had been locked down, with only a lone groundskeeper and his family assigned to watch over it. The groundskeeper was a middle-aged man whose hair was thinning slightly on top. He was surprised to see her, but let her in without protest.

'You and your family attended to my husband while he stayed here, did you not?' she asked as she wandered from room to room.

'Yes, Lady Tan—my apologies. I meant, Bao *Furen*.'

He addressed her by her married title as Bao Yang's wife. A pang of regret struck Jin-mei as she entered the bridal chamber. The red sheets and decorations had all been cleared away. The bed itself was bare and cold.

She closed her eyes. She remembered sitting on the bed and waiting for Yang. They were supposed to consummate their marriage that night. Perhaps coupling would be as awkward as it appeared on the bronze mirror or as profound and ephemeral as it sounded in poems. Regardless of what it would be, she had been excited to be discovering the answer with him. Excited and frightened and happy.

If she stayed any longer, her heart would shatter into a hundred pieces. Gently, with great care, she closed the door as if shutting it on an invalid on a deathbed, not wanting to disturb what little rest might remain.

'Did you attend the wedding?' she asked the groundskeeper.

The man was following behind her solicitously. For all he knew, her visit was nothing more than the whim of a grieving widow. For all she knew, maybe it was.

'No, my lady. Magistrate Tan freed us from our obligations that day. We went into the city to visit family.'

She continued through the rest of the villa. The banquet room had been swept and all the tables cleared and stored. On the other side of the house, the side facing the woods, she entered a spacious chamber with a canopied bed. This bed had also been stripped of all curtains and bedding. At the foot of the bed, beside one of the legs, was a speck of something. She knelt down to retrieve it, closing two fingers around a candied lotus seed.

There had been lotus seeds scattered on her bed the night of the wedding to symbolise fertility and good fortune. Lotus seeds in two places. Two bridal chambers?

On the night of her wedding, Yang would have left the party, ushered away by the well-wishers who were guests at the banquet. By tradition, they would lead him to her bed in case he was too drunk to make it there himself. But Yang had never appeared in her chamber. Instead, the next time anyone saw him, he was being chased into the woods.

In the story of the tragic wedding, the greedy woman

had continued to live for years as a widow, wealthy with her late husband's fortune. No one knew that there was actually a tunnel connecting the two houses. And that the groom hadn't thrown himself into the river that night. He hadn't left the house at all. Years later, the constables found a corpse hidden in the tunnel, still dressed in his wedding robe.

What if the guests had never intended to escort Yang to the bridal chamber? Maybe they had taken him to another room, one with a hidden compartment just as the case record had described.

And maybe, with the suspicious lotus seed in hand, she was standing in that other room now.

Jin-mei searched along the floor for some sort of trapdoor. Next she searched over the walls, feeling all along the wood. Her breath caught when she found a raised edge in the wall.

It couldn't be true. Jin-mei prayed that it wasn't true. Holding her breath, she pulled the panel open.

The enclosure was empty, but Jin-mei felt no relief as she stared into the hollow space. On the ground, a dark mark stained the wood like a spill of blank ink. Her head tried to deny what she was seeing, but her instincts wouldn't be quieted. Blood had been spilled here. Her entire wedding night had been an elaborate ruse, and no one was more deceived than she.

Chapter Five

When it came to matters of commerce, Yang had a reputation for knowing who to trust and how far, but lately those instincts were failing him. He should have known it was a mistake to try to negotiate a deal with a crooked magistrate and an even worse mistake to return after the staged wedding to try to confront the villain. He'd only managed to get into the same room with Tan at the drinking house before being chased off.

He'd simply wanted answers, but apparently Tan Li Kuo was an even greater scoundrel than he was.

With his initial plan abandoned, Yang stood alone at the ferry crossing while the transport ship approached. For a river vessel it was an impressive sight: three masts with sails unfurled to catch the wind. The vessel was a floating fortress that had seen more than one battle in its lifetime.

The ship cut through the deep waters of the Min River and dropped anchor near the bank. Within moments, the gangplank was lowered.

'Could that be the infamous Bao Yang?' a female voice called from the deck.

A familiar face greeted him from the bow and he

let himself breathe. He'd angered both a warlord and a magistrate and had precious few allies left. After ascending the gangplank, Yang was met on deck by the captain herself.

'Lady Daiyu,' he greeted.

'Mister Bao.' Daiyu was smiling at him, though her mouth was tight about the edges. 'I hear General Wang wants you dead.'

She was dressed in men's clothing; in loose trousers and a tunic that stopped short of her knees. Her hair was swept to one side, the black lightened to a reddish, rosewood colour by exposure to the sun.

'I heard that you had been killed.' A booming voice came from the other side of the deck. 'I was ready to celebrate.'

A huge ox of a man approached. His broad jaw was roughened by a thick growth of beard and a scar cut near his mouth, making his grin widen to a sneer.

'Kenji,' Yang greeted curtly.

'Yang.'

There was no cordial bow exchanged between them.

Kenji was a foreigner, originally from the island nation of Wa. No one knew exactly why he chose to never return, but it wasn't hard to imagine he was no longer welcome in his homeland. Lady Daiyu tolerated him and he was one of the few on board who did not serve as crew. As far as Yang knew, Kenji knew nothing about sailing. He was kept strictly for protection and commanded a handful of fighting men. Lady Daiyu would be in an unfortunate position if that beast ever decided to try to wrest control.

Yang did spare a bow for the young attendant who stood dutifully beside Daiyu. 'Young Miss Nan, are you taking good care of your mistress?'

She fought to keep her composure, though she was obviously pleased by the acknowledgement. 'I try to, Mister Bao.'

Nan was slight and willowy, but her eyes held a warrior glint. She blushed at him with all the softness of a young tigress.

Kenji snorted. 'Too bad you can't charm the general.'

'I seem to have lost my gift for it,' he had to admit. He'd foolishly hoped Magistrate Tan would protect his family, but the truth was Yang could only depend on himself now. 'Are you certain you want this fugitive on board?'

Lady Daiyu's smile remained fixed even while her eyes hardened. 'I have no fear of General Wang.' She sent the girl and the hulking Kenji away, and her tone warmed when she faced him. 'It's been a long time.'

'You're still as beautiful as a spring flower.'

'Sweet talker.'

'I'm in trouble, Daiyu,' he said in all seriousness. 'I made a mistake.'

Daiyu was older than him, but her age could only be seen in the finest of lines along her mouth and eyes, barely visible unless one was allowed in close quarters to her. And Yang, at one time, had been allowed in very close quarters.

Pretty was too soft a word for her. She was nearly as tall as he was. Handsome rather than beautiful and as confident and at ease with herself in bed as out. She was also sharp and not one to waste words.

'You used to be formidable. A shrewd and careful businessman. Never too greedy and always a step ahead.'

Yang knew where he'd gone wrong. It wasn't in trusting Magistrate Tan too much, nor in making an enemy of a powerful warlord. He'd gone wrong from the moment he started letting emotion guide him rather than reason. Every choice he'd made since then had ended in disaster.

'I need a safe place where my family can hide,' he began. 'One that Wang Shizhen with his entire army wouldn't think to find.'

Daiyu frowned. 'You can go into the mountains. The Wuyi region hasn't fallen to the warlord yet.'

'Yet,' he echoed grimly.

The plan had some merit. There were many small villages and settlements tucked away in the remote region. Wang would have to scatter his army to find them.

'It's been years since I've spoken to my brother,' he went on. 'I'll need to go to him and convince him to go into hiding. It could well be that the general knows my identity by now, and I can't risk their safety.'

'I understand.' Daiyu nodded sympathetically. 'Family is everything.'

At that, the lady captain offered to take him as far as he needed—for three times the usual fare.

'You're a true friend,' he said out of the corner of his mouth.

'Times are hard,' she replied with a shrug. 'And you're trouble. You said so yourself.'

'Lady Daiyu!'

The girl Nan was looking over the bow as she waved her over. Yang remained by Daiyu's side as she went to investigate, standing perhaps a bit too close to her out of old habit. Much of the crew had known the two of them had been lovers and likely assumed he would resume that role, which wasn't an unpleasant prospect.

Except he was married now and standing on the bank was his wife.

'Don't let her aboard,' Yang said beneath his breath.

Daiyu looked at him with surprise. 'She looks like a poor lost kitten.'

Jin-mei looked nothing of the sort. She stood with a travel pack slung around her shoulder. Her cheeks were flushed and her hair fought against its pins. His heart did a little lurch as their gazes locked. The hard set of her jaw warned him that he was in trouble.

This was no coincidence. She'd followed him. Immediately, he scanned the surrounding area. What could Jin-mei possibly be doing out here alone?

Despite his warning, Lady Daiyu beckoned her aboard. 'Come up, Little Sister! What brings you here?'

Jin-mei was out of breath by the time she ascended the gangplank, but she wiped her brow and straightened her shoulders.

'Mistress, I wish to buy passage aboard your ship.'

She had assessed, quite correctly, that Lady Daiyu was the one in command and not the burly Kenji who had come to stand beside her.

'Where do you wish to go, Young Miss?'

'Wherever you're destined.' Jin-mei flashed a sideways glance at Yang before returning her attention to the lady captain. 'I hope that this will be sufficient as fare.'

She produced a bolt of green silk from her travel pack and extended it to Daiyu, who looked it over without touching it.

'This is very fine quality. Quite expensive. Are you certain that passage aboard this ship is worth so much?'

Daiyu barely held back her amusement as Jin-mei fidgeted. 'I don't want to waste more time negotiating.'

For all her boldness, the girl was staring nervously at the rough characters around her. Yang was tempted to go and put a protective arm around her, but she was still Tan Li Kuo's daughter and no amount of wide-eyed innocence would make him forget that the magistrate was dangerous.

'Miss,' Yang began evenly, 'this ship is not where you want to be.'

Her eyes narrowed on him. They were lovely, expressive eyes that spoke louder than words. They told him that she blamed him for all that had happened. That somehow, he had abandoned her.

'This is exactly where I should be,' she said coolly. Then to Lady Daiyu, 'I wish to avoid the local authorities, and this ship has some experience doing so, I believe.'

'And why do you need to flee?' Daiyu asked gamely.

'I was married to a man who wasn't what he seemed,' Jin-mei replied, shoving a strand of hair away from her eyes. She was certainly growing bolder as the conversation progressed. 'I didn't wish to be his wife any longer, so I had him killed.'

Yang nearly choked at that. Lady Daiyu and Kenji burst into laughter.

'Welcome then, Little Sister.' Daiyu tucked the bolt of silk beneath her arm and directed Nan to take her to a sleeping berth. Jin-mei shot him a pointed look before disappearing below deck.

Yang waited until he was alone with Daiyu once more before speaking. 'She's lying.'

'Seducing girls from good homes now, Yang? Did she become so smitten with you that she killed her husband?'

He was about to protest that *he* was her husband, but that wouldn't serve any purpose. Especially when he was trying to convince Daiyu to evict Jin-mei from her ship.

'Her father is the head magistrate in Minzhou. He'll
be looking for her.'

'Even more reason to keep her on board. It's obvious
she has been pursuing you. If I let her go, she's likely to
lead the magistrate to us.'

He gave her the evil eye. 'I suspect you're siding with
her because she's a woman.'

'Think what you will. I'm allowing her to stay because she's paid me quite handsomely.' She patted the
roll of green silk beneath her arm and gave the order
to lift anchor. 'And I could hide ten runaways on board
and it wouldn't be as dangerous as harbouring one Bao
Yang.'

The girl who called herself Nan led Jin-mei down
into the lower deck to the sleeping area. She continued
along to the far end.

'More privacy here,' Nan explained.

The berth looked like a low shelf built into the wall
of the ship. There was a small window cut high above
the sleeping area to let light and air through. Other than
that, the sleeping quarters were dim. At the other end of
the deck, Jin-mei could see several men lounging. They
looked ragged, unkempt, lawless and unruly.

When evening came, she would be sleeping inside
a ship full of strange men. Jin-mei shuddered at the
thought.

'I can bring you a curtain, Miss. So you don't have
everyone staring at you.'

Nan watched her as Jin-mei eyed the crew suspi-
ciously. The girl looked no more than fourteen years
of age, though her eyes seemed older. If this tiny reed
of a girl could survive on board, then surely this ship
wasn't such a frightening place. Jin-mei thanked her,

and Nan promptly turned and wove her way back to the upper deck.

She had done it.

Jin-mei finally let out a breath. She had run away. She had reunited with Yang and was on a ship that would take her far from her father's lies and schemes.

But she no longer had a home. A lump formed in her throat. She no longer had a father either.

Broken and exhausted, Jin-mei climbed on to the berth and tucked her belongings into the far corner. There wasn't a lot in the pack she'd bundled up. Jin-mei didn't have much of a plan beyond her escape. She'd brought what little money she possessed, and only a single change of clothes. It had been hard to leave Lady Yi and her brothers, but fleeing was easier than having to face her father.

In the space of one afternoon, he'd completely changed in her eyes. And he'd taken the entire life she knew away with him. Suddenly she was trapped in a lie.

He was a corrupt official. A murderer—well, an attempted murderer since Yang wasn't dead. But how many other crimes had her father been involved in? How many times had she been fooled by his talk of justice?

Jin-mei hooked her arms around her knees and let her head sink on to her arms. There was a slight lurch as the boat began moving along the current. Gradually, she accustomed herself to the feeling of being adrift. She closed her eyes and willed the answers to come to her. What was she going to do now? What next?

'I'm curious.'

Jin-mei jumped up, startled. Yang stood beside the berth with a bundle of cloth beneath his arm. He didn't appear angry at her, or startled the way he had been when she'd first set foot on the ship. As usual, he maintained a steady, slightly bemused expression. She wondered if he always masked his emotions so perfectly.

'I'm curious as to whether you were involved in your father's scheme,' he continued as he draped the sheet over a set of hooks around the sleeping area.

'No, I wasn't,' she murmured. 'I thought you were dead. I...I mourned.'

He paused with his back to her and his arms raised to attach the curtain. She watched the rise and fall of his shoulders as he let out a breath. 'It would probably be best if you went on with your life as if I were dead.'

'It would be best for me never to know the truth?'

It was still a shock to see him alive, but it only proved beyond a doubt her father had tricked her. She was still dressed in her pale mourning robe. The rough cloth scratched against her skin.

'Do you know why he wanted me gone?' Bao Yang's eyes were cold when he turned to face her.

Jin-mei shifted uncomfortably. 'I don't know anything about my father any more.'

Yang remained standing while she sat, staring at her hands. With the curtain in place, they were alone for the first time since their wedding. She could feel her pulse skipping as he continued to stare at her.

'How did you possibly find me, Miss Tan?'

'I saw you outside the drinking house yesterday,' she explained, surprised at how casual they both sounded. 'I knew you'd come by the river and would be looking to leave the same way.'

'Ah, that simple.' He sat down on the berth opposite hers. It was obvious Yang didn't want her here, but presently his demeanour was cordial, even pleasant. 'You didn't run into any trouble travelling alone from the city?'

'I'm dressed as a widow and apparently widows are considered the most unfortunate creatures on this earth. No one troubled me at all.'

'Impressive. But I could have guessed from the moment I met you that you would be resourceful.'

'Why do you say that?'

He smiled. 'Because of the way you lured me beneath that bridge.'

'I didn't.'

Well, she hadn't lured him, but she hadn't exactly been beguiled by him either. Jin-mei had done exactly what she wanted, just as she was doing now by tagging along after him.

'Can you swim?' Yang asked suddenly.

'No.'

He looked thoughtful. 'Oh.'

She stared at him across the sleeping berth. He seemed a bit disappointed, crestfallen even.

'You were thinking of throwing me overboard!' she accused.

'Of course not.'

'If I could swim safely to shore, then you would be absolved of all guilt.'

He made a face as he inspected his nails, but gave no answer.

'You're a scoundrel,' she huffed.

He nodded gravely. 'I know. You should leave me. Preferably at the next port.'

Jin-mei wanted very much to have something to throw at him. 'I'm curious as well,' she replied, in not nearly as pleasant of a tone. 'You don't seem very upset at having your life threatened. Did you and my father conspire to fake your death? Was our marriage a ruse from the beginning?'

Yang frowned. 'I was quite convinced we were married.' He smoothed a hand over the front of his robe. 'I remember looking forward eagerly to our wedding night until your father tried to kill me.'

She let out a shaky breath. It was all her father's doing then. She hadn't been absolutely certain of it until now. Father had hosted the wedding to fool her as well as Yang. He was not a diligent and honest public servant, nor was he the caring and doting father she'd assumed he was.

'Jin-mei, why are you here?' Yang asked, watching her with a serious expression.

'You're my husband,' she replied, her tone flat. 'I go where you go.'

'It's not that simple.'

She looked away from him, towards the wall. 'What if you had been taught from birth that honesty and truth were more important than air and water? What if you had been told there was no sacrifice too great to make for the pursuit of justice? And then one day you found out everything was a lie. Could you stay and pretend that you didn't know?'

With a shuddering breath, she tried to compose herself as the tears threatened to fall. Maybe some small part of her needed to remember what it had been like to be that trusting. To be that innocent. That warm and sheltered place could still exist in her heart, but only if she left it behind. Intact.

'We were both his puppets,' Bao Yang said soberly.

But the difference was she was his daughter. She could never go back and could never see her father again. Because the moment he opened his mouth, she would now know his words meant nothing and what was left of her fragile world would completely shatter.

'This isn't simple,' she echoed. 'This is the hardest decision I've ever made.'

For a long moment, he said nothing. She thought that he might have moved closer to her. She could feel heat rising up the back of her neck at the thought of the two of them being alone together.

'The world of rivers and lakes is a dangerous place,' he warned.

'I've made my decision,' Jin-mei said stubbornly, her voice thick with emotion. It hurt to see the world in this harsh new light. 'So rivers and lakes are what it will be from now on.'

Pulling a spare robe out from her pack, she rolled it to create a pillow and lay down. The lurch of the water kept her from truly resting, and Yang was silent for a long time as he watched her.

'I am very exhausted myself,' he said finally, stretching out on his berth.

'You're staying here?'

He turned just enough to regard her with one eye. 'Of course I am. You're my wife and we're among dangerous individuals.'

She rolled on to her back, staring up at the ceiling while her heart thudded inside her chest. They were only husband and wife in name, and only barely that. Their marriage had not been consummated.

Not too long ago, she had dreamt about being wed to this dashing and successful associate of her father's. The handsome young man with the laughing eyes and the crooked nose. It might very well have been a mistake to follow him, but where else was she to go? A woman belonged to her father first and then her husband. But more importantly, she couldn't stay knowing what she knew about her father. She'd rather risk the danger of bandits and thieves than bite her tongue and pretend that she was still ignorant.

This is an adventure, Jin-mei told herself firmly. One that she hoped she wouldn't regret.

Chapter Six

Jin-mei woke up lying on her back, stiff and unable to move. Where was she? She was confused until the lap of the water against the hull reminded her she was on a river ship.

Rolling on to her side, she saw the berth next to hers was empty. At first she was afraid to venture outside the curtain. She could hear the sounds of the crew moving about on deck. Everyone was in motion, going about their duties, while she alone was sitting still and waiting for—

She wasn't sure what she was waiting for. All she knew was that a proper young lady should probably remain secluded and out of sight of strangers.

After an hour of being proper, she poked her head outside the curtain. The berths were empty and she wandered through the deck. The girl Nan intercepted her at the foot of the stairs.

'Miss, the morning meal is already finished,' she scolded.

With that, the girl beckoned for Jin-mei to follow while she moved on nimble feet through the corridor. The galley and kitchen were located towards the front of the ship. Nan disappeared inside and, after some shouting, returned with a bowl of rice porridge.

'Remember, the first bell always rings at daybreak.' She thrust the bowl into Jin-mei's hands before hurrying off.

Back in her berth, Jin-mei ate alone with the curtain drawn. The rice porridge was thick and flavored with a salted egg. Though it was a simple meal, she took her time finishing it. There was nothing to do once she was done. Loneliness set in like a thick fog around her.

There was no use wallowing in regret. She had left home because she had to. This emptiness would fade with time. She finished her meal and climbed the steps on to the top deck.

Sunlight flooded all around her. A strong breeze filled the sails, and the shore was no more than a sliver in the distance on either side.

A group of crewmen were lined up on the deck and armed with bamboo poles. They appeared to be running through fighting drills, executing strikes and blocks. The eastern barbarian, Kenji, led the men through the exercise while Lady Daiyu watched from the prow.

All around her, everyone had a place and a purpose, either adjusting the ropes on the sails or cleaning the deck. Jin-mei had paid for her passage and could hardly be expected to engage in the upkeep of the ship, yet she found herself wishing she had some task to occupy herself.

Jin-mei took a deep breath and forced herself to approach Kenji. His shadow engulfed her and his hands looked large enough to crush rock.

'May I practise with you, Master Kenji?' she asked.

It was a ridiculous request, but she was in a strange predicament. At first the foreigner didn't even acknowledge her request. It was like speaking to the silent mountains.

'Miss, this is not for show.' He turned his back to her to watch over the drills. 'We are training here.'

Her first inclination was to disappear back into the sleeping quarters and spend the day with a needle and thread, something familiar to her, to calm her nerves. But if she was going to survive outside the four walls of her father's house, she would need to be stronger and bolder. She straightened her shoulders, taking what little extra height it gave her.

'The world of rivers and lakes is a dangerous place,' she said, echoing Yang's words. 'I want to learn how to defend myself.'

Kenjii laughed. Rudely. 'What do you know about rivers and lakes?'

'Be hospitable to our guest.'

The lady captain spoke from the other end of the deck. Yang was at Daiyu's side and he leaned in to tell her something. A knot formed in Jin-mei's stomach at the sight of the two of them standing so closely. The knot pulled tighter as the other woman approached.

Daiyu held out her hand to one of the crewmen and he surrendered his staff to her. She turned the bamboo around in her hands, as if testing its weight, before holding it out to Jin-mei. Tentatively, Jin-mei closed her hands around the pole and tried to mimic how the men were holding it. Yang met her eyes with an amused expression on his face, before turning to look out over the water.

She felt better without him watching. After a brief show of protectiveness the day before, he now seemed to mock her with every look. Lady Daiyu stood beside her, keeping her apart from the men as she corrected Jin-mei's grip on the staff.

'Hands at shoulder-width,' Daiyu instructed. 'Not too wide. It feels more natural that way, does it not?'

Nothing about this felt natural. Jin-mei was standing with the wind blowing around her, the sun beating down on her head, while surrounded by strangers. And she had never held a weapon in her life, not even a kitchen knife.

Before she could learn how to fight, she apparently had to learn how to stand. While the men swung and blocked and parried, all she did was stand there with her shoulders back and knees bent, holding the staff up in front of her.

Even standing still was a challenge. She had to steady herself against the roll of the deck beneath her. Before long, the muscles in her legs and arms were burning and her forehead was damp with perspiration. She had been holding the stance for no more than twenty counts.

She felt like a fool. Not just for joining the practice session, but for everything. But it would be more embarrassing to stop now, especially when Lady Daiyu was taking the time to instruct her.

'If your stance is not strong, your defence will crumble. Your strikes will have no power,' Daiyu said. 'Let us try some blocks.'

The captain retrieved another staff and turned to face her. Yang regarded them over his shoulder and even the surly Kenji stopped to watch.

Daiyu led her through a drill, repeating the same blow while Jin-mei deflected. With each repetition, Jin-mei gained more confidence in the way her body moved. The tiredness receded as her muscles warmed and she stopped thinking about everyone else, blocking out the curious stares of the crew and even Yang's smug look.

'Don't get lost in the rhythm,' Daiyu warned. 'Stay focused.'

Jin-mei winced as Daiyu struck her upper arm with the bamboo. It hurt!

Daiyu altered the pattern, moving slowly and deliberately so Jin-mei would have time to react. Gradually she increased their speed until the techniques flowed naturally. The captain was light on her feet, graceful as well as powerful. How freeing it must be to be able to move like that, with such control and precision.

'What are you looking at?' Daiyu's weapon came down fast. Jin-mei parried at the last moment, with her staff lengthwise and her full weight braced behind it.

'Your eyes,' Jin-mei replied, breathing hard.

That was what Father had always said, wasn't it? The eyes revealed what the mind was hiding.

'My eyes will deceive you,' Daiyu warned her. 'Watch the elbows. The knees. Where they move, the hands and feet must follow.'

Jin-mei raised her staff as Daiyu came at her like a wind storm. She tried to watch her elbows and knees, but it was impossible. The other woman was too quick. Jin-mei deflected two strikes only to have the third crack across her hands. With her knuckles throbbing, she stepped back and held up her hands in surrender.

Daiyu propped the end of her staff against the deck, signalling a pause. 'You move well.'

'No, I don't,' Jin-mei gasped out, irritated. 'You're just saying that to be encouraging.'

The exercise had brought only a slight flush to Daiyu's cheeks beneath her sun-drenched complexion. 'You're right about that, but it is commendable that you wish to learn. Keep practising.'

She threw her staff to Yang, who caught it neatly with one hand.

Jin-mei could still feel the sting of the last blow as

Yang took his place opposite her. His look of amusement was firmly in place.

'Ready?' he asked, raising the bamboo.

She was tired and hot. Too tired and too hot to be embarrassed. On top of that, Jin-mei was annoyed that Yang and Lady Daiyu spoke to one another in sly glances and he seemed so ready to do the woman's bidding.

Shoving her damp hair out of her face, Jin-mei nodded and they began in earnest. He attacked while she tried to defend. His smug expression disappeared as soon as they started practising. Instead, he became focused and serious. He was also a surprisingly attentive instructor. In a lowered voice, he pointed out the openings in her defence and reminded her to keep the staff in front of her at all times.

'Never lower your guard. In a real fight, there is no period of rest.'

'Did you learn how to fight from our captain as well?' she asked acidly.

His expression was inscrutable. 'I think you're not skilled enough yet to talk and fight at the same time.'

'And I think you stand a little too close to that woman.'

'Focus,' was his only response, though as he turned away, he appeared to be biting back a grin.

They went through round after round of drills. Yang wasn't as graceful as Daiyu had been. His movements were rougher, more forceful, though still controlled. Jin-mei also found out that he wasn't being easy on her. The end of the staff slipped past her guard to strike her against the chin. It wasn't at full strength, but the blow was enough to bring tears to her eyes. She reeled backwards, and the bamboo clattered to the deck.

'Always keep your weapon in hand,' Yang lectured

with a glaring lack of sympathy. 'You can't let a graze like that render you defenceless.'

Glaring at him, she rubbed a hand over her chin as he bent to pick up the staff. When he came close, his eyes fixed on to her and his gaze moved over her face to rest on her mouth. The rest of the world receded and, for that moment, Jin-mei no longer felt the sun, the wind, or the throbbing of her jaw.

'Did that hurt?' He leaned forward, reaching out to touch his fingertips lightly to her cheek.

She shook him off. 'No.'

'You should know that anything that was between Lady Daiyu and myself is in the past,' he said quietly. His palms lingered over hers as he placed the weapon back in her hands. The touch resonated down to the pit of her stomach.

She looked up at him, feeling vulnerable for making her jealousy known so openly. His past affairs shouldn't matter. As unconventional as their situation was, she was his wife now. And she was the one he was looking at without blinking. His knowing smile was replaced by a thoughtful expression.

'I've learned something about you, Bao Yang. You like dangerous women, don't you?'

He didn't answer as they returned to their starting positions. She raised her staff, determined not to let him through her guard so easily this time. 'Well, you should know I'm dangerous as well.'

'I believe that,' he said softly. 'I believe that wholeheartedly, Jin-mei.'

After their practice match, Yang disappeared while Jin-Mei's pulse was still racing. She didn't see him anywhere on the main deck and had to descend down below to continue her search. Her skin was still flushed from their sparring. Her muscles ached, but her body had been awakened.

As Jin-mei ducked through the curtain to her sleeping area, she heard her name spoken softly. So low that the sounds resonated against her spine.

'My warrior woman.'

Yang came from the darkness and his arms circled around her. Suddenly she was pressed tight against him.

Their first embrace should have been awkward, all hands and limbs and not knowing how they should be with one another. But as Yang pulled her close, her body moulded to his. Her lips parted to say something. She didn't know what, but it didn't matter because she was caught in a kiss that was hard and urgent and made her knees go soft.

'Yang.'

She meant for the utterance to be a protest or at least a question, but it came out the sigh of his name, deep in her throat and unexpectedly sensual. She had never been kissed like this before. She had never been kissed at all. His mouth pressed against hers, urging her response with so much passion that there was no opportunity to doubt or question. It was like the rush she'd felt during their match, but so much faster and stronger. By the time their lips parted, her head was spinning.

'Hold on to me,' he said.

Her hands grasped the front of his robe while she stared at him, confused. Her heart was beating hard and every part of her felt flushed.

'Hold on to me,' he repeated in a low murmur against her earlobe. He bit into the soft flesh, and heat flooded her veins.

Jin-mei hooked her arms around his neck and held

on tight. If she hadn't, she would have crumbled to the floor. He lifted her with his arm secured around her waist and another hooked beneath her knees. The ship spun around her. She found herself with her back against the hard wood of the berth, though it somehow seemed more welcoming with Yang's weight pressed against her, shoulder to hip. *Made to fit one another*, Lady Yi had told her.

He was kissing her again, his tongue stroking over her lips. She thought of the bronze mirror and the bodies clasped so wickedly together. But what he did next took her completely by surprise.

Yang touched his lips tenderly to her chin. 'You're going to have a bruise here, darling,' he said, trailing a path of kisses along her jaw as soft as flowers on the wind.

She could feel the desire that vibrated through him, pulling each muscle taut and darkening his eyes. His chest heaved above her. Though he had appeared controlled and indifferent during the sparring match, he was consumed now with hunger.

'Do you mean to make up for our lost wedding night?' she asked breathlessly.

He met her eyes with a heated look before taking her mouth again. With Yang, kissing wasn't merely the touching of lips, but so much more. Breath and pulse and taste, sweet as honey and wicked as wine. It was a kiss that started things.

But he pulled away. She tried to follow, straining up towards him, but Yang held her back against the berth.

'We aren't alone,' he protested, though his fingers worked at the knot of her sash. 'And I don't know how loud you are in bed…yet.'

Such scandalous things he said. She wanted to hear more. 'Then why are you removing my clothes?'

'You looked very warm outside,' he replied, fixing his gaze on the opening of her tunic. He pulled back just the edge of the grey cloth to reveal her bodice. 'Ah, blue,' he declared with an air of satisfaction. 'I thought I might have seen a hint of silk while you were acting the warrior woman. I nearly dropped the staff.'

'You're lying.'

'Some lies are completely acceptable. Stay quiet a little longer, dear.' He barely gave her warning before pulling the bodice down and closing his mouth over her nipple in a warm, wet caress that made her back lift off the berth. She closed her eyes in abandon as every sense within her awakened. She was a puppet on a string and willingly so.

Yang certainly didn't believe in slow, gentle introductions. Not while sparring and not in this either. He pleasured her with his mouth, flicking her nipple mercilessly until she wanted to beg. As scandalous as the figures on the mirror were, this was so much worse. So much better. Yang teased her with lips, tongue, then the light scrape of teeth over her flesh that made her sob. She couldn't stop the sound, even when she bit hard on her lower lip.

Suddenly the pleasure ceased.

'Not here.' His voice was rough. 'Not like this.'

'Why not like this?' They were husband and wife and she was burning inside, every part of her alive and wanting.

Yang watched her with a thoughtful expression. She could see the rapid rise and fall of his chest and hear the catch in his breath. His mouth was no further than a kiss away.

'There are many things you don't know about me,' he insisted. 'Things you should know.'

She rose to a sitting position and placed her hand flat

against his chest. His heart pounded against her fingertips, steady and strong. Holding her breath, she trailed
her hand downwards and a dark look flickered in his
eyes. The corners of his mouth lifted, but the smile froze
as she pressed against the hard outline just above his
waist.

A knife. She'd thought she felt something when they
were crushed together.

'Do you always have this on you?'

'Always.'

Yang closed his hand over hers and moved it away
from the weapon before letting her go. It was enough to
remind them both of the treacherous circumstances that
had brought them together. For a moment, they both sat
at different ends of the berth, no longer touching while
they gathered their thoughts. She righted her clothing
and closed the front of her robe. Yang's gaze wandered
downward, she thought with a look of regret, before returning to her face.

'Is this a pirate ship?' she asked finally.

'No, but there are frequent pirate attacks on these
waters.'

No wonder everyone was armed and ready to fight.
Even Lady Daiyu and the girl Nan. It was the first time
she had seen women with weapons in their belts.

Jin-mei swallowed, gathering her breath for the next
question. 'Are you a smuggler?'

'I'm in the salt trade,' he answered pleasantly. 'The
private salt trade.'

Suddenly his wealth made complete sense as well as
his visits to her father over the years. Salt smuggling
was rampant throughout the province, fed with a chain
of payoffs and negotiations and bribes to imperial officials who also profited. Father had told her that there

was more illegal salt sold than sanctioned salt. She had just always assumed he wasn't part of the corruption.

'I went back to the villa where we were married,' she began. 'There was a hollow in the wall of one of the rooms—I found blood on the floor.'

'The assassin who had been hired to kill me,' he answered without hesitation. 'I killed him first.'

Her throat went painfully dry. 'But there was no body when I came.'

'Your father must have had the body removed for which I am grateful. I wouldn't have wanted you to see that.'

Her father had served as magistrate in Minzhou for many years now, yet he was the worst criminal of them all. The thought of it made her heartsick.

Jin-mei wrapped her arms around herself, as if she could hold the pieces together. 'Is it difficult? Killing a man?'

He let out a sigh. 'We shouldn't speak of this.'

'Did my father try to kill you to silence you?'

'Enough, Jin-mei.'

There was no use remaining quiet any more. 'Don't you want revenge for what happened? You won't report my father for what he did?'

'Report him to whom? Who would take my word over the honourable Magistrate Tan?'

Perhaps not the word of a privateer, but the officials would take the word of a magistrate's daughter. She couldn't speak out against her father when she knew it would mean his execution. Yet she couldn't stay silent and remain his dutiful daughter either. Another reason she had to go.

'I can't afford to make an enemy of your father,' Yang went on. He paused to consider his words. 'To make *more* of an enemy of him than I already have. It's best that he and I go our separate ways.'

She fell silent for a long time after that. When she finally spoke, it was with an air of determination. 'Your path is my path as well, from here on forward.'

'Jin-mei—' he started, then stopped, pausing to search for words. 'You're a reasonable woman. You know this is a poor decision. *I'm* a poor decision.'

Yang hadn't stopped himself from making love to her just because of the time or the place, she realised. He didn't want to tie the two of them irrevocably together.

'You're still trying to be rid of me,' she said bluntly.

'What I wonder is why you're not trying to be rid of me,' he countered.

'Because I chose you.'

He snorted at that, and Jin-mei glared at him. If she had a bamboo staff now, he would have been the one nursing a bruise as well as a cracked skull.

'I chose you that day in the park,' she said firmly.

It was true she was sheltered. Her father had protected her and kept her away from the harsh realities of the world. But now that her eyes were open, she needed to decide what to do. Return home and pretend as if nothing had happened? Or move forward into the unknown? If it was the latter, she wasn't going to do it with Yang mocking her.

'I'm not as easily tempted or as blind as you think. And I've never been reckless, yet within moments of meeting you, I followed you alone into the shadows. I knew what the consequences might be.'

'I remember.'

His gaze was dark on her, and she could feel her skin warming. 'How did you do it?' she asked curiously.

From what she remembered, Yang hadn't used any

sweet words or been particularly persuasive. He certainly hadn't tried to kiss her which she now knew would have had her clinging to him. Her cheeks flushed hot and she tried to ignore them.

'I've always had a natural skill.' A line appeared between Yang's eyes, as if he was trying to figure it out himself. 'I spoke with a potter once. He said that he could feel the clay and sense where it was pliable, where it would bend and move. It's the same thing, feeling your way gently with words, with touch, finding the way a person wants to move.'

'And pushing them in that direction,' she finished for him.

'I only asked you to do what you already wanted to do.' He didn't seem happy about that conclusion.

She had wanted to make an impression on him that day. She had wanted him to think of her as important, so Yang had made her the most important person to him in that moment. *Your life is in my hands*, he'd said.

'You didn't lie to me,' she pointed out. 'And you haven't lied to me since.'

He had been starkly honest about everything from the beginning; the illegal source of his family's wealth, his hand in salt smuggling, and her father's true nature. She had to believe he had been sincere in his intentions to marry her. She also believed in the concern he was showing for her now.

'So I choose to go where you go,' Jin-mei concluded. 'Or if you won't have me, then I'll find my own way. But I'm not going back to my father.'

Chapter Seven

Yang inspected the map laid out over the table in the main cabin. The rivers and waterways were etched in dark lines over the landscape. Lady Daiyu stood beside him, her arm just brushing his sleeve as she pointed out a juncture where a tributary joined the main waters of the Min.

'Our next stop is here. We might be able to find a shipment to take all the way to Sanming.'

He shook his head. 'That port is a snake's nest. We can't leave her there.' He followed the thin line of ink upstream. 'What about here? That's a respectable town. I can find someone to take her back to her family.'

'Impossible. The port authority there is known for being strict. They'll board us as soon as we drop anchor. We can make a stop at Stone Pavilion Crossing.'

Another wasteland. Yang moved away from the map to slump down on to the wooden settee.

'You *are* conspiring against me,' he accused. He picked up his tea and drank it with ill humour.

'Circumstances are conspiring against you,' she corrected. 'You're too soft-hearted to abandon your lady in an unregulated port and it's too risky for us to go where some diligent official is going to try to confiscate my ship and have you arrested.'

'Anchor the ship at a safe distance and I'll take her inland by boat,' he suggested. 'And I'll pay you for the trouble.'

'With what money?' Daiyu made a show of looking at her hands, turning them over and then back to show empty palms. He was a fugitive now and low on funds.

'You know you can trust me for it.'

She shook her head, a coy smile on her lips. Daiyu had never had any problems accepting his word in the past. She was indeed conspiring to keep him and his wife together.

'The girl reminds me of myself twenty years ago,' she admitted.

Retrieving her tea from the table, she sat down beside him. Her profile was striking with the high arch of her nose and the well-defined contours of her cheekbones. The two women were nothing alike. Daiyu was sharp and tough with a will made of iron. Her figure had the same whip-thin quality, almost harsh in its beauty. Jin-mei was soft, small in the waist and full in the hip. She was wide-eyed and innocent and as lost as a sparrow blown off course by a storm.

Yet for all her outward softness, Jin-mei possessed a rather sharp tongue. He had to admit, he was quite taken with it.

'Have you considered that it might be useful to keep her with you?' Daiyu asked.

'Once we head north, I'll be in constant hiding from General Wang's forces. It's no life for a lady.'

And Jin-mei certainly was a lady. He might have been a suitable match for her years ago, but he'd been living a lie then. Gathering wealth and influence as if it was enough to make him worthy.

'You can pretend to be married. Wang's soldiers are less likely to suspect a man travelling with his wife.'

'Jin-mei is already my wife,' he said drily.

Daiyu's eyes flashed with amusement. 'It must be fate then. You have a better chance of appearing respectable with her at your side. And I have a sense that she's audacious enough to figure out what to say in a rough situation.'

He recalled Jin-mei climbing on to the deck with her hair in damp strands about her face and barely able to catch her breath. Yet she'd stood tall and attempted to sound worldly as she'd negotiated her passage on to the ship.

'There's one very important reason Jin-mei can't stay with me,' he said soberly. 'Everyone who knows me is in danger.'

And those who trusted him would suffer the worst of it.

Daiyu's smile faded. 'Your concern is touching. But your young wife seems to have made up her mind.'

He had always had a skill for making connections and forming alliances, but lately he had an affinity for making enemies out of friends. Magistrate Tan wanted his head now as well as General Wang. He wasn't in a particular mood to appease Tan by returning his daughter, but Jin-mei didn't belong out in the world of dust and roads and outlaws. The sort of women he befriended were like Lady Daiyu.

Dangerous women, Jin-mei had accused. He smiled, thinking of how she had faced him so defiantly. There was no denying she was as crafty as her father.

'You're thinking of her,' Daiyu remarked, seeing his grin.

He closed his eyes and reclined his head back on the seat. 'Yes.'

'I never thought you would be married to someone so…well mannered.'

'Well mannered?' He opened one eye to peer at her. 'She was up on deck swinging a bamboo stick at me.'

'But I could tell she was a gentlewoman. She wielded the staff so…politely. How did such a thing happen between the two of you?'

'I think she tricked me into it.' He closed his eyes again. She had been fearless beneath the bridge that day. So lovely. 'Or I tricked her into it. I don't know.'

Daiyu laughed. 'It would have had to happen like that.'

Jin-mei. Spirited little Jin-mei with her soft curves and sharp tongue. Every once in a while, Yang dreamed of living a respectable life and maybe she was part of that dream.

'Can she stay with you?' he asked. 'I'll come back for her once…once all this is done.'

She made a scoffing noise.

'If I don't return, you can ransom her back to her father.'

'You're a snake-tongued demon,' Daiyu scolded.

Maybe he was. He didn't even know what respectable was any more.

'Do you think it's any safer aboard this ship than with you? Piracy is rampant on the Min and the past year has brought hard times for everyone. There are days when Kenji can barely maintain order.'

'Kenji is the one you should be worried about,' Yang said with a scowl. 'It's dangerous to have another authority aboard your ship with his own men to command.'

He stopped himself as Daiyu eyed him over the rim of her teacup. It was her ship, her decisions. Daiyu was also correct that the only way he could protect Jin-mei was to keep her by his side. But Yang didn't have a friend in the world who wasn't dangerous and now he was suffering the consequences of that.

Jin-mei didn't understand what it meant to stay by his side. He was in constant danger, and he'd brought it upon himself. He couldn't burden himself with worrying about Jin-mei. With caring for someone who was vulnerable and innocent and had no place in his treacherous world. If he lost another soul to it, it would destroy him.

Jin-mei was starting to become accustomed to life on the ship, following the wind and water. Every day when she woke up, the view from the bow had changed. Water was drawn from the river for washing and baths and nets were set out to catch fish to feed the crew. With the triple masts and adjustable sails, the ship was always able to find a breeze to propel it forward, cutting through the river efficiently.

Most mornings, she would lean upon the bow to watch the shore go by in a blur of green and brown. Hours would pass like the blink of an eye.

She did the same today, thinking of how her father would worry about her. Perhaps some time in the future, when the pain was not so sharp, she would write a letter to him to tell him she was safe.

'It's calming, isn't it?' Daiyu was suddenly beside her. 'The breeze, the water, the sun above.'

'Yes,' Jin-mei lied, but then felt bad for doing it, so she added a truth. 'The river is very beautiful. It's no wonder why you've chosen to make your home on it.'

'It's not always an easy existence, but it's a blessed one. A life of freedom.' The captain breathed deep and rested an arm over the bow with a proprietary air.

The truth was Jin-mei was sore from the hard wood of the sleeping berths. The food consisted of the same gruel of rice porridge and salted fish nearly every day unless the nets brought in a good catch, in which case the salted fish was replaced with fresh fish. Yet, despite a little discomfort, she was grateful for the haven of the ship.

For the moment, the world outside the river didn't exist. It floated by. Here, she was someone else. A reckless young wanderer who could boldly practise staff fighting alongside men in the mornings and stay up late into the evening to watch the glow of distant lanterns from other boats.

'We'll be docking tomorrow at the Peaceful Waters Bridge, at the juncture of two rivers. It's a busy port. We'll only be ashore for a few hours, but it'll be time enough for you to procure any necessities.'

'Thank you for allowing me on to your ship. And for your hospitality.'

The other woman shrugged. 'You've paid for it. Paid very well, I might add.'

But Lady Daiyu had been kind to her from the start when she had no reason to be.

'How did you come to be captain?' Jin-mei asked, too curious to hold back. 'Every man on board obeys your command.'

'This was my husband's ship.' The corners of her mouth lifted though her eyes were sad. 'When he passed away five years ago, it became mine. I could have sold it and found some small village to live out my years, but I had been on the river long enough for it to seduce me.'

Jin-mei looked back out on to the water. 'You must think me weak to chase after Bao Yang like a lovesick maiden.'

'I don't think that of you at all. I worked in a brothel before taking to the river. My husband was a paying customer then, one who liked to proclaim his deep affections for me whenever he was in town.'

A streak of heat rose up the back of Jin-mei's neck while she tried to contain her embarrassment. Lady Daiyu had no need for bronze mirrors with amorous engravings to instruct her.

'One day, when his ship was set to sail, I took my belongings and ran away from the brothel to join him. I chose my own destiny.' Daiyu faced her. 'So you see, I couldn't turn you away when you came to me. In a way, we are like sisters.'

But the difference was that Daiyu had fled a life of servitude for one of freedom. Jin-mei had left a life of privilege behind.

'I didn't come all this way only to follow my husband,' Jin-mei confessed.

The breeze blew through Daiyu's hair, brushing it back from her face. Strength resonated through every line and curve. 'Neither did I.'

The wooden bridge spanning the breadth of the river overlooked a busy port which was crowded with transport boats and smaller fishing vessels. Beyond the dock area, Jin-mei could see several lanes of shops and buildings. A bustling town had emerged, feeding off traffic from the river.

Yang disembarked before her and waited at the end of the plank. Jin-mei set foot on solid earth for the first time in days and stared at the crowd at a loss.

'Say nothing to anyone,' he warned, scanning the crowd. 'Your father could have informants here.'

His stride was confident as he pushed forward, as if he navigated such ports all the time. She supposed he did as a salt merchant. Or a privateer...or whatever he was.

They passed by a two-storey building with a green-tiled roof and windows draped with pink curtains. Two ladies in gauze robes with red painted lips greeted men as they walked by. Jin-mei was entranced, so much so that she had fallen behind and hurried to catch up with Yang.

'Mister...Yang,' she began.

It would be strange to call him Mister Bao now that they were married, but she didn't yet feel comfortable enough to address him as 'Husband.' Her awkward compromise was worse than either of the other two forms of address.

'Jin-mei.' Yang smiled at her as if nothing was amiss.

'There are some...matters I need to attend to.' Her pause should explain enough. These were private things, womanly things.

He looked uncertain at first, but relented. 'Nan can go with you. Do not forget the ship will sail at the start of the next double hour. Our lady captain has no qualms about leaving stragglers behind.'

They made arrangements to meet at the dock before parting ways. Little Nan took her side without complaint.

'Have you been here before?' Jin-mei asked.

'Once, Miss. But all of these dockside towns are the same.'

'Do you know where I might find a place to sell some things?'

'A pawnshop, you mean?' Nan glanced about before stopping a passer-by to ask for directions.

The girl was so confident walking the streets among strangers. Jin-mei had lived in many different places due to Father's various promotions and appointments, but her knowledge was nothing compared to Nan's experience.

'One lane over,' the girl said, already moving in that direction.

Jin-mei followed after her, finding it a little odd to be reliant on someone so young as her guide. But as the girl cut through the crowd, Jin-mei took special note of her demeanour. She moved with purpose, without hesitation. No one questioned her presence or gave her more than a quick glance even though she was young and small. There was a lesson to be learned there.

The signboard in front of the pawnshop was decorated with a dragon carving. A string of coins hung from his mouth. The owner greeted them from behind a counter as they entered the modestly sized shop.

Jin-mei pulled a robe from the pack slung around her shoulder. 'Sir, how much for this?'

Her wedding money as well as a few dowry items were securely bundled in the pack, but she didn't know how long this journey would take or what else she'd require.

He expertly rubbed the material between two fingers. 'Twenty cash.'

'It's quality silk,' she insisted without flinching. Nan glanced at her with interest from the corner before turning her attention back to the shelf.

'Yes, but there's not a lot of use for quality like this here.'

'With so many travellers passing through, Uncle? And silk is as good as silver.'

'She wants silver now, hmm?' the owner remarked, but he smiled crookedly.

Father had come from peasant folk and had been skilled at the art of negotiation. She had learned a few things herself. This was a private merchant as opposed to a government-run establishment. There was certainly more room to haggle.

She countered with a higher price, determined not to be taken advantage of simply because she was a woman. Pawnshops were notorious for paying women less than men.

'And a few items here in trade,' she added, gesturing towards the counter of discarded goods.

The owner raised his scraggly eyebrows at her, but she knew he'd agree to it. Silk could be exchanged readily for money, whereas those forgotten items were difficult to resell for any value at all.

'You're practically stealing from me,' he complained, which she knew wasn't true. It was standard banter for any shop.

Finally they agreed on a price, and Jin-mei palmed her coins before selecting a plain tunic woven from hemp and cotton and loose trousers. The colours were drab without any adornment at all, but the garments appeared sturdy without tears or holes. Yang seemed to be masquerading as a peasant and these would match his level of dress better than her silk.

Next they found a bathhouse, and Jin-mei spared an extra coin for Nan. Together they soaked in the steaming waters of the communal pool.

'I knew you were a fancy lady from the look of you.' Nan hadn't stopped grinning since the pawnshop. Jin-mei suspected the girl found her endlessly amusing.

'How long have you lived on the ship?' Jin-mei asked.

'Many years now, Miss. Lady Daiyu was a friend of

my mother's. She took me in after my mother fell sick and died.'

Nan spoke as if losing her mother were just something that had happened, as if it were nothing at all, yet Jin-mei still felt a small tug in her chest. 'I lost my mother when I was young too.'

The girl shrugged. 'It was a long time ago. I don't remember her much.'

They lingered in the steam for half an hour, luxuriating in silence and solitude. On a river boat, one was never alone. Jin-mei felt her muscles relaxing and loosening in the bath. For the first time since running away from home, the tension left her shoulders, and she dared to think of the future.

She was with her husband now. They would travel to the other side of the province and begin a new life.

Perhaps this was a good time to send a message to her father. A port town like this one must have a relay station. If not, she could hire a messenger to bring her letter to one.

After a moment's consideration, Jin-mei decided against it. There was no predicting what Father would do if he found them. And what other atrocious crimes had he committed that she knew nothing about?

In Father's study, there was a scroll on the wall with only two characters painted on it. He always brought it with him when they moved. Once, when she was little, Jin-mei asked what they said.

'Good fortune,' Father told her. 'I've always been lucky. Lucky to marry your mother. Lucky to pass the exams.'

He always chuckled when he said it and much later she learned why. Father was lying. The characters weren't the ones for 'good fortune.' Together, those two characters meant 'persistence.'

Jin-mei had come to understand that her father made his own luck. Now she would do the same.

As they left the bathhouse, Kenji stormed around the corner. Nan tensed beside her at the sight of the rugged warrior. Her easy smile from earlier was replaced by a wary look.

'Where have you been?' His expression was grim beneath his beard.

'We were told to be back at the dock at the end of the hour,' Jin-mei protested with as much politeness as she could summon in the face of such a brute.

Kenji snorted. 'We need to leave now; captain's orders. Where's Bao?'

Jin-mei looked helplessly at Nan who could only look helplessly back at her. Yang hadn't told her where he was going, and she hadn't asked.

Kenji didn't wait for an answer before marching off and they had no choice but trail after him through the streets, fighting with their shorter strides to keep up with his long ones. Wherever he went, the townsfolk quickly stepped aside.

'Is something wrong?' Jin-mei asked to Kenji's back, but Nan shook her head to hush her. Apparently the giant simply got his way when he was in a mood such as this one.

'Bao Yang might be at a tea house,' she suggested. 'Or a wine shop.'

Kenji ignored her suggestions and went directly to the two-storey building with the coloured banners that they had passed earlier. The plaque over the front door read, 'The Pavilion of the Singing Nightingale.' Kenji disappeared inside while Jin-mei stopped at the threshold. Surely a pleasure house was no place for a lady.

Nan stayed beside her as they peered into the interior. The furnishings were opulent, garishly so. Jin-mei recognised they were made to look expensive by layers of lacquer and paint. The brushwork paintings on the wall were similarly ostentatious. Imitations of more famous works done with a heavy hand. And she supposed the liberal use of red lanterns was meant to invoke an atmosphere of celebration.

Yang appeared with, predictably, one of the pleasure-house courtesans on his arm. Her robe was barely a robe and her shoulders were scandalously bare, with nothing but a thin shawl of gauze over them. Kenji barked something at him while Yang moved forward as calm as ever.

He disengaged himself from the courtesan, taking her hand in his as he removed it from his arm. Then he turned, and Jin-mei met his gaze from the doorway. She made a point of narrowing her eyes at him.

As soon as Yang was out the door, he took her arm, just as he'd done with the courtesan. His cheek brushed against her hair as he leaned in close. 'You smell nice.'

Her hair was still damp from the bath. It had been combed and pinned in a chignon that was fitting for a married woman.

'You smell like cheap perfume,' she told him through her teeth. 'A lot of it. It's giving me a headache.'

'She's a friend,' he explained, which only made Jin-mei grit her teeth harder. 'She had news for me. A messenger arrived in town just yesterday. Magistrate Tan has notified the authorities in three counties to be on the lookout for us.'

'Which is why we need to go now,' Kenji said.

So they went, hurrying back on to the ship to set sail.

'She was just a friend,' Yang insisted once more as they pulled away from the shore.

Jin-mei snorted. 'You seem to have a lot of friends.'

Chapter Eight

'You should know, I didn't go to the courtesan at the Nightingale Pavilion for companionship.'

Yang had taken Jin-mei above deck after the evening meal to the stern of the ship where they might have some privacy. Three days had passed since they'd left the river junction. A favourable wind had picked up and they were making good time.

'It is not for me to say a thing if you had,' Jin-mei remarked curtly, her mouth pursed. 'I'm not a controlling sort of wife.'

'You're just the sort of wife who has her husband killed and flees to the river,' he noted with a grin. She looked pointedly out to the water which was much calmer than her mood that evening. Her shoulder jutted out towards him, clearly unwelcoming.

'I went to Lotus strictly for information,' he went on.

'Oh, is that her name?' she asked breezily.

Jin-mei was certainly a spirited creature. There would never be a dull moment between them should they ever be able to settle in as husband and wife. They would be eighty years old and still sparring with one another.

The thought sobered him. Though they had been wed,

they had yet to share a marital bed. He was hesitant to bind her to him, though the reason had nothing to do with courtesans or other women. He only wished their obstacles were so mundane.

'Your father is not the only person I need to avoid,' he began. 'Lotus told me there's a price on my head. A rather generous price.'

She turned and her gaze narrowed on him warily.

'You should know everything, Jin-mei. Several months ago, I attempted to kill a very powerful man; the warlord Wang Shizhen. I failed and now he wants revenge. He has the power to take away everything I hold dear.'

She frowned. 'Then why did you take the risk?'

'Hatred.' He smiled crookedly, but it was a cold expression. 'What else could make a rational man act so impulsively? You can step carefully all your life, but one mistake can take it all away. Everyone I know, everything I touch, is now in danger.'

He could see her thinking, considering the weight of what he'd revealed to her. It was his hope that she was rational enough to leave on her own. They were far enough away that her father couldn't immediately track him and by the next river bend they would be within General Wang's domain. It was time for a decision.

'There is a temple not far from here. Secluded enough that you can remain there safely. General Wang has no knowledge that I've married, so we can send word to your father—'

'No.'

'It's a Taoist temple,' he continued persuasively. 'Less strict than a Buddhist monastery.'

Her gaze narrowed.

'Your father is no worse a man than I am,' Yang pointed out.

'Have you ever used those closest to you in your schemes? Betrayed their trust?' she challenged.

Her words were an attack, though not directed at him.

'No. I haven't,' he replied soberly.

'Then you're not the traitor my father is.' She swung back to the horizon, her soft features as hard as he'd ever seen them.

Her conclusion didn't absolve him. His brother and sister had known exactly who he was: over-ambitious, a swindler, a bastard. He had even claimed that everything he did was for the sake of the family, but nothing they said could stop him from leading them into ruin. An honest bastard was still a bastard.

There was a reason he preferred dangerous women, as Jin-mei had stated. His pursuits were risky and his own life always in danger. The women and truly all the people he associated with were ones who could handle themselves. No matter how wilful she was, Jin-mei was a proper lady who had been sheltered and protected, though she was fierce in her own way. And stubborn as well. The more he refused, the more she'd insist. If he abandoned her, she would track him down as she'd done before, putting herself in more danger.

'If you won't go to the temple, then we have a side trip to make in two days' time,' he told her, setting the argument aside for the moment. 'We'll travel on foot. The roads will be small and not well marked.'

'Just you and I?'

'Just the two of us.' He didn't know if she was nervous at the prospect of being alone with him or travelling out on the open road in such an isolated area. 'I don't expect trouble, but one should always be careful when travelling.'

She was thinking, considering the possibilities. As headstrong as she was, Jin-mei was also practical. 'Where are we going?' she asked finally.

'To see my younger brother and his family. There's also a gathering of sorts nearby. Some people I've arranged to meet.' He wasn't certain of how to explain the second part, but fortunately Jin-mei didn't seem to notice his hesitation.

'I didn't know you had a brother,' she said, her face brightening.

He nodded. 'Tien is much smarter than I.'

'Did you bully him as a child?'

'Of course.'

She laughed, and he could see how her expression grew soft and wistful at the mention of family. The knots in his stomach relaxed as well and an iron weight lifted from his chest. Had they truly spoken of nothing but plots and schemes since they'd met? He took in a cleansing breath and found the air was cool and damp from the river.

'If your brother is the clever one, then you must be the handsome one,' Jin-mei said with a sly glint in her eye.

'To your good fortune, being my wife.'

He leaned against the bow beside her, as close as he possibly could without touching. She closed that last small gap between them as she shifted. She kept her eyes focused in the distance while her arm brushed against his in a touch that could have been inadvertent, but wasn't. His heart beat faster.

Even scoundrels could dream.

'What are those lights?'

'River pavilions,' he replied. 'They're built to mark

ferry crossings or turbulent waters. Lanterns are hung at the top of the tower to light the way for boats on the river.'

Her voice floated over him as if in a dream. 'So they warn of danger ahead.'

'Or provide guidance and shelter for travellers. Some are thought to house friendly spirits.'

'Can we visit one some day?'

'Some day,' he promised.

She seemed satisfied with that.

They were speaking of nothing really. Yet Yang breathed easier than he had in a long time. A slow, spreading warmth filled his chest.

There could be an advantage to having a wife by his side when he went to see his brother. Jin-mei gave him some semblance of respectability. As if he were any other man who still had a chance at happiness.

The ship dropped anchor beside a wooded area. Lady Daiyu came to see them off, but she bypassed Yang with barely a glance in his direction. Instead, she approached Jin-mei and handed her a bamboo staff along with a few whispered words. Jin-mei nodded, accepting whatever advice had been given quite seriously.

For some reason, the scene made Yang uneasy. The two women were his former lover and...and he supposed his wife. The thought was still new to him.

'We'll meet three days from now at the Stone Pavilion Crossing,' was all Lady Daiyu had for him. 'Don't delay.'

Jin-mei held on to his arm with an iron grip as he helped her into the boat attached to the side of the ship. They would need to be rowed ashore.

'My brother and his wife have a child,' Yang said by way of distraction as the crew began to lower the ropes.

'Oh?' She was making a concerted effort to not look down.

'She should be two or three years old by now.'

'When was the last time you went to visit your brother?'

'Years ago,' he managed after too long a pause. He hadn't expected the ache in his chest. 'I sent along a gift when their child was born.'

'I look forward to meeting them.'

Jin-mei mercifully stopped asking questions after that. His brother Tien had sent along a brief letter to inform him when the child was one month of age. Yang had replied with a much longer message accompanied by a generous amount of silver for Tien and his wife. Yang had taken an entire evening composing the letter which emphasised their bond as brothers and the importance of family. He'd invited his brother and his wife back to live in their home town, so that their children could one day play together. Of course, Yang had no plans for a wife or family then, but it had seemed the sort of notion that would appeal to Tien.

His attempt to finally make peace had gone unanswered.

The boat was on the water now and Jin-mei exhaled slowly. The crewmen released the ropes and began rowing towards shore.

'What did Lady Daiyu say to you back on the ship?' he asked.

'Womanly things,' she replied cryptically.

The current was gentle in this part of the river and they reached the bank without incident. Yang had deliberately chosen to come ashore in a secluded location where they wouldn't be detected. The two of them set off into the woods.

'Have you been this way before?' Jin-mei asked, hefting her pack on to her shoulder. He held out a hand to take it from her, but she declined.

'Once. The closest village is a few hours' walk from here, but my brother lives beyond it, on a secluded strip of land that belonged to our ancestors.'

'He doesn't work in the family business?'

'The family *shipping* business?' he asked pleasantly. She narrowed her eyes at him.

'Tien preferred to go out on his own,' Yang replied.

Only Yang remained to oversee the salt wells that the family had built their fortune on. He still sent money to his brother several times a year, but it was met with the same resounding silence.

Yang set a steady pace. Jin-mei followed alongside him, using the bamboo staff as a walking stick and keeping up without complaint, even when she was breathing hard.

At midday, when the sun was highest, they stopped beside a well to draw water and take a meal. Several flat boulders had been moved near the well to provide a place to sit, and Jin-mei sank on to one with a sigh.

'I can see why your brother would want to come here,' Jin-mei said. 'It's peaceful. A place away from all the headaches of the world.'

She tilted her head to listen and he did the same, hearing the buzz of cicada song from the surrounding trees. They unwrapped the bundles of rice and fish wrapped in lotus leaves that the ship's cook had steamed that morning. While they ate, Yang had a chance to watch her.

A scarf was tied over Jin-mei's hair and she wore a grey tunic and slippers. The clothing itself might pass for a peasant's garb, but her complexion was pale and smooth and she appeared too well fed and soft for a woman of the lower class.

'You can't run away for ever, Jin-mei,' he said finally.

She kept her head down as she cracked and peeled a longan. 'Do you ever intend to see my father again?'

'Of course not.' Magistrate Tan had plotted to kill him.

'Then if I stay by your side, I can indeed run away for ever,' she replied matter-of-factly, handing him the half-peeled fruit.

He bit into the longan. The juice of it was sweet on his tongue. 'I'm a means to an end, then.'

Jin-mei shrugged. Wriggling her slipper loose, she rubbed at the sole of her foot. The gesture was unexpectedly erotic; the sight of a pale foot and bared ankle, offset by a startling glimpse of colour on her toes. Her nails were painted in a red lacquer and he was beset once again by images of what could have been on their wedding night.

When he looked again, the slipper was back on. Yang let out a breath, more than a little disappointed to no longer be glancing at a delicate foot and wondering exactly why he was fighting so hard not to make Jin-mei his wife in every way.

Chapter Nine

The sun was nearing the horizon, casting the sky in an orange light when they reached the old wood mill. The river that had once fed it had dried to a small stream. Long ago, Yang's ancestors had abandoned the property rather than digging the ditches and canals that would have been required to keep the mill in use.

The building was a family dwelling now, surrounded by patches of vegetables. A young woman knelt among the rows with a basket. Beside her was a girl with a stick in hand, digging in the dirt. The woman and child stood at once, regarding him with wide eyes. The girl held a dirt-covered radish. The woman was slender in frame, but with a strength that came from toil.

'Shou-yun,' Yang called to the young mother by name.

It took a moment for recognition to light up her face. 'Bao Yang! How have you been, Brother?' Then she looked at Jin-mei expectantly.

He exchanged a glance with Jin-mei before speaking. 'Tan Jin-mei. My wife.'

'Little Ling, greet your aunt and uncle properly,' Shou-yun instructed.

The girl bowed politely, her hands still covered in dirt.

She was a beguiling creature, with dark eyes and hair that was tied in a wispy topknot. Embarrassingly, she was also much older than the two years he had assumed.

More time had passed than Yang had realised. Perhaps in his mind, he'd tried to remove the distance between him and his brother.

Shou-yun set aside her gardening and invited them inside. Little Ling hurried to wash her hands in a basin while her mother lit an oil lamp. Yang and Jin-mei were left standing uncertainly inside the door.

The interior of the mill was a single room. Some of the stonework and structures that had once been part of the mill were still intact, but the furnishings of his brother's home had been laid around them. There was a sleeping area off to one side and a storage area in the back.

'Come in.' Shou-yun waved them forward and gestured towards the stools at a low table. She ladled water into a pot and set it on to the cooking stove, presumably for tea. 'We didn't know you'd be coming, Elder Brother. Tien will be surprised.'

Not happy, Yang noted. Surprised. 'Have you been receiving my letters?'

'Yes, yes. My husband reads each one.' There was a forced brightness to her tone. 'We are always very grateful to receive them.'

Shou-yun was the daughter of a tradesman from their hometown. Her parents had assumed she'd married into wealth when she joined the Bao family. Instead she lived in squalor, all because of the rift between Yang and his brother. The sight of the rundown mill left a hollow pit of shame in his stomach. He wanted to apologise, but Shou-yun was regarding him pleasantly while she spoke of this and that.

'It's quiet here,' she said. 'Life has been treating us well.'

The windows and doors of the mill remained open to make use of the last of the daylight. Shou-yun had just set down the tea before them when a shadow fell over the doorway.

'Baba!'

Little Ling went running, the patter of her feet on the dirt floor the only sound for a few beats. Everyone else went silent including Jin-mei beside him. Shou-yun straightened with the teapot still in her hands.

Yang rose to face his younger brother for the first time in a long time. 'Tien.'

His brother was dressed in a drab brown robe of a peasant farmer. He took the time to remove his bamboo leaf hat before replying, 'Elder Brother.'

Tien was his equal in height, but naturally leaner in build. Five years separated them. They had always been similar in appearance, with Tien being thinner in the face, his forehead more pronounced. A sign of cleverness, they had always said.

In contrast to what Shou-yun had said, Tien didn't look surprised to see him. The corners of his mouth pulled tight and his eyes narrowed. He looked wary.

Shou-yun broke the silence by moving towards her husband. 'Darling,' she cooed. 'Look, your brother has come to visit with his new wife. You look tired. Come sit and we'll all eat together.'

Yang felt a hesitant touch on the back of his arm. Jin-mei looked at him questioningly, but he had no answers for her. The only one who was oblivious to the tension was Little Ling, who tugged on her father's sleeve. Tien scooped the girl up with one arm, and she giggled. Her father didn't share in the laughter.

Tien locked his gaze on to Yang. 'It's been a long time, Elder Brother.'

'It has.'

Yang had a gift for words, for making an advantageous deal, for charming strangers. But none of that would work on his own brother. Instead, Yang found his tongue thick in his mouth.

There weren't enough stools and Jin-mei started to relinquish hers, but Tien stopped her. 'Please sit, Elder Sister.'

His tone was noticeably more cordial when addressing Jin-mei. At the very least, it wasn't cold. He set Little Ling down and pulled over a wooden tub which he overturned to use as a seat. Shou-yun brought him a bowl of tea, which he took with two hands and a nod of thanks.

'Elder Sister, you must have travelled far to come here,' Shou-yun said from the hearth as she assembled the meal. 'You must be tired.'

'It wasn't too much of a hardship. Your home is not too far from the river,' Jin-mei replied.

'Did you stop in Nao Village?'

'No, Little Sister.' Jin-mei glanced briefly at him, as if seeking reinforcement.

'There's a stand that makes an oxtail soup there. I've tried very hard to imitate the taste of it.'

The two women were valiantly working to fill the silence, but no amount of polite chatter could banish the tension between him and Tien. He and his brother made a show of listening to them while they assessed one another.

'Your family looks well,' Yang began finally.

The conversation between the women fell away. Shou-yun went to tend to the food at the stove. Jin-mei sipped her tea, applying more concentration than needed. He could see her shoulders lifting like a fox sensing danger.

'You look the same, Elder Brother,' Tien returned.

'Not entirely the same. Something has happened, Tien.'

'I figured that must be so, seeing you are here.'

His brother's tone was cold enough to chill the room. Shou-yun came to the table, balancing two bowls of stew. Jin-mei rushed to help her, probably eager to escape the death stare Tien was giving him.

They settled down to eat with Shou-yun kneeling on a bamboo mat beside the table and Little Ling beside her in the crook of her arm. Mercifully, she took over the burden of the conversation.

'When were the two of you married?' Shou-yun asked while scooping more stew for her girl.

'Earlier this month,' Jin-mei answered for them.

'Are you from Taining County as well then?'

'Minzhou prefecture.' Again she shot him a questioning look. 'But Yang and my father have known each other for a long time.'

Shou-yun smiled warmly. 'Do you have plans for children then?'

To his surprise, Jin-mei replied without reservation, 'I've always wanted a big family. At least two boys and two girls.'

'Really?' Yang raised an eyebrow, while Jin-mei barely batted an eyelash. They hadn't yet established what would become of this marriage, so there certainly was no talk yet of children.

Shou-yun laughed at his confusion. 'I've been thinking Little Ling needed a brother or a sister. Cousins would be happy news. Imagine them playing together—'

'Elder Sister,' Tien interrupted, making a show of

addressing Jin-mei rather than him. 'It is good to meet you. We are all family here now so perhaps my brother can say what needs to be said.' He set aside his bowl of stew though it was only half-finished. 'And then he can go. Yang has always been a very busy man and you have a long journey ahead of you.'

'Tien!' his wife scolded. 'They'll be staying the night. There's no question of them leaving. It's dark and the village is hours away.' Then she turned to them. 'I apologise, Elder Sister. We so rarely have visitors.'

Tien nodded. 'I do apologise and mean no disrespect towards you.'

The *you* was emphasised without subtlety. All these years apart hadn't softened his brother towards him one bit. Tien still blamed him for everything.

'General Wang wants me dead,' Yang told him bluntly.

'Wang Shizhen,' Tien intoned. He did not appear particularly surprised by the news.

'The general controls nearly the entire prefecture by now. His word is law and once he discovers my identity, if he hasn't already, he'll send his men everywhere searching for me. I've tried to send word to our associates.'

'You still speak as if I have a part in this business of yours.' Tien folded his hands before him, fingers laced tightly together. The barrier he created was more impenetrable than the Wuyi Mountains.

'It's the Bao family business. Our legacy.'

'Not mine.'

If Tien had chosen to engage in commerce, he would have been a formidable negotiator. Whereas Yang relied on charisma and cleverness, Tien was level-headed and impenetrable.

'Elder Sister, will you come help me with the sleeping area?'

Shou-yun, ever the peacemaker, tried to draw Jin-mei away from the confrontation. As understated as the exchange appeared, there was no mistake that it was a confrontation. A quiet war that had started between them years ago and had never been resolved.

'Let her stay,' Tien said. 'You as well, Wife. We're family and this concerns all of us. What my elder brother is telling us is that our lives are about to change. That we are no longer safe here, on our farm. On the land that we have worked with our own hands.'

His brother paused, challenging Yang to deny it. He couldn't.

'You were always ambitious, Elder Brother,' Tien accused. 'Never content with what you had. Yet your decisions affected all of us in irrevocable ways.'

'I've tried to set things right.' Yang's chest drew tight and he could feel all the old wounds opening. 'I wanted justice for An. For our family.'

'You wanted revenge,' Tien corrected. 'Not justice. And now we all must suffer.'

This was the first outward sign of anger he had seen from his brother in years. He wished Tien would curse and shout. Then they could fight like brothers did and resolve their differences. But Yang's younger siblings had always treated him with respect, as was his due. In return, he'd destroyed everything.

'I cannot let that man continue to draw breath,' Yang said. 'Not after what he did to our family.'

Tien shook his head. 'It was always about you. Only you, Elder Brother. Never talk to me about family obligation.'

By now, Shou-yun was clutching Little Ling to her,

and Jin-mei had moved closer to them to soothe both mother and child. Yang was truly alone, lowlier than a dog. Everything his brother had said was true. His own vanity had brought them to this.

There was no use in arguing any longer. Nor was there any use in him trying to regain any sense of honour. He would always be a villain in his brother's eyes, a worse human being than even the warlord.

Yang had to think of the present; of the task at hand and what needed to be done.

'You must leave as soon as possible and go into hiding,' he instructed. 'General Wang will come after everyone close to me. Anything I've touched.'

'How will he find us here?' Shou-yun asked tremulously. 'This is a remote area.'

'It's no secret that I sent messengers here every year.'

All the gifts and money he had sent them, seeking atonement. The letters would lead Wang's men straight to Tien and his family. The realisation left a bitter taste in his mouth.

'Wang Shizhen is known for being cruel to traitors,' Yang explained. What he was about to say would only frighten Shou-yun further, but he needed Tien to accept his help, as much as his brother hated it. 'He will exact vengeance in the form of the Nine Exterminations. Not only does he execute his enemies, but the general considers their entire families guilty by association.'

By law, the Nine Exterminations was reserved for those who had plotted against the Emperor, but Wang Shizhen was a warlord who made his own laws in this corner of the empire.

'You need to come with me,' he continued. 'There will be a ship docked at the crossing to take us somewhere safe.'

'Where on this earth can we be safe while we're with you?' Tien challenged.

'The ship moves quickly and the crew is trained to defend themselves. There are places in the mountains where we can hide.'

'Smugglers' hideouts,' Tien spat.

'This is only for now, until I confront Wang Shizhen for the final time,' Yang vowed.

He thought he saw a look of concern cross his brother's face, but it quickly disappeared as Tien shook his head.

'You've proven that you cannot protect us, Yang. I'll take my family and go where we won't be found, not by General Wang or by you. Go die your honourable death, Brother. All I need from you is an oath that you will not seek us out ever again.'

Chapter Ten

'I will take better care of you than this in the future. I promise.'

Yang's voice came to her in the darkness. They were lying on a mat in the corner of the mill house. Shou-yun had given them a thin blanket to share, but Yang had relinquished it entirely to her.

'This is very comfortable,' she whispered back.

It wasn't a lie. The floor was kept meticulously clean and there were no sounds of rats scurrying about as she occasionally heard at night on the ship.

Tien and Shou-yun were quiet at the far end of the house where they had lain down with Little Ling. Either they were asleep or they were having their own whispered conversation. After the tense meal, Jin-mei had helped her new sister-in-law pack up the family belongings. Listening to Shou-yun determine what to keep and what to leave behind had been heartbreaking. Yang remained quiet the entire evening, watching his brother's family from afar like a stranger.

Apparently Yang wanted to talk or he couldn't yet fall asleep and didn't want to lie awake alone. For some reason, realising that made her heart ache for him. He wasn't as impervious as he pretended to be.

She reached out to touch his shoulder and felt him tense, though he didn't move away.

'I'm cold,' she lied.

The night was warm enough and the mill provided enough insulation to sleep comfortably without a blanket, but Jin-mei shifted closer. Yang obligingly curled his arm around her waist and pulled her against him.

'Better?' he asked.

His voice was low and deep, the tone so intimate that a shudder ran down her spine. Her throat went dry, and she could barely find her voice.

'Better.'

'Good.'

Yang pressed his palm to her lower back and drew slow soothing circles. As if she were the one who needed comforting and not him.

'Who is An?' she asked.

The soothing circles stopped. She was afraid he'd grow silent and pull away, but he answered, 'An-yu is my younger sister. Our sister. She's no longer with us,' he added after another pause.

Jin-mei wanted to reach out to Yang and touch him in some way so that he would know he could tell her everything. Or not tell her. She rested her hand lightly over his heart. Her fingers lifted and lowered with the rising of his chest.

'Wang Shizhen and I weren't always enemies. There was a time when I saw him as a way to gain influence.' He took in a deep breath, trying to compose himself, as if it took all his strength to make the admission. 'He was a strong and capable leader who was building a following, so I married my sister to him.'

Jin-mei held her breath. The darkness felt suffocating around them, and Yang lay unmoving beside her. It was as if each word were a drop of blood from a wound that had never closed for him and now he was drained dry.

'It ended badly,' he whispered finally, his breath catching.

Her chest pulled tight with dread. "What happened?"

Yang was silent for so long that she thought he wouldn't answer. When he spoke again his voice was faint and absent of any emotion, but she could sense the struggle within him.

'I didn't see my sister again for half a year after the wedding, but when I did she looked so pale I thought she must have been ill. When she spoke, she could only answer in a few words. Even though I was concerned for her, it was much later before I realized what was happening. Wang had broken her. He'd taken her will until she was too frightened to escape. When he saw my concern, he used her against me, threatening her so I would do whatever he wanted.'

'You said your sister was no longer with—'

'She took her own life.' His voice broke on the last word. 'I didn't realize how bad it was for her until then. Otherwise, I would have tried to take her home…I tell myself I would have at least tried.'

The sad truth was once a woman was given away in marriage, there was little she or her family could do. Her happiness depended entirely on whether her husband was kind or cruel. Jin-mei could have told Yang he'd only done what he thought best. That he couldn't have known what would happen, but there was nothing she could say to free him of his guilt.

'I should have known Tien wouldn't come with me,' Yang continued. 'He hates me. With good reason.'

'Your brother doesn't hate you. You wouldn't notice how he looks at you because it's likely how he's always looked at you. Tien loves you.'

There were things only an outsider could see. Or perhaps only a woman, who had to base so many decisions on trust and unspoken affection. Tien had certainly been angry with Yang. And Yang had been angry as well at his brother's stubbornness. It was hard to see clearly through pain and old wounds.

She didn't know if Yang believed her, but he didn't protest or deny it. Eventually he did fall asleep while Jin-mei remained awake with her thoughts. Even when his breathing became deep and heavy, he kept one arm draped around her.

This simple embrace wasn't one displayed on the marriage mirror. It was too intimate and revealing to depict.

Jin-mei felt as if she'd just closed her eyes and dozed off for a minute before she was awakened by the sound of a pot boiling on the stove. Pale light streamed in through the windows while Shou-yun roused Little Ling from her pallet. Yang and his brother were nowhere to be seen.

Jin-mei rose to splash water over her face before going to help Shou-yun. The morning meal consisted of thick rice porridge accompanied with scallions and bamboo shoots. The two of them ate seated at the table with Shou-yun's daughter beside her.

'I finished organising the kitchen,' her sister-in-law said. 'We have sacks of rice and jars of pickled vegetables. Those will last for a while. My husband has gone to harvest what he can from the fields.'

Shou-yun's eyes were dry, but her voice was pitched too high and she spoke rapidly to fill the silence. She concentrated on scooping scallions into Little Ling's bowl with her chopsticks, brushing back her daughter's hair, pouring tea.

'I'm sorry,' Jin-mei said quietly.

'Don't be sorry. This is the way of things for us women.' Shou-yun looked quickly away. 'We create our lives wherever we can. We endure.'

Jin-mei felt the weight of her statement deep in her chest. Fathers and husbands could make whatever decisions they saw fit. Then it was a woman's task to change course, flow around obstacles and adapt. No wonder the *yin* element was water.

They continued eating in silence. Even Little Ling was more reserved than the day before. Though she probably couldn't understand what was happening, the child could sense that her mother was unhappy and that something was changing.

'Perhaps it would be better for you to come with us,' Jin-mei suggested. She might be overstepping her bounds, but Shou-yun was frightened. She didn't want to go. 'We are sailing on a large river boat. You won't be alone.'

'Thank you, Elder Sister, but my husband will take care of us,' she replied soberly.

The two men didn't return until their meal was finished. They set down two baskets filled with yams and other vegetables, still caked in dirt. Jin-mei went to rinse out the bowls as Yang and Tien seated themselves.

The two men said nothing to each other as they took tea and the silence was far from companionable. Yang barely glanced up at Jin-mei as she passed by to carry the kitchen goods outside. He had become as closed off as his brother.

An ox cart was hitched up at the front of the house. After everyone had eaten, they made a few trips back and forth into the house to pack the cart full. Then, with nothing else to do, Yang stepped back and watched as his brother prepared to leave.

'Please reconsider.' There was no force behind Yang's final appeal, but he had to make it.

Tien shook his head. 'Farewell, Elder Brother.'

'At least take this money. You'll need it on your journey.'

Instead of a reply, the younger man stepped away to tend to the ox cart, too stubborn, proud or angry to accept the offering. When Yang turned to Jin-mei, the corners of his mouth were pulled downward. There was genuine anguish in his eyes.

'We're done, then,' he told her. 'Let us go now.'

As if it were too painful to stay and watch his brother disappear into the woods to some unknown place.

He couldn't give up so easily. Where were his negotiating skills now? 'It's dangerous out there,' she protested. 'Surely you can convince him.'

'It's no use. Tien won't accept any help from me.'

Shou-yun lifted her girl on to the cart while Tien finished securing the last of their belongings inside. Neither party, not Yang nor his brother, was willing to push any further. They were resigned to this fate.

Jin-mei could see how much his brother meant to Yang. She could sense the longing within him. What he probably didn't notice was how much his brother longed for him as well, but she had seen it from the very first moment Tien had stood in the doorway, looking on to his elder brother for the first time in years.

Yang didn't resist as she pried the satchel of money gently from him. The coins had been wrapped tight under layers of sackcloth and lay heavy in her hands as she approached the ox cart. Jin-mei slowed her step and caught Shou-yun's eye.

Shou-yun broke away to approach her. 'I am sorry that we were barely able to speak. It's so good to see family.'

In her look of wistfulness, Jin-mei could see a hint of the loneliness of living in isolation. The more subtle consequences of the long-time rift between the brothers.

Jin-mei reached into her pack and searched around until her hand closed around a packet of folded paper. She pulled it out and placed it on top of the bundle of silver that Yang had tried to hand over to Tien earlier. 'This is for Little Ling.'

Shou-yun shook her head. 'We can't accept that.'

'Are we not sisters now?' Jin-mei was insistent, thrusting the items into the other woman's hands. 'You must. My feelings will be hurt if you don't.'

Finally, Shou-yun nodded. She opened the red-paper packet and her eyes lit up at the sight of the jade bracelet inside.

'For when your daughter is older.'

The bracelet was another of her wedding gifts. Jin-mei had never had a sister to share such things with so she'd felt an immediate bond with Shou-yun.

'We'll see each other again,' Jin-mei promised as if she could will it so.

Shou-yun nodded and clasped her hand in farewell before returning to the ox cart. Jin-mei breathed deep as she watched the other woman climb into the back of the cart. Finally she returned to Yang, who hadn't moved a step from his position in front of the door.

'She accepted the money.'

He nodded solemnly. 'Thank you for that.'

They stood side by side, watching the ox cart as it rolled down the path away from the mill house. Tien did not look back, but the little girl turned to wave at them, calling them 'Uncle' and 'Auntie.' Jin-mei hoped that the couple would be able to find a safe place to settle once again and that their child would never have to know anything of warlords or blood feuds.

Once the cart had disappeared into a tiny dot on the horizon, Yang started off in the opposite direction.

'What did you two speak of this morning out in the fields?' she asked, walking alongside him.

'Nothing,' he replied, his tone neutral. 'We haven't spoken for four years and he didn't have anything to say to me.'

'Did you say all that you needed to say to him then?'

She hadn't meant it as a challenge, but Yang grew quiet.

Jin-mei thought of Lady Yi and her two brothers at home. Father had named them Ji Fa and Ji Dan, after the two great heroes of the Zhou Dynasty. Fa, the older boy, was studious and eager to please, whereas Dan could not be told anything.

Brothers could fight like cats and dogs and be as different as night and day, but that wasn't the case with Yang and Tien. They were too similar, harbouring the pain of an old grudge deep inside, each in their own way.

There was so much she wanted to know about the man who was now her husband, but she didn't want to pry. Yang and his brother spoke of tragedy and vengeance and death as if all three had been hanging over them for a long time. Just like last night, she waited for him to tell her.

'You can still turn back,' he said instead, keeping his gaze on the road. 'You can return to what your life was before I disrupted it.'

'There is no turning back. And you didn't bring this

upon me. Wang Shizhen and all these dangers you speak of were always present.'

'But you were protected from all of it.'

'Was I?' How safe was she when her father was involved so deeply in such subterfuge and treachery? But her eyes were open now. 'You cannot unknow something once known. I always knew my father was ambitious, but I didn't think that he was dishonest or that he was capable of murder.'

'But he still loves you.'

She was taken aback by the quiet fierceness of his reply.

'You were his treasure,' he continued. 'Your father might have been a scheming, lying trickster, but he would move mountains to keep you safe. Especially against the likes of someone like me.'

'You're defending him for trying to kill you?'

His lip curled. 'I probably deserved it. I've done plenty of things I should have died for.'

A dark cloud moved over her. 'That isn't funny.'

'I didn't mean—'

'Life and death isn't a game, Bao Yang.' Jin-mei turned to go. 'You surround yourself with cutthroats and outlaws and act as if it were nothing. As if there were no consequences for your actions.'

'I was just trying to tell you to be a little more forgiving of your father.'

She bit back her reply and focused on the ground beneath her feet. Yang was holding back from revealing what had happened with his sister, but there were secrets she wasn't ready to tell him either.

After the sickness had taken Mother, her father had become her only friend and confidant. When he came home from his travels, her world would brighten. He could make her laugh and make her think, but there was no one else in her world. No siblings or cousins or playmates.

Yang insisted that her father still loved her. She still loved her father too, the father she thought she'd known, and that was exactly why she couldn't stay.

She turned swiftly to walk away but the terrain had become rocky and uneven. As she started down the slope, the soft earth gave way and she began to slide. She tried to use the bamboo staff to brace herself, but couldn't find her balance. Immediately, Yang was beside her. Taking a firm grip on her arm, he led her down to the foot of the hill.

'Thank you,' she muttered beneath her breath. Being rescued had certainly taken the fire out of storming off.

'I live a dangerous life,' he began sombrely.

His hands closed over her shoulders, willing her to look up at him, but she couldn't. She forced herself to take a deep breath before she replied, 'Your brother cares about you.'

'I wish I could believe that.'

'I...' Jin-mei paused. How did one say something that was just supposed to be taken for granted? 'I care about you too.'

Yang didn't answer immediately. He still held on to her, though it wasn't quite an embrace. The space between them felt like a chasm. She had never felt so vulnerable and so aware of his presence beside her.

'I know,' he said finally.

All of the sudden, her heart was pounding and her breathing grew shallow even though she was standing still. They were married, but to admit such feeling when there was so much she didn't understand about him frightened her.

'Can we rest?' she asked because it was something to say. And because her knees had become weak.

They stopped to rest beneath the shade of a tree, sitting side by side on a fallen log. She rested the bamboo walking stick beside her. Yang passed a gourd of water to her, and she took a sip before passing it back.

'Are we headed back towards the river?' she asked.

Though she wasn't certain of their direction, it appeared as if they were moving away from the water, not towards it.

'I told you there were some people I had to meet. Important people.' He let out a breath as he rubbed a hand over his temples. The morning had already exhausted him. 'I'm not just a salt trader, Jin-mei.'

She stiffened. Was there no end to the schemes and underhanded dealings?

'The attack on General Wang wasn't merely my doing. There were many others involved gathering information, planning—'

'My father,' she realised.

'Yes.'

Now that she knew her father had no qualms about plotting murder during his only daughter's wedding, there was obviously no limit to what he was capable of.

'I heard of that incident,' she told him. 'But I never imagined that it was planned by you and my father.'

'And many others,' he pointed out. 'Wang Shizhen is a bloodthirsty tyrant. Many people want him gone.'

It had been a shocking scandal. Two important officials attacked during a banquet by killers masquerading as entertainers. The assassins had all escaped and the next day the head of the prefecture had committed suicide for reasons unknown.

'I don't doubt you or the righteousness of your cause.

I just wish—' She sighed, suddenly feeling very tired herself. 'I just wish you weren't at the heart of all this.'

Just because her father had kept her sheltered before didn't change the reality of the situation. She could turn away like Tien and Shou-yun and refuse to be a part of it all. She'd even tried to do that when she'd run away from home, hadn't she? But corruption and treachery were everywhere. She couldn't avoid seeing them.

'What do you need to do?' she asked.

'Regroup. Whether or not the attack succeeded, all of the faction leaders agreed we would meet again to plan our next step.'

Factions. Leaders. She felt dizzy. 'Where is this supposed to happen?'

'At one of the salt wells my family used to run. It's been abandoned for a long time and not likely to draw attention.'

Unlike Yang's dealings with his brother, there was no hesitation in him now. Every word from his mouth was single-minded and confident.

She stared at him in shocked comprehension. 'You're not just another pair of hands, are you? You're the leader of this rebellion.'

'There is no one single leader,' he denied, leading them away from the dirt path and into the wilderness. 'But I have been very persuasive.'

Chapter Eleven

They were still on the road when the sun dipped below the horizon. Jin-mei was nervous to be travelling in the dark on a deserted route, but Yang seemed unafraid. He lit a lantern as the sky darkened. The flicker of it soon provided the only light in the wilderness.

'The well must be close,' he assured her. 'It was one of the smaller of our family's operations and not well known.'

Jin-mei gripped her bamboo staff tighter and strained to hear through the night sounds for a stray footstep or any sound that would indicate an intruder. She didn't know what she feared worse: an attack by a wild animal or an encounter with bandits. As a magistrate's daughter she had heard too many stories about wrongdoers and outlaws.

Of course, many of her father's stories were also about ordinary people who met misfortune in ordinary settings. She was just as much in danger in her own house as she was on the road, she told herself. Why, most crimes were committed by neighbours and so-called friends who schemed against you. It might actually be safer out in the wild among foxes and wolves and tigers—

'Jin-mei,' Yang interrupted softly.

She froze. 'What?'

'You're whispering to yourself.'

'It's a habit,' she confessed. 'When I'm nervous.'

With a chuckle, he drew her in close, his arm around her waist. She did feel a little better closer to the lantern and also pressed to his side.

'There are no wolves in these parts,' he assured her. He suppressed a laugh. 'Or tigers.'

She tried to jab him in the ribs, but he was holding her too close.

It was into the early part of the evening when they started climbing what Yang claimed was the final hill. Jin-mei didn't want to complain, but the huff of her breath as he tried to reassure her for the tenth time was very clearly a protest.

As they reached the top of the slope, she could see a clearing in the basin below. A group of buildings stood at the edge of a lake. From afar, it appeared to be a commune surrounded by a bamboo wall.

'Something feels wrong,' she remarked as Yang moved forward.

He nodded, but said nothing more when she came up beside him. His pace had slowed considerably. At the edge of the clearing, he came to a stop within the cover of the bamboo forest.

'Stay here. It will be all right,' he added firmly when she started to protest.

Jin-mei didn't want to be left alone, but had no choice. She huddled close to the towering stalks and told herself there was nothing to be afraid of. Yang had taken the lantern, and she followed the path of the light as he moved towards the gate of the compound.

She held her breath as the lantern disappeared within the gates. A short while later, Yang came out.

'There's no one there,' he reported. 'It's safe.'

Having shelter was better than sleeping out in the wilderness, yet every muscle in her remained tense as she followed him to the gate. They slipped inside like thieves and Yang paused to bar the gate behind them.

The interior was dark and silent. They moved past storage houses and work areas. There were large, shallow troughs where she assumed salt used to be collected. Tall structures built of bamboo towered high above the ground. It was eerie walking through the abandoned space which had once been a site of so much activity. Everything appeared to have been left exactly where it was, the tools laid down without thought. One moment in use, and the next discarded.

'The sleeping area is at the back, away from the water,' Yang said.

The quarters were also constructed of bamboo and consisted of one long bay. They entered in through one end at a compartment that had been sectioned off. Jin-mei assumed they were once the foreman's quarters.

There was a low bed fashioned from teak in the corner, but any blankets or coverings had been stripped. Still, there was a roof overhead along with walls to hold back the wind and keep insects out. And tigers as well.

Jin-mei sank gratefully on to the bed. Yang took a few moments to prepare the room, lighting the brazier which still held a small amount of charcoal. He rummaged through the other quarters and retrieved an oil lamp, lighting it and setting it on to the bench. Finally he sat down beside her with her pack between them.

The compound looked large enough to house fifteen to twenty. She knew little about the workings of trade and commerce, but given that Yang had described this outfit as one of their smaller ones, Jin-mei was beginning to understand the scale of his family business.

'You're responsible for quite a lot of people. Not only your family, but many other families as well.'

He nodded, appearing deep in thought.

'You could have just as easily embarked upon a legitimate business,' she pointed out.

'There's more money in salt and it's easier to come by.'

'Than farming the land or...or making pots?' Her argument wasn't holding up very well considering she'd never engaged in any sort of trade herself. She knew little beyond what she purchased in the market.

'It's easy because the imperial government wants to control the salt trade so they tax it heavily, creating a place for those of us who sell it for just a little less. It's money created out of air. An illusion,' he explained.

'For that argument to work, then the imperial administration must be an illusion too, including any need for law or cities or officials.'

'Every official I know is corrupt,' he said with a smirk.

She slitted her eyes at him. That was uncalled for.

'It's not like I'm a bandit!' he protested.

Jin-mei sighed. 'Hard on others, but easy on himself.'

He scowled at her. 'What do you mean by that?'

'You've admitted to being a smuggler.'

'A private salt-trader,' he corrected.

'Words,' she dismissed with a wave. 'Who are you to criticise bandits?'

'A bandit takes something that isn't his. A smuggler sells something he isn't supposed to sell,' Yang argued. 'The difference is night and day.'

'The thief who shouts "theft",' Jin-mei remarked blandly.

He opened his mouth to argue, but then stopped himself. The gleam in his eye transformed from a spark into something smouldering. 'I married a magistrate's daughter,' he reminded himself with a half-smile.

Her pulse jumped, and he moved to stand right before her, looking down at her fondly. What was it that they had been arguing about? Bandits? The price of salt? It was just like their meeting beneath the bridge. Jin-mei wasn't trusting by nature, but somehow Yang managed to disarm her with a few words, a look, just the lightest lift of his mouth.

As quickly as his heated look came, it disappeared to be replaced with a serious expression. 'Why are you still here, Jin-mei? With me?'

She picked at the hem of her tunic nervously. A thread had somehow worked its way loose. 'I had to go with you,' she replied slowly, eyes averted. 'A woman belongs to her father first, then her husband.'

'The Three Obediences.' He sat down beside her on the bed. 'I wouldn't think a woman as daring and independent as you would adhere to those rules so strictly.'

'I'm not rebellious by nature, I want a tidy and ordered life.'

'With two sons and two daughters,' he said, echoing her sentiments from the day before. Yang shifted closer to her as he spoke and his tone was full of warmth and good humour, something that she had been missing from him since they'd left the river.

'I never had a brother or a sister when I was a child so I wanted my children to each have a companion to be paired with,' she explained, his presence warming her so much more than the coal in the brazier. 'That way, no one would ever be lonely.'

He tilted his head curiously. 'Were you often lonely?'

If there was any trace of mockery in his voice, she would have snapped at him, but there was none. His expression could even be considered fond. Her face heated beneath his careful scrutiny.

'I was rarely alone,' she said hastily. 'There was always Amah or the other house servants. Father also hired tutors to teach me.'

Yang nodded and was kind enough not to mention that she hadn't answered his question. 'Two sons and two daughters then,' he acknowledged, reaching over to brush back her hair. The spot where he touched her cheek radiated warmth until her whole face was flushed.

She hadn't been merely lonely, she had been desperate for companionship. Someone to share her thoughts with. She longed for *someone* so much that her fourteen-year-old self had been infatuated with Yang immediately after meeting him. Even when he didn't know she existed.

Yet now he was here after all those dreams and unbelievably he was her husband. It wasn't the poetic love story that Mother and Father had shared, but she and Yang had chosen each other all the same. At least she thought he had chosen her.

'I used to always dream of marrying well,' she admitted. 'I would be a good wife and my husband would cherish me.'

'What does being a good wife require?' he teased.

She made a face. 'I don't know.'

They both smiled at that, and for a moment the desolation and fear lifted.

'I would run a harmonious household,' she continued, quite serious. 'And raise my children to be studious and dutiful.'

Yang nodded. 'All admirable accomplishments.'

'And I…' What else? What else did it mean to be a wife? 'I would make sure my husband's clothes are mended and that he's well taken care of. I would bring him tea while he's up late in his study.'

With each mundane task she listed, her chest constricted more and more, as if caught in a tight fist. That was a thousand *li* from the life they were destined for. They had begun their marriage in turmoil and were now completely separated from the ones they loved.

'I must have found myself the perfect match,' Yang said quietly.

His words made her eyes fill with tears. She blinked them back furiously. She was being silly.

'Jin-mei?' He reached for her, confused.

She waved him away, but he only moved in closer with a look of concern on his face. He tried to hold her, his arms closing around her as gentle as a bird's wing, but she tore out of his grasp.

'None of this is possible, is it? All those small, peaceful moments. The diligent husband, the dutiful wife.'

Yang didn't answer, which was answer enough.

They were bantering about marriage and children as if they weren't fugitives. As if they had any chance for a future together.

Yang had spoken to his brother about continuing to seek revenge. That was why Tien had insisted on going his own way. She should leave as well, but Jin-mei couldn't bring herself to go. Yang could charm the moon and the stars.

He reached for her again, but this time she let herself

be drawn in. He eased her head gently down on to his shoulder. There was something so natural about how his arm encircled her. Yang did everything without hesitation, without apology, so that it always seemed as though his way was the right way. The way things should be.

The connection between them was almost palpable, a force in the air like the coming of a storm. Yet he didn't do anything more than hold her.

Jin-mei could feel her palms sweating. She wanted very much for him to kiss her. She wanted him to do more.

When Yang did reach for her, she jumped, but he only placed his hand over hers. 'You should prepare for bed. We've had a tiring day,' he said gently.

She nodded. It was obvious that Yang was experienced in the bedchamber while she was a complete innocent. Aside from a few lurid engravings, she had only the memory of his mouth on her skin to educate her. His possessive touch when he kissed her.

She was even too inexperienced to know how to reach out to him in invitation. Should she wind her arms around his neck and try to kiss him as he'd done to her on the ship? Her stepmother, Lady Yi, had assured her that men and women were made to fit together, but she'd said nothing of them being of one mind. It all was very, very confusing.

With disappointment pressing down on her, Jin-mei pulled the spare robe from her sack and bundled it up to use as a pillow. Her slippers she took off, one after the other, and placed them carefully by the foot of the bed. Her feet were sore from all the walking they'd done. As she rubbed her hand over the soles, she turned to see Yang watching her, unmoving.

Hastily, she climbed on to the wooden frame of the

bed, turning away as she reached up to undo the wooden pins from her hair only to find Yang's hand there, his fingers closing gently over hers. She hadn't heard him move. Couldn't hear anything over the rush of her pulse.

'This is the first time we've been alone since our wedding.' His voice stroked over her like a caress, sending a shudder down her spine.

'Was it truly a wedding?' She was unable to keep her voice from trembling. For the life of her, she couldn't find the courage to turn around and face him. Even though he barely touched her, Yang filled her senses. 'I was beginning to wonder.'

Carefully, he withdrew the pins. Her hair fell about her shoulders, tickling against her neck. She could feel every strand as he brushed it tenderly aside. His next words came very close to her ear.

'It was a wedding,' he said, low and serious. There was no lightness, no careless flirtation there. 'Except for one very important part.'

His lips captured her earlobe, sucking gently in a move that shocked her and sent a streak of heat straight down to her toes. Jin-mei didn't realise she'd fallen back until he caught her. His mouth moved to the side of her neck, and a moan escaped her lips as he first kissed her and then nipped at the soft skin there. She melted against him, pooling in his arms like warm water.

Jin-mei watched in a haze of desire as his hand closed over her breast, his thumb circling. With that touch, every nerve ending in her came alive. Her skin heated and her body dampened down below.

'Will you ever look at me?' he asked huskily.

Jin-mei turned her head like a puppet on a string. Yang was smiling at her, a knowing, possessive smile. He held her securely in his arms and continued to tease her nipple in slow circles that made it impossible to think or form words. At that moment, she truly did feel that she belonged to him. All it took was his slightest touch and the softest words for her to yield.

Reaching up, she touched her fingertips lightly to his jaw. And then what had seemed so awkward and un-fathomable a moment ago became as natural as breathing. He bent his head to her. She raised herself to him until their lips met. His mouth was harder on her this time. Hotter.

He worked her sash loose and her tunic open with one hand. His other hand was tangled in her hair, holding her to him as he took her mouth. Suddenly she felt his hand on her bare nipple, his fingertip rasping lightly against the peak. It was the same movement as before, but this time the tiny stroke was enough to send her back arching off the bed.

'Yang,' she gasped out his name as her hands fisted into the front of his robe.

Impatiently, she tore at his clothes. That much she knew had to be accomplished, but her fingers were clumsy. With a laugh, Yang moved to help her. It took only a moment to free himself from his robe. The fire-light danced over his bare torso as he took her in his arms again.

She placed a hand on the centre of his chest, feeling the heartbeat just beneath his breastbone. She had never seen a man naked before, or even half-naked. His skin was lighter beneath his clothes, but not much, and his chest and shoulders were taut with muscle. She ran her hand down over his stomach, fingertips grazing against his ribs.

'You have such a look of concentration on your face,'

he marvelled. 'A little frown line here.' He kissed her between her eyes.

'Does it make me look very strange?' she asked, suddenly aware of her half-dressed state.

'It makes me feel that I can't wait much longer.'

She didn't know exactly what he meant, but when he pulled her hand to his lips for a kiss and then rolled her beneath him, she started to get an idea. Yang pulled her tunic away as well as the trousers beneath, then removed the rest of his clothing with the same efficiency.

This was the part when nature was supposed to take over and everything was to move inevitably towards its end, but she was still confused. No invisible instinct guided her. Yang laid himself over her and lowered his mouth to her once more, his tongue slipping into her mouth in a way that was both strange and beautiful.

She was unaware his hand had moved downward until it closed around her hip. And then he touched her, first with just his fingertips against her sex. Then he parted her, stroking gently, then circling, then she didn't know what he was doing because her eyes were closed and her head thrown back. Nothing had ever felt so good. Nothing.

'Yang,' she said again, this time panting. She never wanted him to stop.

'Jin-mei,' he breathed. 'My wife.' His fingers moved over just barely, enough and not enough. She strained towards him.

The sensation ceased to be, replaced with the feel of something blunt and smooth pressing against her. She hadn't dared to look for too long at him when he'd disrobed, but she knew it was him. The male part of him. He stroked against her with a short movement of his hips and the pleasure returned, somehow *better* now that it was more than just his fingers.

'Such concentration,' he remarked once more, capturing her mouth as his hips rocked and his organ glided against her sex.

Then gradually, bit by bit, he began to ease himself inside of her. She could feel the resistance of her body, tight around him and giving only slightly with each thrust. Despite what he'd said about not being able to wait, Yang seemed to be endlessly patient, kissing her lips, her neck. Watching her as he finally pushed fully into her and then he had to close his eyes as well. The look in them bordered on pain before he laid his head into the crook of her neck. He murmured her name again, this time rough, guttural.

Her eyes widened as the mystery was finally resolved. This was how men and women came together, with pleasure, with pain. With her taking a part of someone else into herself. She could barely move with Bao Yang's weight on top of her, with him embedded inside her. It was overwhelming. It was confusing.

His arms closed around her, lifting her off the hard wood as he began to move in small thrusts that gradually grew stronger as he held her tighter. Then, somehow, in the midst of everything, he was touching her again, his hand pushed between their bodies, the touch rougher this time and propelled by the movement of his body over hers. But her body welcomed the directness of it. Though part of her was sore with his intrusion, another part of her strained against him, seeking more of whatever it was he was doing. All she could do was hold on as a wash of heat and pleasure took her. She cried out with surprise as her entire body tightened at once, desperate and straining. Yang seemed to know what had taken her

over, because he immediately took hold of her hips and
began to move faster, his muscles pulling tight as if he
were made of stone. Then suddenly he held himself rigid
over her and she could see the muscles straining in his
neck. His body pulsed inside her.

A moment later it was done. He was lying beside her
with his arm draped over her shoulders. Their skin was
slick with sweat though they had barely moved. His chest
heaved and his eyes were half-closed.

'I was given a mirror as part of my dowry,' she told
him when she finally caught her breath. Her cheek was
pressed against his shoulder and she never wanted to let
go. 'I have it here with me. It's engraved with…pictures.'

'Oh?' There was that smile on his lips again. Crooked
and self-satisfied. 'What sort of pictures?'

'They were instructional.'

'Perhaps I should take a look at this mirror.'

'It failed to address the finer points,' she concluded.

The smile turned into a laugh. He grabbed her and
held her tight, his laughter ringing out and filling her
heart until she forgot the hardness of the bed and the
sparseness of the room. It was as if they were in their
bridal suite, becoming husband and wife, as they'd originally intended, and all the turmoil that had happened
since did not exist.

Yang slept lightly as a rule, especially in a situation
such as this one when he needed to remain vigilant. As
a result, he was wide awake before first light. There was
little to stir the air of the abandoned camp. Only the chirp
of crickets and the low buzz of insects.

Jin-mei was asleep beside him, curled up on her side
with her hands folded beneath her rounded cheek. Her
tunic was draped over her shoulders, but remained open

in front to reveal a glimpse of smooth, pale skin. He did his best not to wake her, even though the sight of her heated his blood. Yesterday had been a gruelling trek, and Jin-mei was high born and gently raised. Completely unaccustomed to spending a day on her feet beneath the hot sun.

Having Jin-mei so close was another reason his body had barely gone to sleep before it was awake again. He was keenly aware of her lying barely a breath away. His wife.

When Yang had first agreed to the marriage, it seemed the only reasonable course of action. Yang had needed Magistrate Tan's aid and wedding his daughter would only strengthen their alliance.

Since then he'd learned Jin-mei was as clever as her father. Her mind was quick and efficient, cutting immediately to the heart of the matter. She was also conscientious, possessed a keen sense of right and wrong, and was unforgiving when betrayed. And she had one particular look of determination, with her eyes narrowed and chin lifted, that always made him want to grab her and kiss her.

He knew all this before last night. Before he'd learned how she felt in his arms, how her flesh would tighten and yield around him, and how much his body would crave more of hers. Now that Jin-mei was his, truly his, Yang was starting to doubt himself. Was this path of vengeance truly worth it? Maybe it had been an ill-fated plan from the start. Maybe it was finally time to forget it.

Except he couldn't. He closed his eyes and saw another girl who had trusted him. His sister. He owed her his very soul and now that she was gone, there was only one way to repay the debt.

Jin-mei shifted beside him, and he held his breath in hopes of looking at her for a moment longer. He'd been enamoured by other women in the past, but they had come and gone. Jin-mei was different. She belonged to him, and he was surprised how much that changed everything. He could no longer spit in the face of danger. He couldn't march up to his enemies without a care in his heart to plunge a knife into theirs.

Jin-mei had accused him of falling for dangerous women. She was the most dangerous woman of all, in the worst and best of ways. He'd become afraid. Afraid for her, afraid of losing her. Afraid to hurt her.

There was no place for fear in a blood feud. He had to be hard, cold and relentless just like the warlord.

But that was for later once he reunited with his associates. Yang caressed his fingertips lightly over the swell of Jin-mei's breasts. Her generous and beautiful breasts. Apparently his restraint had reached its limit.

Her eyelashes fluttered open and the moment her gaze found him, his heart started pounding.

'I'm glad you came with me,' he said with a quietness that belied the quickening of his pulse.

She blinked sleepily. 'I had to go with you. We never had our wedding night.'

'And now we have.' Yang laid his hand over the curve of her waist. From there, it was natural to draw her closer until their legs were intertwined.

'This is only the beginning. We'll have many days and nights, won't we?' She pressed her cheek into the crook of his arm, nestling closer.

'Perhaps, Jin-mei,' he said softly. 'If fate will allow it.'

She came awake at that, pushing up to sit beside him. 'You don't need to go after General Wang.'

He closed his eyes. 'I do.'

'You had your chance, but fate wouldn't allow it. It was a sign,' she insisted.

'You know I have to do this.' Pain lanced through him, surprising him. He'd always managed to make decisions dispassionately, following the most advantageous course of action. When he acted on emotion was when he faltered, as he had during the assassination attempt. 'It's not merely revenge any more. It's also about self-preservation. The only way I can keep my family, the only way I can keep you safe, is to be rid of the general.'

Her chin tilted stubbornly, and he could see the argument hovering on her tongue.

'I will succeed, Jin-mei. You trusted me enough to come find me. Trust me in this as well.'

The doubt in her eyes gutted him. After all, it was a reflection of his own private fears.

'He commands an entire army,' she pointed out. 'He's a warrior who's survived battle after battle to be where he is now.'

'But I'm not alone. There are many others with me, some of them closer to Wang than you would ever imagine. He is a lot weaker than he appears on the outside.'

'And you're much stronger?'

She reached out to rest her palm against his chest, feeling every beat of his heart against her fingertips. He couldn't claim to be strong at that moment. Not when his soul had been laid bare.

They were bound to each other now, mind and body. He knew it would weaken his resolve, but he wouldn't have had it any other way. Jin-mei had chosen him and even now he could see she wanted to believe, even though she wasn't willing to remain silent and let him march to his death.

'You've given me a reason to succeed,' he reassured

her. At least he hoped his words were reassuring. 'Even if my fortune is gone, even if I have nothing left but the clothes on my back, I want to live my life with you, Jin-mei. It will be the start of a new life, with all the wrongs of the past washed away.'

Jin-mei looked deep into his eyes, holding his gaze. Seeking the truth. Then her expression softened. In the back of his mind, he knew that he'd uttered exactly what she wanted to hear. Whether or not it was possible, it was true enough for now. He believed it enough for her to believe it.

It was morning and they would have to rise soon, but he kissed her passionately before entering her again, stroking deep as she took him inside of herself, enclosing him in heat.

He watched her face as he possessed her for the second time. He wanted to fill her mind as well, that mind that was always thinking and questioning.

His thrusts were slow, deliberate. Holding back the tide of his own pleasure so he could watch hers. Jin-mei's eyes fell closed and her lips parted as desire built within her. He could feel her body closing around him until the sensation became exquisitely excruciating. Yang gritted his teeth. He wanted to prolong their lovemaking. Soon they would have to part and at least he would have this to remember. They could both remember.

It was impossible to hold back. He shut his eyes as well, trying to maintain control. But her hands dug into his back insistently. He could hear the pant of her breath and those lovely breasts were pressed against him, her legs lifting to curve about his hips. All the while, down below she was so tight. Wet. A fist around him.

Something tried to intrude at the edge of his awareness, but he pushed it away. Every sense he had was focused on the woman in his arms and the joining of their bodies. His arousal, her surrender.

His release came in a flood, blinding him. Deafening him as the blood rushed through his body like the surging of the tide.

Chapter Twelve

Jin-mei woke up to the grey light of morning and an empty space beside her. The coal in the brazier had burned to ash, leaving a pervasive chill in the room. She sat up with the blanket clutched to her.

Yang wasn't far. He was sitting at the edge of the pallet near her feet, but he might as well have been on the other side of the mountains. He was fully dressed and sat with his head bent, elbows propped against his knees. She wondered how long he'd been like that, so quiet and still.

Husband, darling, beloved…no, certainly not that. Yet.

Once again she went through a list of endearments and forms of address in her head. He'd taken her to bed, they were husband and wife now in body as well as spirit, wasn't that so?

'Yang?' she began tentatively.

He turned to her. 'I didn't want to wake you.'

'I… You didn't. I mean, it wouldn't matter if you did. I don't mind.'

They spoke gently. Bedroom voices, though she had never shared her bedroom with anyone besides her amah when she was young. She would have thought there was nothing left for them to be shy about, not after last night. The sensual memory of Yang sliding deep inside her made her stomach flutter.

'There might be a child,' he said quietly.

She blushed. 'I know.'

Heat travelled up her neck and left her palms damp, not that she was embarrassed by what they had done, but—well, she was just blushing and couldn't help it. She wished very much for Yang's typical teasing and disarming manner to appear and rescue her. Instead he sat watching her while she had a thin blanket pressed over her breasts.

'If there is, I'll make sure he— I'll make sure the child is taken care of, no matter what happens to me,' he promised.

'Don't talk like that.' Jin-mei looked away, breathing deeply against the sudden panic rising in her.

'I just wanted you to know that I have thought of the future. I wasn't being reckless last night.' He reached out to squeeze her ankle once, his touch warm through the blanket. Then he released her and straightened his shoulders. 'If my associates do not arrive within the day, we'll need to leave. This camp won't be safe for long.'

He stood to go to the windows, and Jin-mei hunted down her scattered clothing and dressed quickly. 'What happens then?' she asked, twisting her hair into a haphazard bun before pinning it.

'We rejoin Lady Daiyu's ship. Continue north.'

His frown had deepened. There was something he wasn't telling her. 'What about your associates? What if something has happened to them?'

'There's nothing I can do. We just continue on and I make new allies.'

Was it too much to hope that he could reconsider his quest for vengeance? She started to reply, but bit her tongue. This was Yang's world and it was foolish of her to think marrying or making love to her would change it. She stood next to him now, close enough to touch, but not touching.

'When does it stop, Yang?'

His expression remained blank as if he hadn't heard her.

'We take a boat north. You make new allies, co-ordinate new attacks, but when does it end?'

He smiled. 'You have a way of always asking all the hard questions.'

As an attempt at charm, it was a poor one. She narrowed her eyes at him and his smile faded.

'There is only one way this ends: when Wang Shizhen is dead,' he said bluntly.

He turned to start gathering their belongings. Yang tossed such words around so easily: danger, sacrifice, death. Her heart pounded and her palms began to sweat.

'Or you are?' Her challenge came out forced and thin, but she wasn't going to be dismissed so easily. 'When he's dead or you are, you mean.'

Yang paused. 'Yes. Him or me.'

He couldn't face her as he said it. A sick feeling twisted in her gut and part of her wished she hadn't pushed him to say the words, but he was acting as if such a vow meant nothing. As if it didn't affect him and every single person whose life was intertwined with his. That included the workers in his salt refineries, his traders, his so-called associates and certainly his family. And now her.

'Maybe you need some time to consider a new plan,' she suggested as desperation set in. 'The general just survived an attack. He'll be more watchful now than ever before.'

Yang paused, and Jin-mei thought he might have been considering her plea, but she realised he was standing too still and staring at the paper panes of the windows. More specifically he was staring through the thin sheet at the shadows moving on the other side. Someone was there, in the camp.

Yang pressed a finger to his lips to urge her to remain quiet, but it was hardly necessary. She couldn't move a muscle as her throat closed tight. Raising his hand, Yang motioned her for her to stay where she was while he left the room. Jin-mei gathered up their packs quickly and took hold of her staff. Her hand shook so hard that she doubted she'd remember any of Lady Daiyu's combat instructions, but holding on to something solid did make her feel better. There was nothing else to do but wait. She held her breath.

A moment later, Yang reappeared, moving quickly. 'Out back,' he whispered. *'Go.'*

He remained close behind her as they hurried through the sleeping cabin. The back door opened out into the cold morning and the stillness of the camp became more eerie now that she knew they weren't alone.

Yang appeared deathly calm as he took the lead. The hand he placed over her arm to guide her was surprisingly steady while her heart was pounding so hard that she could barely make out his instructions.

'To the lake,' he whispered.

The first sight of the intruders stopped her heart. They were wearing soldiers' uniforms and she could see at least three of them. One of them started climbing the ladder into the guard tower.

Without even a moment's pause, Yang redirected them

behind a storage shack. Then he wound them around the buildings towards the back wall. She followed him without question, gripping the staff so tightly that her knuckles turned white.

As they neared the lake, Jin-mei could see an opening cut into the wall where a bamboo pipeline had been set up to transport water from the lake into holding basins. Yang squeezed her hand once before boosting her on to the rigging. The bamboo structure creaked beneath her feet, but seemed to hold.

She climbed towards the opening while Yang kept watch. From behind them, Jin-mei could hear what sounded like a crackling noise. She didn't have time to ponder it before squeezing through the small opening to emerge outside the compound, just over the lake.

With a splash, she landed in the shallow water below and her feet sank into the soft mud. They made a sucking sound as she pulled free. Yang landed beside her, splattering her tunic. Her clothing was the least of her worries. She could sense movement all around them and hear voices from within the compound, shouting.

They waded towards the opposite bank, the water rising up to her knees. By the time they climbed on to dry land, the crackling, popping sound had increased. Jin-mei turned around to see black smoke and orange flame rising from the thatched rooftops in the compound. The soldiers were setting it on fire.

Yang pushed forward into the surrounding brush. The compound was crawling with General Wang's soldiers. There was little cover near the lake where the saltwater prevented growth and they would be easily spotted. They had to find refuge in the forest quickly.

Only when the trees rose thick around them did he

allow himself to look over his shoulder. Wisps of dark smoke poured into the sky and orange flames licked over the walls, leaving a cold, sick feeling in the pit of his stomach.

His father had established this well. Built this compound. Even though it had been abandoned, Wang Shizhen wanted it destroyed. The warlord would seek out everything Yang called his own and burn it to ash. This was the meaning of a blood feud.

Jin-mei said nothing while she trudged on beside him, but he could hear the catch in her breath. The terrain was growing steeper and she was struggling to keep up. She was also very frightened.

This was not how most people lived their lives; always running from danger.

There was a rustle from somewhere to the left. Something larger than a rabbit or fox. Yang slipped his knife from his belt into his hand for quick access. Jin-mei's sharp eyes caught the movement and she bit down on her lip as she stilled, waiting for him to tell her what to do. The problem was he didn't know; Jin-mei wasn't one of his workmen or his brothers-in-arms. She was an innocent.

Two figures came rushing through the trees dressed in soldiers' garb and there was no time to ponder it. Yang grabbed a throwing dagger from his belt and let it fly. In the next breath, the blade had embedded itself into the lead man's shoulder. He clutched at the wound while the second soldier drew his sword. With a shove, Yang pushed Jin-mei towards the cover of the woods.

'Run!' he shouted.

Her grey tunic blended into the surroundings, disappearing into the shadow of the trees. Hopefully there weren't any more soldiers waiting there.

Yang turned back to see more soldiers approaching. He'd never been much of a fighter and he didn't have any illusions about being able to match trained soldiers. Flying knives were stealth weapons, good only at the beginning of a fight for the element of surprise. He usually focused on outwitting rather than overpowering his opponents, but there was no outwitting fifty soldiers bent on his capture.

More men appeared ahead. *On his grave*. They hadn't seen him yet, but once the alarm was sounded, they would swarm over him like a pack of wild dogs. Desperate, Yang lunged for the closest pair. One hand locked around his opponent's wrist to prevent the sword strike while his knife hand shot forward, punching beneath the ribs. He pierced through cloth and then muscle before dragging the knife out.

The first soldier slumped forward while his partner lunged. He hit Yang squarely in the chest, knocking him on to his back. Yang tried to wrestle free only to find himself pinned. The soldier hovered over him, snarling. The hilt of the throwing knife protruded from his shoulder.

Yang opened his mouth to negotiate. It was instinct, or at least his particular instinct. Odds weren't in his favour, but it was his last and only weapon. Before he could speak, another shadow rose over both of them. The soldier turned just as Jin-mei raised her arms overhead. She swung downward with all her might and there was an audible crack before the man fell aside. Yang scrambled to his feet and gave him an additional kick to the ribs, leaving the soldier in a moaning heap on the ground.

Jin-mei clutched her bronze mirror as she stared at him. 'Yang—' she began in a shaky voice.

There was no time to celebrate, but he fell for her a little bit harder right in that moment. 'Run, Jin-mei.'

She dropped the mirror and ran, panting. 'Where are we going?'

'I don't know. Just run.'

No soldiers leapt out at them, but for all Yang knew there could be patrols surrounding the entire area. Jin-mei staggered, picked herself up, then staggered again.

'Go,' she told him, out of breath. 'I'll slow you down.'

'Nonsense.' He pulled her forward, willing her to continue.

His lungs were burning as well. There was a small burst of speed as they both pushed past exhaustion, but soon after Jin-mei truly reached her limit. He pulled her behind a fallen tree where they both crouched, gasping for breath.

For several long minutes they waited, listening for the sounds of pursuit. Jin-mei was pressed close to him, trembling. He put his arm around her, holding her tight as if to keep her from breaking into pieces. 'I think we're safe.'

He wasn't certain of that, but it was what Jin-mei needed to hear.

She pressed a fist to her chest. 'What…do we do…now?'

'The river. We have to get back on to the ship. We'll walk to conserve our strength until we need it again.'

He stood and held out his hand to help her up. She hesitated before taking it.

'Thank you.' Her dark eyes fixed on to him when she was on her feet. 'For not leaving me.'

'Did you think I would?' he teased.

A strange feeling knotted in his chest. She wasn't like the men he commanded or his co-conspirators. His breath caught in his throat just looking at her with her cheeks flushed and hair wild as he added, 'Who else would I find foolish enough to marry me?'

She rolled her eyes at him and pushed her hair out of her eyes before plodding forward. At least his jest had the intended effect; Jin-mei looked a little less frightened.

There were times when he closed his eyes and could almost see a future with her. Jin-mei was clever, fearless and headstrong enough to put him in his place. She had seen him for who he was and she hadn't run away.

Even though they were still surrounded by danger, he reached out to touch a hand to the small of her back. He had to, if only to remind himself that Jin-mei was real and she was worth fighting for. He would do anything in his power to keep her safe—and that meant ridding the world of his greatest enemy.

Jin-mei wasn't accustomed to a life of violence, but sometimes bad deeds were needed to accomplish good deeds. She would understand after he had won this war. Only then would he finally be free.

Chapter Thirteen

Jin-mei was learning quickly that her husband was fearless. Not only with the courage required to escape from armed soldiers—that was merely for survival and every animal possessed such instincts. Apparently Bao Yang had no fear of ridicule, gossip or sidelong, disparaging glances.

Even though they were rumpled and splattered with mud, Yang smoothed his hands over his sleeves as if there was nothing amiss but a few wrinkles and entered the business office with head held high. The signboard over the door labelled it as a shipping company.

At the front counter, he asked the clerk for a Mister Shen. They didn't have to wait long before they were beckoned into the inner office.

Inside, a portly, middle-aged man stood to greet them. 'Mister Bao, welcome!'

The two men exchanged pleasantries while Jin-mei took a seat on the stool in the corner. She stared at her ruined slippers and wondered whether she looked more like a beggar or a madwoman. At home, she wouldn't have been seen outside their four walls in such a state, let alone in a public building.

'My wife and I are headed for the Lintai valley,' Yang was saying. 'If you could offer us transport, I would be grateful.'

'Lintai?' The merchant looked through his record book. 'The area is remote, but I do have a caravan headed to a stop nearby in two weeks.'

'Two weeks is a long time. Is there any way we can get there sooner?'

'You would have to go by water.'

It didn't take long for them to work out the details. Once they were done, Mister Shen wrote up a few instructions which he handed off to the clerk to deliver. 'Everything will be ready by tomorrow morning.'

'Efficient as always,' Yang commended.

The merchant beamed at that. 'So what business do you have in Lintai, friend?'

'Funny, you've never asked about my affairs before.'

Jin-mei had stood as they were about to take their leave, but the slight hardening of Yang's tone took her aback. She glanced at him to see he was still smiling pleasantly.

Shen had stood as well. 'Just conversation, Mister Bao.'

'I apologise.' Yang gave a light laugh. 'Lately I've been wondering if anything has changed between myself and my old-time acquaintances.'

Apparently the matter was far from closed. Shen straightened to his full height, which was still half a head shorter than Yang. 'I have long done business with your father as well as yourself. Yet I consider you a friend as well as a business partner. It would be my hope to go to my ancestors still calling you a friend.'

'Mine as well,' Yang replied, his expression grave. 'Do you know of what's happened?'

'I don't need to know.'

The merchant broke off the tense exchange to look at Jin-mei. She stood stiffly behind Yang's shoulder.

'Bao *Furen*. I apologise for not attending your wedding,' he addressed her by her married name. 'If you would please stay at my house tonight as my guest, I can feel as if I have made up for not being there on your day of happiness.'

'Of course, sir. We're grateful for your hospitality.'

She was uncertain, even as she spoke the words, whether or not it was the right response, but Yang seemed to harbour no ill will as they left the office.

'What was that?' she asked beneath her breath.

'Just conversation,' he said, echoing the merchant's response.

'What do we do? Do you trust him? Do we flee again?' She shushed and her heart skipped a beat as Mister Shen appeared outside the door. With a sweep of his arm, he pointed down the road before taking the lead.

'We go have tea and get some rest before tomorrow,' Yang answered cheerfully, as if the tense exchange inside had never happened. 'And you must do a better job of appearing to be my wife.'

'I *am* your wife—'

He smiled at her before taking her arm and pulling her close. Then they fell into step alongside Shen. Jin-mei tried to follow along as they discussed their various journeys and she wondered how many such friends Yang had throughout the province. Associates he could impinge upon at a moment's notice, yet whom he still didn't trust.

The merchant Shen's residence consisted of a square courtyard with living quarters arranged around it—

luxurious for the country, but still simple. They were brought into the main parlour and indeed there was tea. It was brought to them on a tray alongside dishes of candied ginger and lotus seeds. Jin-mei didn't realise how much she'd longed for a little touch of civility until she took her first sip of the fragrant brew.

This was the life she had been prepared for: quiet parlours and cups of tea.

'Bao *Furen*,' Shen began cordially. 'We may have just met, but I already know you must be the most kind and forbearing of women to be married to this scoundrel.'

Yang bit back a grin, a dimple forming in his cheek, while the older man wagged a finger at him. It reminded her how she had first become enchanted with him. Yang was at ease in any surrounding. Certainly he was clever with words, but his silences were even more endearing. He could charm with a glance or a mere quirk of his lips.

'I tricked him into marrying me,' she declared, earning her a raised eyebrow from Yang.

Shen belted out a laugh. Her response seemed to earn his approval and he turned to her to continue the conversation. 'Where are you from, little one?'

'Minzhou prefecture, sir.'

'And your family?'

She looked to Yang for any instruction, but he merely gave a nod of encouragement.

'My father is the county magistrate.'

Shen went silent, then his grin returned. 'Ah, Mister Bao. Fortune smiles upon you.'

'Indeed, I'm very fortunate.' Yang met her eyes and a small thrill went down her spine. 'But I must remember to take care of my wife. She's very tired.'

Jin-mei frowned. 'I'm not very tired.'

'So selfless, my dear wife. We've had a hard journey. You look as if you can barely stay awake.'

Her eyes narrowed at him. He reached over to pat her hand—a very deliberate tap.

'I suppose I am quite tired,' she relented.

The merchant watched their exchange, amused. 'My housekeeper will show you to your room.'

She had no choice but to leave the two of them to whatever secret and underhanded matters they had to discuss. Even a hot soak in the bathhouse couldn't relieve the tension that made her stomach knot and her head ache. She returned to the guest room in a fresh change of clothes and lay back on the bed.

Half an hour later she was still staring at the ceiling when Yang entered.

'What did you and Shen speak about?' she asked.

'This and that.'

'Old times?' she offered archly.

'Exactly that.'

Jin-mei shot up to sitting position. 'Will I have to listen to half-truths for the rest of our lives—why are you smiling?'

'Even though you're angry at me, you said "our lives".' He sprawled on to the bed with his head in her lap. 'I find that endearing.'

'I am angry,' she agreed. 'And you're still filthy.'

His hand rounded her knee, squeezing gently in a way that made her toes want to curl tight. She wouldn't let them.

'You smell nice.' He inhaled, closing his eyes. She thought he might be falling asleep, holding her in this awkward embrace with a contented look on his face. A tiny, invisible fist squeezed around her heart.

'What did the two of you talk about?' she asked

again, fighting the urge to tuck a stray lock of hair from his face.

'You're very precious to me, Jin-mei. I'll do anything to keep you safe.'

It took her a moment to find her breath. He'd stolen it away. 'You told Mister Shen that?'

'No.' He opened his eyes and looked up at her. His hand tightened on her knee. 'I'm saying this to you now.'

If that was all Yang had to say, she would have taken her soul and handed it to him with both hands, but he continued. 'If there are things I cannot tell you or matters that I must hide from you, it's only to protect you.'

Immediately the warmth in her chest was replaced with ice. 'If you want my permission, you won't get it.'

It had been the same with her father—more secrets and lies than truths between them. She nudged Yang from her lap, and he had the audacity to look wounded.

'I told Shen the truth,' he admitted. 'I informed him of my failed attempt on General Wang and warned him of the danger of being involved with me. I offered to dissolve all ties to him from here forward.'

'Just like that?' she asked incredulously.

'Quick and clean.'

'But you appeared to be…to be good friends.'

'There are friends of the heart; you know they would die by your side and you by theirs. There are friends of the mind. You know you can trust them, but you cannot ask them for more than they're willing to give. Then there are friends by circumstance alone who will cut your throat if it's to their advantage. Shen is the second sort. I can only ask him for so much.'

A sinking feeling pulled at her from inside. 'And what sort of friend was my father?'

Yang's eyes became cold, and he abandoned any attempt at humour. 'With all due respect—which is none— your father has already tried to cut my throat. I no longer consider him a friend of any kind.'

She felt a sharp pang in her chest, as if his words had severed her last tie to her father. 'What is it Father wanted from you?' she asked bitterly. 'Money?'

He didn't answer.

She let out a breath, defeated. 'What did you want from him?'

'Any bargain worth making is made for power,' Yang admitted. 'Sometimes all he needed to do was turn a blind eye. At other times, he was able to make things happen.' He climbed off the bed and straightened with a long sigh. 'You know I'm no better than him. No better or worse.'

He was wrong. Yang wanted revenge for his sister. He wanted to right what he'd done wrong. Her father had taken a position of power in order to abuse it.

When she'd made love to Yang in the abandoned salt well, she'd made a choice with her body. She was Yang's wife for that night and for the rest of her life, but that meant she was no longer her father's daughter. Perhaps it would have been best if Yang had kept the truth from her after all.

Chapter Fourteen

True to the merchant's word, their transport was ready early the next morning. The boat was a small vessel with a shelter built over the hull. It was the sort of boat a fisherman could work as well as live on as he floated along the river. With the sun not yet fully risen, they would actually be setting out at the same time as the morning fishing boats.

Yang offered his hand to Jin-mei, who stumbled a little upon first setting foot on the swaying vessel. She righted herself and went to sit beneath the awning that had been rigged up to provide shade from the sun.

'Do you know how to sail this boat?' she asked as he untethered the vessel.

'My ancestors built their fortune by the river.' Yang used the wooden pole to push off from the dock. 'My family has its own fleet of boats.'

'Which you now use to transport salt?'

'Among other things.'

The water was shallow there with very little drift. He wedged the pole against the river bottom and used the leverage to propel them forward. In the adjacent boats, fishermen stood to do the same, using small, efficient movements to guide their vessels along. As time went on, each of the boats floated farther apart until they were isolated upon the river.

Eventually Yang caught a current and the flow of the water took over, allowing him to sit down. With his shoulder pressed to Jin-mei's, they watched in silence as the sky brightened into day.

'Do you intend to keep smuggling?' she asked him finally.

'No.'

'No?'

He wished she didn't sound so surprised. 'Do you think I can't change?'

She played with the embroidery on her new slippers, tracing the fish pattern with her finger. 'I don't know if you really want to change.'

'Jin-mei.'

Something in his tone must have warned her. She finally looked up.

'I intend to spend the entirety of my ill-got fortune on toppling Wang Shizhen,' he promised. 'And when that is done, I can become a peasant farmer if you like.'

'If you were a farmer, you'd swindle the landowners out of their property somehow,' she retorted.

It was hard not to break out into a grin. He rather liked her picture of him. Despite her claim otherwise, he was the one who had tricked her into marrying him, and at that moment, he didn't regret it at all. Because he was a scoundrel and because a man like him couldn't have won a woman like Jin-mei through honest means.

All wooing was a bit of a con game. Jin-mei already knew him for what he was—Yang just hoped very much to be honest with her where it mattered.

'So what is in Lintai?' she asked.

'Pottery.'

She frowned at him, but he didn't leave her to ponder for long. 'Deep in the valley, there's a remote village inhabited by labourers and craftsmen all devoted to the creation of ceramic pottery. There are several such villages hidden throughout the area. It's the ideal place for us to hide while I try to re-establish communication with our allies. Something happened to prevent them from showing up at the meeting as we'd planned.'

Instead, Wang's soldiers had swarmed the salt well and burnt it to the ground. Fortunately, his fellow conspirators hadn't been caught up in the raid. They'd known to stay away. Either they'd been cautious enough to scout the area or...

'Do you think there was an informant among them?' Jin-mei asked, echoing his thoughts.

His mood darkened. 'Hard to trust anyone these days.'

Even though the merchant Shen knew where he'd gone, the valley was wide and surrounded by dense wilderness. The villages were far beyond General Wang's reach and it would be difficult for his scouts to figure out which village they were hiding in.

'There's a friend in the remote village who will take us in,' he continued. 'Or at least I hope he will.'

'You have friends everywhere,' she remarked drily.

'It's good to have friends.'

'You use that word too carelessly.'

He nodded. 'Perhaps I do.'

The journey would take several days. Eventually they would leave the main river and follow tributaries deep into the valley. At night, they anchored near the shore to sleep inside the cover of the boat. From early morning until sundown, they floated steadily along the current towards their destination. By the middle of the next day, there was neither a boat nor a person in sight. Only the hovering dragonflies and the occasional splash of fish in the water kept them company.

One afternoon, while the sunlight danced lazily over the water, Yang found Jin-mei checking the fishing nets that she had cast over the side. He went to stand over her, watching as she bent over the prow to dip her hands into the water. Her hair was tied into a single braid that trailed down her back and she had rolled up her sleeves to her elbows.

'We have enough food to last until we reach the village.' The meals had been simple and sparse, but Shen had supplied them well.

Jin-mei continued with her task, undeterred. 'I saw the nets and the days can get a little long out on the water. I thought I could learn something new.'

Her hand had become trapped within the woven fibres. Desperately, she tried to shake it loose which caused water to splash over the deck. A warm feeling settled in his chest as he lowered himself beside her.

'The harder you struggle, the more entangled you'll become. Nets are designed that way.' Gently, he took hold of her wrist to free her from the mesh. 'See?'

Her hand looked pale and delicate in his. He held on for longer than he needed to, massaging his thumb over her wrist and feeling the skip of her pulse in response. With an intake of breath, Jin-mei slipped out of his grasp to return her hands to the water. Colour formed high on her cheeks.

'I know there's fish in the river,' she said in a rush. 'I can see them swimming when the water's clear. With any luck, we'll have fish for dinner.'

Jin-mei dragged the net from the water bit by bit.

When it came up empty, the forlorn look on her face made him want to grab her and kiss her hard.

She glanced up as a choked sound escaped his lips. 'Are you laughing at me?'

'No.' Yang placed his fist over his mouth. 'Not at all.'

'You *are* laughing!'

'The boat's moving.'

Her eyes narrowed at him, and he could see her mind working. The days out in the sun had cast her pale skin in honeyed tones, and her hair was on a constant quest to break loose from its braid. If he was captivated before, he was enchanted now.

'Explain,' she demanded, still glaring at him.

Jin-mei was a properly educated young lady: calligraphy, embroidery, the arts. Before throwing her fate in with his, she had no need of the basic knowledge any child living along a riverbank would know.

He tried to keep his tone neutral, lest he be pushed into the water. 'The movement of the boat disturbs the water around it. Fish don't usually swim into a moving net.'

Her blush deepened. 'Well, that makes complete sense.'

By now there was more than a ball of warmth in his chest. It was decidedly hotter and the location decidedly lower.

'We should get out of the sun,' he suggested, his throat dry with desire.

'Oh?' They were still kneeling, but Jin-mei stood quickly, staggering a bit with the sway of the boat.

'Yes.' He stood to take her side, steadying her with a hand against her hip. 'Your skin is soaking up the sunlight. You don't want to burn.'

He was burning. Curling his arms around her, he pulled her close. At first it looked as if she might try to escape, though there was nowhere to escape to. As soon as he pressed his mouth against hers, Jin-mei melted into his embrace.

'But...' She gasped and caught her breath between kisses. 'But we're outdoors.'

'No one will see,' he assured, his voice deep.

He took her mouth again, pushing his tongue past her lips. A shudder went through her, and he pressed her against him to absorb every response. She caressed his tongue with hers, her touch tentative. Sweet.

The thought came to him that he should take her into the shelter, but in the next moment they were already on their knees on the deck. He laid her gently on to the wooden planks, the sun illuminating her face. Heavens, she was beautiful.

'You have a spot here,' he said, kissing a newly formed freckle on her nose. 'And here.'

He touched his lips to her cheek and then the curve of her throat as she arched upward, turning her entire body into a collection of sensual, sinuous lines that made him hard with desire.

'I must look so unladylike,' she murmured, her voice sounding as though it was floating. Her eyes were squinted against the sun; distant and glazed with passion.

'Very unladylike,' he agreed huskily.

His shadow moved over her. Her eyes came into focus as he laid himself alongside her. With one tug of her sash and a few deft manoeuvres, his hand was pressed against the soft skin of her inner thigh. Then he stroked his fingers between her legs, finding the slick, sweet wetness that told him she was burning for him as well.

Her eyes widened as he dipped within her womanly cleft, searching the small knot of flesh at her centre. There was pleasure to be found in the petals, but he knew he'd found the bud when her eyes squeezed shut and she shuddered, hips thrusting against his hand.

His next kiss was against her earlobe before he spoke to her. 'Will you take me inside you? All of me. Here.'

He slid his longest finger between her folds, feeling her swollen flesh part for him. Her head moved restlessly in what might have been a nod, but his name was on her lips, encased inside the sweetest sound of surrender.

Jin-mei moaned again when he circled his thumb gently over her bud. Below, her muscles clenched around his knuckle. She would be sensitive and tight. He'd have to be gentle. He would try to remember that if he had any rational thought left when he was inside her.

Jin-mei made a small sound of protest when he pulled away, fuelling his impatience even more. With heavy-lidded eyes, she watched him undress. First himself and then her, until there was nothing but skin between them.

He could have accomplished the deed without removing every bit of clothing, but they had the luxury of time, of seclusion. And he wanted to feed his senses with her. Yang laid himself over Jin-mei and, with the sway of the water beneath them and the bright sun above, pushed his body fully into hers.

Her head fell back and her lips parted in a silent cry. Yet he heard it deep in his bones and in the hard, responding throb of his body. Inside, she was dampness and heat, closing around him like a cruel fist. He tugged off the ribbon tying her braid and dug one hand harshly into her hair to drag her up to him for a kiss. There was no sense to his actions other than that he wanted more.

Her flesh squeezed tight around him, responding to his claim with its own. It would be fast, too fast. He could already tell from the tension gathered at the base of his spine. Holding his hips as still as he could, he lowered his free hand between them to find her centre once more. It was harder with the crush of their bodies, but Jin-mei moaned into his mouth when he connected, rough fingers against sensitive flesh.

He moved in tiny strokes, as light and fast as he could, willing himself not to climax. It was madness, this fight. All wooing was in part a con game, except for this, when he was without words to negotiate, without pride and without shame.

'Jin-mei,' he choked out. It was a plea.

His last control over his body was slipping, and her flesh was relentless, squeezing him tight, slaying him. His finger worked her pearl faster; no longer gentle, but in pure desperation. When he felt the first pulse of her body in response, elation swept through him. He watched her through her release, nothing more than one heartbeat in time, but a long one. Stretched out.

Then his body would not be held back any longer. He lifted his hips and thrust, once, twice, and in three short strokes he lost his essence inside her, releasing all that he was with no strength left within him to hold anything back.

Chapter Fifteen

At the moment of her release, Jin-mei's vision went black, leaving her in darkness where all she knew was the feel of Yang's body around her and inside her. Once she could see again, Yang's head was tucked against her neck, and she squinted up at the too-hot sun bearing down on them.

Laughing, they gathered their clothes and retreated beneath the shelter. Once she was in the shade, Jin-mei tried to dress, only to have the tunic snatched from her hands and tossed aside. Apparently, she didn't know what it meant to have a new lover, especially if that lover was also a husband.

Yang curved his hands around her breasts, running his tongue and sometimes even his teeth over sensitive skin. Every other part of her felt appreciated as well. The valley of her stomach and the slope of her waist. In response, she ran her hands down over his chest and arms, appreciating the flex of his muscles as he held himself above her.

As her explorations became bolder, Yang rolled on to his side. A smile formed on his lips.

'Curious?' he murmured.

'There's always too much happening to stop and look,' she admitted.

His grin widened as he lay back. 'Look all you want.'

She did look her fill. And touched as well, roaming over the strong, lean contours of his body. Clothing hid so much of these subtleties. Clothed, a body could be anyone, but naked this could only be Yang. Her husband. His skin was slightly damp from their exertions, yet burned with an inner heat.

Yang's gaze darkened as he watched her and she could see the rise and fall of his chest deepening with each breath. Her pulse skipped in a silent response. His organ began to thicken between his legs, even though her hands were nowhere near. The reaction no longer caused her to blush. This was merely the language of their bodies. One that she would study for the rest of their lives.

Emboldened, she climbed on top of Yang to straddle his hips. With her heart pounding, she felt between their bodies, searching for him. There was a moment of fumbling, and she became keenly aware of her own inexperience. The only knowledge she had of this position was laughably from an engraving upon a bridal mirror, but Yang didn't laugh. He settled his hands over her hips. His thumb moved in a slow circle to caress her inner thigh, soothing even as his gaze burned into her.

And soon none of the preliminaries mattered any more. She eased the head of his manhood to her entrance and sank down slowly until they were once again locked as one. The soreness from their first coupling was a temporary discomfort, immediately replaced with a new build of pleasure. She wrapped her legs around Yang's hips and held him tight to her, revelling in the sense that he was hers. Secret things that were secret no more.

Yang watched her face as he thrust gradually upward to deepen the penetration. The first few times they had made love, or rather, when Yang had made love to her, she was too overwhelmed with the sheer newness of it as well as the discovery of untold pleasures. There was hardly time for her to understand what she was feeling, but now he wanted her to experience every moment of it.

'It's taking longer this time,' she said, revelling in how different it felt to be the one to direct their movements.

His intense look broke into a grin. When he laughed she could feel it through his entire frame as he lay beneath her. She could feel it where their bodies were joined. The sound was both warming and sensual.

'Yes, longer this time,' he agreed ruefully. 'As long as you need.'

Jin-mei wasn't sure what he meant by that, but she would learn.

Yang tightened his hands on her hips, lifting then lowering her on to his thrusts which remained deliberate and languid. She braced her hands against his chest and closed her eyes, savouring every slow slide of their bodies. It was beautiful.

Overcome, she cradled his face in her hands and lowered herself to rain kisses over his jaw, his chin, his mouth. Yang returned her kiss softly at first, and then harder. Then all her thoughts fled when he lifted his head and closed his hot mouth over her breast.

Her body tightened with need as he circled his tongue over her nipple in a wet caress. With a cry of surrender, she bucked against him, riding him hard. Her sex flooded, and Yang must have sensed the increase in her arousal. With a groan, his thrusts became shorter. More forceful.

The sensation built in coils and spirals. Her toes curled tight, and her hands dug into Yang's shoulders. Her climax came as a low throb this time; not as intense, but more prolonged. Yang joined her in bliss shortly after, every muscle in his body tensing as his hips jerked beneath her. She watched every emotion play over his face while he gave himself over to the pleasure.

'Let's stay here on this river for ever,' she said much later, sinking sleepily into Yang's arms.

He chuckled and held her tight. They were under the cover of the shelter and wallowing in the last dregs of the afternoon. The sway of the boat on the water lulled her into a restful state.

'Could you live like this?' she asked, serious this time.

'How do you mean?' Yang stroked the pad of his thumb absently over her arm.

'At the far edge of the province, away from the main thoroughfares and headaches of the cities.'

Yang made a sound that might have indicated he was thinking of it. Jin-mei stared at the light filtering into the shelter while she waited for his answer.

'Certainly. Some day,' he answered evasively.

They were both avoiding the obvious. The obstacles that awaited them were much more than headaches. For her, it would be a decision to sever her ties to her father. A pang of loneliness struck her at the thought of her father never knowing what had happened to her. Maybe after some time had gone by, she wouldn't feel the pain so keenly. One thing was obvious. No matter how many years passed, Yang would never forget that her father had tried to kill him. She wouldn't be able to forget either. Or how her father had lied to her.

As for Yang's part, he would have to put aside his hunger for revenge.

'We could start a new life, just the two of us together,' she urged.

Yang nodded beside her. 'It does sound peaceful. My brother Tien had wanted to do just that.'

If it was one thing Jin-mei had learned about Yang, it was that he rarely disagreed. He avoided confrontation and instead somehow managed to bend everyone around him to his will.

'Please consider it.'

He gave her arm a squeeze. 'I will.'

Yang sounded sincere, but Jin-mei didn't know whether she'd changed his mind one bit.

That evening when they were anchored, she did manage to catch a fish. It was a tiny little thing that flopped on to the keel of the boat. With cupped hands, she scooped it up to release back into the water.

'My kind-hearted and merciful wife,' Yang mused.

The truth was she didn't want to ruin the moment by bringing harm to any living creature. The day had been too perfect. She watched the flash of silver as the fish took to the water and disappeared down beneath the cool surface.

Signs of life began to appear along the banks of the river, bit by bit. There was a line with clothes hanging on it to dry. Baskets floating in the water to catch fish. At one point, Jin-mei thought she heard the distant sound of laughter. Maybe children playing.

It was as if they were emerging from the clouds back into civilisation. They reached a bend in the river where the bank circled around to form a shallow basin. Several small boats had been tethered nearby and a group of women were taking out the wash in baskets.

The women looked up curiously at their approach. Yang acknowledged them with a nod that already had the women smiling and nodding back. He certainly had a way about him.

'We are here to visit a friend. His name is Liu Yuan.'

'Ah, yes, Liu Yuan.' They pointed in the general direction of the village. 'Look at the clay pits.'

'They seem friendly,' Jin-mei murmured, taking Yang's side as he thanked the women with a wave.

As Yang had described, the entire village was dedicated to the making of pottery. Arrangements of bowls and cups were laid out in the sun to dry. Beneath covered awnings, Jin-mei could see artisans painting designs on to the ceramic and an entire section of the settlement contained a long row of mounded structures made of brick.

'Kilns,' Yang told her when she mentioned them. 'For firing the pottery.'

The workmen who tended the kilns gave them little notice as they passed by. This was a safe place, with no fear or suspicion of strangers. It was in stark contrast to Minzhou prefecture with its guard patrols and curfews. Over the past year, her father had doubled the number of constables under his employ due to bandit attacks and street crime.

The crimes had escalated when a man had his throat cut out on the street in broad daylight. Then there was the attack at the banquet and the prefect's mysterious death shortly after. She shuddered. Sometimes being a magistrate's daughter made her thoughts wander in morbid directions.

'Have you been to this village before?' she asked Yang.

'Only in passing.'

He stopped at a hut to ask an elderly man out front about the clay pits. They were promptly directed to the hills that surrounded the village. It wasn't too far a distance and she rather enjoyed the walk through the tall grass after being on water for the past few days. The passage of feet from the villagers had created a natural path through the grass which they followed to the foothills.

There they found basically a lot of mud.

The clay pits were exactly that. A shallow basin had been dug all around the base of the hills and a pool of water had collected at the bottom of it. A crew of workmen bent to scrape clay from the sides and collected it into large carrying baskets. They wore leaf hats to shield themselves from the sun and remained barefoot as they worked in the dirt.

Jin-mei stood beside Yang on the outskirts of the pit and waited patiently while the sun seemed to burn brighter and hotter with each passing moment. One of the workmen finally glanced up from the far end of the pit. His gaze locked immediately on to Yang. The man set down his tools and started towards them.

He removed his hat as he came close, revealing long, black hair tied back in a topknot. His face was rough in appearance, with a layer of stubble shadowing his jaw. But it was his eyes that took her aback. They were set deep in his face and piercing, like the eyes of an eagle. His gaze was very far from welcoming.

'Bao Yang,' he remarked in a tone that at best might be called wary.

'Liu Yuan.'

The man's gaze focused on her next. His expression didn't exactly warm up or even soften, but he did look slightly less feral.

'My wife,' Yang introduced.

Liu Yuan managed a nod. *'Furen.'*

'There is something we need to discuss,' Yang began.

The eagle eyes shifted back to him. Without another word, Liu Yuan went to gather his sandals.

'How good of a friend is your "friend"?' Jin-mei asked in a low voice.

Yang gave a shrug. By then the man had returned. Liu Yuan beckoned them back to the footpath and in the same gesture handed her his hat so she could shield herself from the sun. Jin-mei stared at it in surprise. The gesture was done brusquely. The underlying gallantry of it was at odds with the rest of his demeanour.

Yang's friend struck her immediately as a man with thick walls around him; distrustful and suspicious by nature. She knew by the way he refused to take the lead, keeping them in his sight at all times. Yang remained at Liu Yuan's side, continuing on in a conversational tone. This left her in the awkward position of being at the head of the group, though she didn't know where they were going.

'I didn't know if I would still find you here,' Yang was saying. 'You seem to have settled in well.'

'Well enough.'

'This village is so peaceful and quiet. It suits you—'

'Bao,' Liu Yuan interrupted him with a curt address to his family name. 'If you're here, then I know there's trouble.'

Jin-mei glanced back at them. Yang met her gaze before turning to his friend or whatever Liu Yuan was. 'Wang Shizhen survived the attack.'

Liu looked to her. 'Does she—?'

'My wife knows everything there is to know about me. There is no need to keep secrets around her.'

Jin-mei didn't know if she should be touched by that or not.

'General Wang wants revenge now,' Yang continued. 'Mostly he wants my head, but you should be aware so you can stay out harm's way.'

Liu folded his arms over his chest, but otherwise appeared unperturbed. 'You thought he would hunt me down out here? When no one from the authorities even knew my name?'

'Well…there have been some complications,' Yang admitted. 'I was thinking this village would be a good place for us to stay hidden for a little while.'

The other man didn't seem to be happy with this. He didn't seem particularly unhappy either. His face was made of stone. Jin-mei bit her tongue to keep from saying anything. Apparently the two of them had been involved together in the plot to kill the general. Her instincts about this Liu Yuan had been correct; he was a dangerous man.

There was a way about hardened men, Father had told her once. The worst of criminals were caught and punished severely. Usually that either ended their wrongful ways or more likely ended their wrongful life. But those who survived became inured to danger. They no longer feared pain or death the way men were meant to. And thus, they became reckless and irrepressible.

But her father had never been caught or punished for any crime, yet he'd proven himself to be just as ruthless. Life was a mystery. She couldn't presume to be a good judge of anything about anyone now, especially who was right and who was wrong.

'With your permission, if Jin-mei and I could stay in this village, I would be in your debt,' Yang proposed. 'I'm certain that no one here is under the warlord's employ and that we'll be secluded from prying eyes.'

'Permission?' A dark flicker crossed Liu Yuan's face. 'I don't own this village. You're free to do as you please.'

Despite his cold words, Liu Yuan led them to a small hovel outside of the boundaries of the village. He paused outside the door to wash his hands in a bucket that had been left there. That was when Jin-mei noticed that despite the clay and mud caked on to his hands, Liu had worn gloves while he worked. The day was hot and none of the other workers had worn anything over their hands. Furthermore, these gloves had no fingers sewn into them so that only his palm and the back of his hand were covered.

'Bao *Furen.*'

At the sound of her married name, Jin-mei looked up and saw Liu Yuan watching her. He had caught her staring, but said nothing of it as he welcomed them inside.

The hut was built of wood and bamboo and the roof was thatched with straw. The interior consisted of a single room with a sleeping pallet set up in the corner, a tabletop raised just high enough from the floor to sit beside and a meagre collection of belongings that had been stacked along the walls.

Despite the poor state of the hovel, Jin-mei felt a lifetime of good manners pushing her to speak. 'Your home is very—unpretentious.'

She caught Yang stifling a smile. Beside him, Liu Yuan didn't appear offended. 'I built this hut myself and just completed the roof, but we haven't had a big rain recently so it may leak.'

'Built with your own two hands?' Yang asked, impressed. 'You've only been here for a few short months.'

'I was staying with the master artisan and his daughter, but that arrangement was…unacceptable.'

Liu Yuan looked away as if he'd said too much. Restlessly, he moved to tie up the bamboo blinds that lay over the windows. The place improved tenfold with light flooding in.

'I admit there isn't much here in the way of comfort, but you're welcome to stay.'

Yang didn't bat an eye. 'How very generous of you. We graciously accept.'

Jin-mei was about to claim that their boat would be sufficient, but she clamped her mouth shut. It was certainly a finer home than she could have built with her two hands.

'Then it's done,' Liu concluded. 'I must return to the clay pits. The work shift ends at sundown.'

Once Liu Yuan was long gone, Jin-mei finally spoke. 'Explain,' she demanded.

'Liu Yuan and I were involved in a transaction that didn't go as planned.'

She stared at him without blinking, but Yang was shameless. He gestured at the four walls of the simple home his friend had invited them to stay in. 'He had his own reasons for participating, but as you can see, he's now reformed, living a simple life away from the world.'

'He doesn't seem to like you very much,' she pointed out.

'That's how you know you can trust his word,' he returned too easily. 'Liu Yuan isn't easily charmed and makes no effort at being polite.'

She had to ponder that one for a bit.

'We've spilled blood together,' Yang insisted. 'That forms an unbreakable bond with men like him.'

Jin-mei glowered. 'That is somehow not entirely reassuring.'

Unperturbed, Yang took her arm. 'Let's explore the rest of the village, shall we? And remember, you're my wife. Keep up appearances and dote on me a little bit.'

Chapter Sixteen

'Married?' Liu Yuan scoffed. 'Is she really even your wife?'

Liu Yuan took a drink from a jug of wine before passing it to Yang. It was dusk and Liu Yuan had just returned from his work at the clay pits. They sat outside the makeshift house on a wooden bench.

'If Jin-mei heard you say that, I would be in trouble for a long time.'

The other man shrugged. 'Where is she?'

'The women seem to have taken her under their care. And, yes, she is my wife.'

Yang tilted the jug to his lips, rolling the wine in his mouth before swallowing. Millet wine, perhaps unrefined, but certainly not poisoned. Jin-mei was correct that he and Liu Yuan weren't friends in the conventional sense. This must be the first time they'd ever spoken of anything remotely personal.

'Does she know of your past?' Liu Yuan asked after a while.

'She does. At least now she does.'

'But not when you married her.'

'Not then.'

Yang had no doubt that if she had, his life would have

taken a different path. He'd be alone right now, for one. He'd also have less of a reason to succeed in his quest.

'Do you know she's a magistrate's daughter?' Yang asked, not sure why he wanted to reveal that fact to Liu Yuan, who was a convicted criminal.

Indeed, Liu Yuan's spine stiffened at the news. 'That's unexpected.'

'The county magistrate of Minzhou.'

With a snort, Liu Yuan took back the wine and drank. He shook his head as he swiped the back of his hand over his mouth. 'The same magistrate who had us imprisoned.'

'You should know that Magistrate Tan was my contact. He got us into that banquet and put us within striking distance of our enemies. He also made sure there were enough openings for us to escape the prison house that night.'

There had been three of them during the attack at the prefect's banquet. Yang had focused on General Wang while Liu Yuan and his sister had targeted Prefect Guan who had sentenced their father to death.

When plotting the assassination, Yang had determined he needed someone by his side who was trained in combat. Liu Yuan and his sister were both skilled fighters; cold and sharp enough to take a man's life. Overall, it was a brash plan, but it had nearly succeeded.

'And several months later, you married the magistrate's daughter,' Liu Yuan remarked. 'You thought this was wise?'

Yang laid his head back against the wall of the hut, letting his eyes fall closed. 'Things just fell into place that way. The magistrate wants me dead now as well. I can identify him as a co-conspirator, after all.'

'There is no escaping one's past, is there?'

Liu Yuan stared down at his hands before looking out into the night. He had built his home on the far outskirts of the village, in a place where it was hidden within the trees and hills. From what Yang knew, the other man had been a bandit for the past ten years whilst seeking revenge against the men who had destroyed his family. But Liu Yuan was different now. Yang could sense it with every movement and every word, which he chose so carefully. Liu Yuan was trying to turn his life around right when Yang had returned to drag him back into danger.

'We'll be gone within the week,' Yang said instead. 'Your life will resume as it was. No one will know you're here.'

'You haven't asked what you came here to ask.'

'No, but that was a mistake. I won't be asking anything of you.'

'You came here to enlist my help in your rebellion.'

Yang let out a slow breath. 'I came first to warn you that Wang Shizhen had survived, but, yes, my secondary purpose was to recruit you. I've fought by your side. I know what sort of man you are.'

'I'm an outlaw and a murderer,' Liu Yuan said bitterly. 'And that's why you need me.'

Yang didn't want to admit it, but there was no hiding the truth. This was what Yang excelled at. He orchestrated and plotted and brought people together to act on his plans. Liu Yuan had been a dangerous man who cared little for the ruling class. There were few trained fighters in the rebellion and, even more importantly, few who wouldn't shirk at the thought of killing someone who got in his way.

Not many people could deal a death blow without wavering. Yang knew that first-hand now. It wasn't an easy thing, taking another man's life. Even one he hated.

But Liu Yuan had gone from leading a gang of roving bandits to working with his hands in the dirt, building a home in a remote village to try to fit himself into a new life. Suddenly Yang felt like a cold-hearted scoundrel. He'd always prided himself in never bringing anyone into the fold against their will, but he had a talent of finding the places where someone's will could be bent and shaped. Yang could still see those touch points so clearly, but he didn't have the heart for it any more.

'Your blood debt is paid,' he told the former bandit. 'Once I'm gone from here, forget you ever knew me.'

Maybe Yang had changed as well. He wanted to believe there was such a thing as a righteous death. That there was a way, under heaven, for a man to have his revenge and continue on afterwards. Even once there was blood on his hands.

Yang found Jin-mei at the centre of the village, sitting beneath a covered work area with lanterns lit all around her. She had a porcelain bowl in one hand and a calligraphy brush in the other. Another young woman was working beside her, painting a tall vase.

Liu Yuan stepped forward into the halo of lantern light. At that moment, the young village woman looked up and her face brightened into a smile. The former bandit practically stumbled to a halt.

'Miss Shifen,' he greeted, his voice catching roughly over her name.

'Brother Yuan.'

Yang suspected he'd found what, or who, had inspired Liu Yuan to mend his ways. Shifen wore a plain tunic over trousers, both dyed dark in colour. Her hair was tied back in a single long tail that hung halfway down her back and a scarf was wrapped around her head. Everything about her spoke of practicality and simple efficiency, but her eyes shone with an inner light that was more eye-catching than the brightest of pearls—at least they were for Liu Yuan, who looked as though he couldn't decide between looking away or staring at her as if she were the moon.

Shifen turned to Yang next. 'I apologise for kidnapping your wife, Mister Bao. Her calligraphy is so beautiful, much better than mine. And we are behind on this next shipment.'

'There is no need for apology. My wife is headstrong and known to follow her own mind.'

'See how my husband complains about me to strangers?' Jin-mei's eyes remained focused on the task before her. She held her bottom lip between her front teeth as she concentrated on finishing the verse.

'It wasn't a complaint.'

The quietness of his tone brought her gaze up to him. The moment their eyes met, every part of him filled with warmth. A flush came to her cheeks as well and a thought came to him, as clear and pure as ice.

He could make a life with this woman. Jin-mei would change him in every way, but he wouldn't fight it. He wanted to become what he could be with her. All he had to do was get them to a place of safety where their lives could finally begin. And then the dream would gradually unfold. He would will it so.

'Everyone else has retired to their homes except for you,' Liu Yuan was speaking to the artisan.

'I work too late,' Shifen admitted with a laugh.

'You always do.'

Jin-mei exchanged a knowing look with Yang as Liu Yuan and his village miss babbled on.

'The two of you must be hungry.' Shifen directed the

last statement at him and Jin-mei, with a furtive glance thrown towards Liu Yuan. 'Father and I have more than enough.'

In the end, they cleared the work area to make enough room for the four of them. Shifen brought bowls of a hearty bone stew with wood mushrooms and bamboo shoots. A congenial atmosphere took over with the two women carrying the conversation.

'How long are you staying in our village?' Shifen asked.

Jin-mei looked to him. 'I told her we're going to your family home up north, but how you insisted on seeing a good friend beforehand.'

'That's true,' he remarked, picking up where Jin-mei had left off. It was vastly more difficult to keep secrets when two people had to co-ordinate. 'Liu Yuan is like a brother to me.'

Liu Yuan responded to his statement with a stone-cold look—which was likely what Yang would get from his own brother as well. 'Bao Yang assisted our family when we were in need.'

At least the man was trying to put up a good front.

Shifen remained warm and welcoming in every way. 'I'm so happy to meet your friends, Brother Yuan.' It must have been the tradition of the village to address one another with such familiarity. 'And I have never heard a word of your family. Do you know he speaks very little of himself?'

The last part was said to Jin-mei with the conspiratorial air of two females who had become fast friends.

'I have a sister,' Liu Yuan offered gruffly. 'She and my mother live in a tea village north of here.'

'Actually, I believe your sister has returned to Minzhou. She's married that thief-catcher you and I are both acquainted with. He's now apparently head constable,' Yang said.

Liu Yuan stiffened, though his words belied his shock. 'I wish her well. I have no quarrel with thief-catchers or lawmen of any sort.'

'If you would permit it, we would like to stay the week,' Yang said quickly. 'My wife and I are enjoying the forest air and the tranquil atmosphere here is good for balancing out the soul.'

Shifen looked more pleased than Liu Yuan did. 'It is peaceful here in our village. And Bao *Furen* can assist me with her wonderful calligraphy. It's nice to have company while working.'

'I would be happy to,' Jin-mei replied, all the while scrutinising Liu Yuan with a sharp eye. Apparently the remark about thief-catchers hadn't escaped her notice. No detail ever did.

Chapter Seventeen

There were no secrets in a small village like this one. Within the first hour of sitting beside Shifen the next morning, Jin-mei learned that the village sold porcelain pottery to support the inhabitants. There were thirteen households who had for many generations taken the surname of Yan, though they were not all related. And the widow Zhao and Liu Yuan were the only two people who lived alone.

Jin-mei had also learned quickly that Shifen had a soft spot for the mysterious Liu Yuan.

'He came to the village nearly six months ago,' the young woman said. 'We knew he was a drifter and some of the village elders were suspicious of him, but he petitioned the elders to be allowed to stay.'

Though Shifen was focused on completing a border design on a bowl, her cheeks grew pink as she spoke of him. Jin-mei had to push her suspicions of Liu Yuan aside. It was only by Yang's association with him that they were able to stay in the village. She was grateful for the respite and even for the work to keep her mind occupied.

'I don't know much of Liu Yuan,' Jin-mei confessed. 'But my husband thinks highly of him.'

Or at least Yang seemed to trust him, which amounted to high enough esteem in his circles.

'Not everyone in the village is convinced Liu Yuan should stay. He remains so distant. It only heightens suspicion among those who were already uncertain of his origins,' Shifen said. 'But everyone can see how hard he works.'

'He doesn't seem distant towards you,' Jin-mei replied with a sly look.

What was it that turned every married woman into a matchmaker? She didn't even particularly *like* Liu Yuan. Something about him irritated her instincts. She should be warning the young woman away from rough-looking strangers with hidden pasts.

Shifen's blush deepened. 'My father offered him shelter when he first arrived. Everyone warned him against letting him into our home...especially with a daughter, but Liu Yuan has been a gentleman in every way.'

'But now he's brought in more strangers to your village. The elders will be upset over that.'

'Not at all. Our village is very welcoming to all travellers.' Shifen set down her bowl to place a reassuring hand on to Jin-mei's arm. 'If anything, your arrival will help Liu Yuan's cause. You and your husband are so well mannered and well spoken. It's reassuring to see that Liu Yuan has friends.'

Yet they were just as much fugitives as he was. Jin-mei had hoped to escape the feeling of being hunted out here, while they were far away from the main roads.

'Here.' She turned the vase so that Shifen could see. 'I selected a verse that I thought would fit the mood of your painting.'

It was the same vase the other woman had been working on the night before. Apparently Shifen had returned to it after dinner once they had all departed. She must have worked late into the night to finish the waterfall and mountain painting.

'The characters look beautiful, Miss Jin-mei. What do they say?'

Jin-mei was taken aback. 'It's from one of my favourite poems. "Can I dream through the gateway, over the mountains?"'

Shifen replied with a smile, 'It sounds pretty. I'm not as educated as you. I doubt anyone in this village is. All of these inscriptions are merely copies. My father has a scroll with the original inscriptions that we painstakingly duplicate to avoid mistakes. A poetic verse or famous inscription adds to the value of the piece considerably.'

Jin-mei helped her set the vase aside before starting on the next vase. This one was more understated in design. A few peach blossoms etched in blue glaze decorated the front of it.

'You know, I do wonder...' Shifen paused to pick up her brush again. She made a show of being absorbed in her work as she spoke. 'How did your husband come to know Liu Yuan when they are clearly from very different stations in life?'

Jin-mei's brush hovered over the vase. If her speech and the way she held herself didn't give her away, then her calligraphy surely would have.

'My husband meets all manner of people in the course of his work,' she managed. 'He's also the sort who seems to befriend everyone.'

'I can see that. Especially if he was able to befriend Liu Yuan,' the young woman said with a laugh.

Jin-mei smiled weakly. 'He is a bit of a mystery, isn't he?'

Anyone could see the pieces of this puzzle didn't fit.

Once again, that nagging restlessness had taken hold of her. A sense of dissatisfaction.

Yang, Liu Yuan and the constable's wife, Li Feng, were somehow all connected. And within that mix, she could probably find both Constable Han as well as her father. Connections between people didn't break that easily. They tended to linger. Their remnants were visible long after the parties concerned had moved on.

Which led her to the only conclusion possible: they were still all connected. Yang had built his network of associates and allies all over the province, like a spider weaving an intricate web. There was no way for him to untangle himself, no matter what remote little village he travelled to.

After a night spent on a thin bamboo mat and a hard floor, Yang was awoken early the next morning by a sinister-looking Liu Yuan standing over him. Jin-mei was no longer by his side. He vaguely remembered her rising a little while earlier.

'A man with as many enemies as you should be more careful,' Liu Yuan intoned.

Yang pulled himself up into sitting position, one arm propped over his knee as he squinted up at his some-time friend. 'I only have one enemy. He just happens to be a formidable one.'

Well, two enemies if he considered that Jin-mei's father had also tried to have him killed.

'I would have taken you for a light sleeper. Once someone is standing over you like this, there's nothing you could do to defend yourself. That knife hidden in your belt would take too long to reach,' Liu Yuan added for good measure. 'I could have gutted you by now.'

'You are a frightening man. I suppose you're a very light sleeper?'

'When I sleep at all.'

'Right. Anyone who wanted to get to me would have had to go through you and you were right outside the door, remember,' Yang replied with a grin. 'Which is why I got such a good night's sleep.'

Liu Yuan scowled back at him. Or perhaps it wasn't a scowl, perhaps he always wore that expression. Yang had known the man's sister and Li Feng was by far a more amiable companion. Just as deadly, but much more pleasant about it.

Jin-mei was right that he seemed to have a penchant for dangerous women. Until now. 'Where's my wife?'

'She said she wanted to continue her work with Miss Shifen.'

'Hmm.' Yang rose to his feet. 'The lovely Shifen— are you going to marry that girl?'

This time Liu Yuan really did scowl at him, complete with furrowed brow and a hint of teeth. Funny all the varied ways that love manifested itself.

'Work at the clay pits starts soon. The elders might think better of you if you were to join us. That is if you don't mind your hands in the dirt.'

'My hands are rarely clean.'

Yang raked his fingers through his hair to tie it back. Then he shoved his feet into boots and joined Liu Yuan outside the door.

'It is strange to see the notorious bandit leader working as a common labourer,' he remarked as they headed for the foothills. The smell of fresh grass awakened his senses. The air was damp and cool with morning dew.

'I buried my knives,' Liu Yuan replied. 'The man you knew doesn't exist any more.'

'Hmm. Then how were you going to gut me back there?'

'With my bare hands.' There was another flash of teeth that might have actually been a smile. 'Is it true about my sister? She's married the thief-catcher?'

'I rarely lie.'

Liu Yuan stone-faced him.

'I rarely lie for no reason,' he amended.

They continued through the grass to the pits.

'It gives me hope,' Liu Yuan said after a while. 'Li Feng was never as embittered as I was. I should have never involved her in my need for revenge.'

'She made her own decision,' Yang countered.

'That doesn't absolve me of responsibility. I'm her elder brother.'

Yang was assailed with thoughts of his own sister and her eagerness to do what was best for the family. But he was her elder brother. He was the head of the family and ultimately responsible.

They were nearing the edge of the clay pit where the other workmen were already assembled. A few waved in greeting. Liu Yuan introduced him to the rest of the crew. Shortly after, Yang realised he had mistakenly assumed the clay came from the pit. He also learned quickly that a lot more than his hands would be getting dirty.

The morning started with several carts of white stone being unloaded. From there, the workmen, along with Yang, descended into the pit with sledgehammers and mallets to pulverise the rock into the consistency of sand. A different type of rock was carted to them followed by more pounding. By midday, Yang's shoulders were burning. He and everyone else in the pit were covered in a layer of powder. He caught Liu Yuan's smirk as he swiped his forearm over his brow.

'The village elders don't care if I work or not, do they?'

Liu Yuan shook his head with silent amusement before lifting his hammer over his head. With one strong swipe, the rock at his feet fragmented into tiny shards. Apparently the reformed outlaw did have a sense of humour after all.

Once the rock was turned to powder, they carried buckets of water from the stream to mix into the pit. Yang shed his boots and was soon up to his ankles, stomping and mixing the compound into clay. As the end of the day neared, the damp clay was ready to be dug from the pit and deposited on to the cart to be transported to the pottery wheels. By then, Yang was caked from head to toe, the clay starting to harden over him in a shell and turning him into a statue.

'Jin-mei told me you didn't seem to like me very much,' Yang remarked.

'I don't dislike you,' Liu Yuan replied easily. 'And I like you much more now.'

They finished loading the clay on to the carts to head back into the village. Then Liu Yuan directed him to the eastern side of the foothills.

'There's a lake over there. You can wash up while we take this shipment to the potter's area.'

Yang nodded gratefully, feeling no particular need to be proud and stay with the work crew until the end of the day. At least Liu Yuan seemed to have warmed towards him after working in the pit together.

He considered shoving his feet back into his boots, but then opted to carry them instead. His muscles protested as he bent to retrieve them, and Liu Yuan clasped an almost brotherly hand over his shoulder as he straightened.

'You'll likely sleep very deeply tonight. I won't give you any trouble for it tomorrow morning.'

'You're a gentleman indeed.'

The clay was starting to itch. The thought of the lake was very promising at the moment.

'One more thing.' Liu Yuan leaned in close and lowered his voice. 'In regard to Miss Shifen: she's kindhearted by nature. Wouldn't think of bringing harm to any creature, not even an ant. I appreciate you not saying anything to her about the things I've done.'

'I wouldn't think of it.'

Liu Yuan nodded gravely. 'As to your taunt to me about marrying her—'

Yang started to apologise. It had been nothing more than a meaningless jibe, but Liu Yuan wasn't one for jokes.

'That can never happen. I'm a no-good scoundrel,' Liu Yuan continued, looking straight ahead. 'But I'm not that much of a scoundrel.'

Chapter Eighteen

Jin-mei found the lake by first sighting the top of a waterfall through the trees. The lake itself was immediately below it, nestled into the curve of the surrounding hills. Yang was there with shirt removed beneath the cascade of the water. His eyes were closed as water ran down over his shoulders and chest. The sight of him was practically barbaric.

Her heart raced and her breath grew shallow. The view was obscene. Wonderfully obscene.

Liu Yuan had returned to the village with the work crew and warned her to go see that her husband was still able to move. At the time, the warning had sounded strange, but she had been standing by the lake for a few minutes now and Yang hadn't stirred. Even when she called out to him, he didn't answer.

Jin-mei rounded the edge of the river, careful to keep her slippers out of the mud. When she neared the base of the waterfall, she tried his name once again. The roar of the waterfall drowned her out. Cupping her hand beneath the surface, she flung some water at him to get his attention.

Yang's eyes immediately flickered open. 'That was unpleasant.'

'I needed to be certain you weren't unconscious.' She edged a little closer to not have to shout so loud. The tips of her slippers dipped into the water's edge before she righted herself. 'What are you doing there?'

'Thinking.'

He remained halfway submerged in the lake with rivulets of water streaming down his torso. It was distracting, all that skin. And she with nothing to do but stare at it. 'What were you thinking about?' she asked.

'Water wheels, levers, counterweights used to drive a hammer. There are contraptions used in mines that can break rock a lot easier than a crew of men swinging mallets.'

It was all nonsense to her, but it certainly made her curious. 'You are a complicated man.'

He grinned at that. 'My schemes aren't all greedy and self-serving.'

'Are you going to come out of the water? This is hardly a proper place to have a conversation.'

Yang glanced down over his bare chest as if noticing his state of undress for the first time. His lips moved, but she couldn't make out what he said over the falling water.

She inched closer, feeling a light mist spraying over her face. 'What was that?'

He repeated himself, but she couldn't hear much more than before. When she tried to lean in, Yang's hand snaked out to catch her arm. Jin-mei gasped as she tumbled into the water. A moment later she was securely in his arms.

'I said come closer,' he told her, laughter in his eyes.

She tried to jab him in the chest, but he was holding her too tight. 'Scoundrel—'

He kissed her then, his mouth closing over hers possessively while the water poured over them, drowning out everything but the feel of his arms around her and the press of his lips against hers. Something wild and unbidden released within her and she found herself returning the kiss, eager for the soft invasion of his tongue into her mouth. She clung on to his shoulders, and her feet rose up from the lake bottom until she was floating.

'The villagers will be here at any moment,' she warned the moment Yang broke the kiss. Her heart was pounding hard. Pressed this close to him, she could feel Yang's heartbeat as well, a strong and resounding reply to hers.

'Then we'll have to be quick.'

His voice was low and rough, sending a shudder down her spine. She wanted to ask what they needed to be quick about, but her words lodged in her throat as he led her behind the curtain of the waterfall and backed her against the alcove. Inside, she knew what would come next and her blood pulsed hot through her. The roar in her ears had little to do with the fall of water now.

She watched Yang's face as he opened her tunic. His jaw was tight with desire and his eyes dark and sensual, focused on nothing but her. Water glistened on his cheeks. Jin-mei reached out to cradle his face in her hand. Everything was pulled into sharp clarity as if nothing else existed. She took in every line and contour that made him distinctly Bao Yang.

It wasn't quick, as he had claimed. Or maybe time had slowed. Yang bent his head to her breast and took her nipple into his mouth, sucking gently while she curled her fingers into the dark, wet mass of his hair. His hands worked at the tie of her trousers, loosening the knot and then pushing them down over her hips. Cool air breezed over her legs now exposed. She shivered as she stepped free of the damp clothing. Meanwhile Yang licked water from her skin, causing a pool of heat to build low inside her.

With one hand, he tugged his own trousers open and then he was lifting her against the hillside, one arm at her back to cradle her, one hand wrapped around her thigh. Jin-mei wrapped her legs around his hips and a moment later she felt him pushing inside her, penetrating up into her and taking her thoughts away in a rush of emotion.

This was senseless and irrational. Yang was inside her. A cool curtain of mist surrounded them. She clung to him and the muscles of his shoulders flexed and tightened beneath her hands. Raised and pinned as she was, her body and her pleasure was at his mercy.

Yang kissed her again, using the angle of his body to hold her up. His hand stole between the press of their bodies to find her bud. A sweet ache coursed through her when he did, and she moaned into his mouth.

It wasn't comfortable. His thrusts were shallow and grinding, robbed of full movement, and the hillside was rough against her back. She didn't think it was possible for her to find her release in this way, but she was wild and uninhibited. Yang's tongue was hot inside her mouth, his hand rubbed her sex with a sultry, desperate rhythm, and she found her insides coiling and tightening. Jin-mei gasped as the sharp, blinding streak of climax took her over. Unexpected and more intense because of it.

Yang removed his hand from between their bodies and the arm around her back stole away as well. It took only a moment for him to readjust, with his hands both anchored beneath her legs, lifting and opening her to the thrust of his hips. Before long, he joined her in climax, losing his essence inside her as the water cascaded down around them.

'Sometimes my plans are purely self-serving,' he said huskily as she lowered herself back down. Her legs were shaking as her feet touched the ground. Sometimes she didn't mind that at all.

The affair of gathering clothes and making a hasty retreat had a different sort of desperation from the tryst beneath the waterfall. Jin-mei giggled and Yang swore as he tried to help her back into her trousers which were soaked through and heavy with water. By the time they reached Liu Yuan's hut and smuggled themselves inside, they were both laughing outright.

Yang tried to pull Jin-mei into his arms again, but she swatted him away. 'Shameless,' she scolded.

Jin-mei was starting to shiver in her wet clothes which were dripping water on to the floor. Yang was appointed to be the one to procure dry clothing. He made an effort to straighten his appearance, running a hand over his hair and smoothing out the front of his tunic, which only made her smile widen.

'You may be a hopeless cause,' she said, pulling the edges of his tunic closed over the exposed view of his chest.

'Never.'

The gentleness of his reply brought her head up from her task. His gaze locked on to her and she was caught; rendered more naked and vulnerable than when they'd made love just minutes earlier. There was a boyishness to his look, something earnest and fond that hooked deep into her and wouldn't let go.

'Go, you. I'm getting cold.' She tried to sound playfully commanding, but her voice came out unsteady.

He grinned at her once more before disappearing outside. When he returned a little while later, they dressed in silence. A heavy veil had descended over them.

Yang turned to her after dressing and she reached out to straighten the neck of his tunic, though it didn't need straightening. She just wanted to touch him to somehow explain that she hadn't fallen silent because she was upset or ashamed or disappointed. She had just suddenly found herself without words.

Her hands settled on to his chest, and she could feel his gaze on her. She kept her eyes lowered, unable to meet his at that moment. And her heart, her reckless heart, was beating so loud she couldn't think.

'Are you all right, Jin-mei?' Yang's voice sounded low and close and very intimate.

'Yes,' she said, a bit lost.

Yes, I'm in love.

But she didn't say that. If just the thought made her knees weak, how could she find the strength or will to put it into words? Anything she said would be inadequate. Could those sentiments even be spoken out loud? Or were such raw emotions meant to be kept close until they became understood deep in one's soul, without need for words?

Yang took her hand and she twined her fingers into his, letting the silence speak.

By the time they returned to the centre of the village, she felt like a co-conspirator at his side.

All work had stopped and the villagers were gathered on benches set out in the common area. Warm, savoury smells surrounded them and it looked like the beginning of a communal supper. Shifen beckoned to her from the artisans' tent where many of the women were gathered.

The men collected on the opposite side of the main area. Jin-mei gave Yang one last glance before going over to her new friend.

'Oh, good, the clothes fit,' Shifen said as she handed Jin-mei a bowl of soup.

Jin-mei's face heated. 'Yes...thank you.'

All she could think of was how small and close-knit the village was and that a waterfall, and the water itself, was clear, making it a poor hiding spot. And now everyone, *everyone* must know what she and Yang had been doing.

As she took a spot beside Shifen on the bench, Jin-mei glanced about to reassure herself that the entire village was *not* staring at her. Actually, only one person was looking at her and that was Yang, who caught her eye from the other side of the common and smiled before returning to his conversation with Liu Yuan.

'Brother Yuan seems much happier with his friends here,' Shifen remarked.

'Really?'

Jin-mei stole another glance in that direction. Liu Yuan was focused on whatever Yang was saying. His expression remained grim, almost fierce in its intensity. He wasn't an unattractive man, Jin-mei decided. Just an unapproachable one.

She turned back to Shifen in time to see a wistful look cross the young woman's face. 'Usually he doesn't talk to anyone. He just eats his supper and then retreats, no matter how hard we try to draw him into conversation.'

Shifen looked away to take a spoonful of soup, and Jin-mei's heart softened towards her. If she hadn't been there, would Shifen be sitting here alone as well? The girl seemed friendly and well liked, but from Jin-mei's short time there, it seemed as if Shifen spent a lot of time absorbed with her work. Each person had a task to keep them busy within the village, but Shifen's painting seemed to set her apart from the others.

'Does he know about your feelings for him?' Jin-mei asked quietly.

'There's nothing to know.'

For the next few moments, Jin-mei ate her soup and waited for Shifen to say more, which she didn't. She still had her misgivings about Liu Yuan, but if someone like Shifen cared for him, he couldn't be so bad. He certainly didn't have Yang's finesse or craftiness, which meant Shifen's impression of him was likely an honest one.

'You should say something to him,' Jin-mei suggested, perhaps a bit too secure in the fact that she had a husband. 'Would you like me to make a suggestion to my husband? He and Liu Yuan are friends and he can speak on your behalf.'

There was a reason marriages were often arranged with family members and go-betweens, otherwise they might not happen at all.

Shifen smiled and shook her head. 'It's kind of you to ask, but better not to say anything.'

Jin-mei frowned, but didn't push her any further. They spoke of more inconsequential things for the rest of the meal: how long Shifen had been painting, how her father had taught her his techniques. For Jin-mei's part, there were writing lessons, sitting back straight, wrists in the perfect position as she copied out characters, one after the other.

'Look over there,' Shifen said as their bowls of soup were nearly empty.

Jin-mei followed the nod of the other woman's head, but couldn't discern anything in particular from the men's side of the gathering. A few others had gathered around Yang and Liu Yuan now. Yang was rubbing his shoulder with a pained look on his face and the men were laughing. He really did have a way of commanding an audience.

'Nearly everyone here has grown up in this village,' Shifen said. 'I knew those men as boys, saw them grow taller and stronger. When you live in a place like this, you know who you'll marry for a long time before it happens. You fancy it will be a certain boy that you find handsome and maybe all the other girls feel the same way. You'll end up with him or you'll be with the next one, but it's known in some way.'

Jin-mei nodded. 'Like fate, in a way.'

'Fate,' Shifen echoed softly, but her expression looked sad. 'I never imagined myself with any of them.'

'Why not?'

'My father has only me, Jin-mei. My mother has been gone for a long time now and he has no sons. You understand, don't you? I wouldn't be telling you such personal things, but I feel we're alike in so many ways.'

Over the course of the day, they had exchanged many small details as they worked side by side. Though each seemed insignificant in and of itself, put together they formed a larger picture. She had bonded with Shifen over the shared details of their lives.

'You feel you can't leave your father,' Jin-mei concluded.

'I can't go freely to a husband,' Shifen agreed. 'My father is going blind. He's been losing his sight for years. He can still mix colours and do smaller tasks, but he can no longer see well enough to paint. I'll take care of my father for the rest of his life and when he's gone, I'll join the likes of widow Zhao. There will still be a place for me here. Just not alongside anyone else. When

I was younger, the boys used to try to tease and flirt, because they were boys.' She looked once again to the other side, this time focusing on Liu Yuan. 'The men are kind, but they don't come by to ask for me any longer. Everyone in the village knows my story and how it will end, except for Liu Yuan who doesn't know any better. So he looks at me sometimes, the way no one has in a long, long time. And I like it. That is all. There's nothing more to tell.'

'Oh, Shifen. You know that's not true.'

The girl smiled at her, but it was a forced smile, put on to mask the look of loneliness she wore all the time. It was ineffective.

'Now tell me about your husband and how you came to be wed,' Shifen implored, with a playful nudge against Jin-mei's side. 'That's a much better story.'

She was trying to sort out what part of their strange journey she should recount, when a group of five strangers entered the common. Immediately, the mood of the gathering shifted and conversations fell silent.

The men had the look of mercenaries, with leather armour and swords in their belts, but they identified themselves as soldiers on official business. The village headman, one of the elders, came forward to greet them.

Shifen's hand tightened on her arm. 'It'll be all right.'

Jin-mei held perfectly still, though her instinct was to shrink back and disappear into the tent to hide among the vases and bowls, but that would only draw more attention. Across from her, Liu Yuan tensed. His shoulders were drawn up and his body coiled as if ready to spring. Beside him, Yang's posture remained surprisingly relaxed. He exchanged a glance with her that she assumed was meant to be reassuring. She wished she'd remained by his side.

'They've come here before,' Shifen whispered to her. 'Hopefully they'll be gone quickly.'

Chapter Nineteen

Yang had to settle a heavy hand on Liu Yuan's shoulder to keep him from bolting the moment the soldiers arrived. 'Stay calm. We don't know why they're here.'

Liu Yuan sat back on to the bench, though his posture refused to relax. His fingers curled in his lap as if itching for his knives. Yang understood the sentiment. He'd had more than one confrontation with the general's soldiers, though his strategy was to never face them head-on if he could avoid it.

Across from them, he saw Jin-mei among the other women. She appeared pale, but otherwise she maintained her composure. After their tryst at the lake, he and Jin-mei were dressed the same as the villagers and blended in as if they belonged there. Of course, every villager knew they had arrived just two days ago. He had to rely on them to remain quiet. The thought made him uncomfortable. Though the villagers were welcoming enough, he and Jin-mei were still strangers among them. Liu Yuan himself had only arrived several months earlier.

'We're here to collect taxes,' the leader told the headman.

'But our village has already paid to the collector, sir.'

'It says here you haven't.'

The soldier drew out a notice, but Yang knew it didn't matter what the notice said or if it was true. The headman hesitated as he looked at the paper in his hands. Then he gestured at the other elders. A middle-aged man Yang recognised as the head potter disappeared towards a row of houses in the back.

'There's food cooking,' one of the soldiers remarked loudly. 'It's time for dinner, isn't it?'

The headman took the cue to offer soup, quickly ordering one of the worktables be cleared of pottery so the soldiers could be seated. Widow Zhao and a few helpers brought bowls, setting them down before scurrying away. A few of the villagers tried to continue as if nothing was happening, but it was impossible. All eyes were fixed upon the soldiers.

Maybe they had just come to extort tax money and filch free food. Yang surveyed the villagers in case it came to more than that. There were enough strong, able-bodied men to outnumber the soldiers. Though the soldiers were armed with swords, they wouldn't dare try anything more than a few bullying tactics.

The soldiers ate quickly, speaking amongst themselves in loud voices that rang throughout the common, which had fallen silent. After the first bowls were emptied, they demanded more, which was immediately provided.

The potter returned and handed a satchel over to the village headman who then presented it to the leader of the soldiers. Coins clinked dully from inside the bag as the leader rifled through the contents.

'You're short the required amount,' he declared.

Several of the villagers raised their voice in protest, but the headman quieted them. 'That's all we have.'

'Are you certain of that?'

The soldiers stood and started towards the headman's house. Liu Yuan rose from his seat before Yang could stop him and moved into the soldiers' path. On his grave, Yang had forgotten how fast the man could move.

'Who is this?' one of the soldiers demanded. His hand was at his sword and his comrades moved to do the same.

Liu Yuan eyed the swords briefly, but remained unmoved. 'He said there's no more money.'

His hands remained loose by his sides, but Yang recognised the stance. Liu Yuan was prepared to move quickly if he had to.

'I hear there are fugitives in the area,' the leader said, loud enough for all to hear. He stood from the dining table and strode across the common, coming to a stop in front of Liu Yuan. 'Rebels in hiding. Perhaps you're one of them.'

That, too, was a blind statement, just like the demand for taxes. The warlord's thugs didn't care who was a rebel or if taxes had been legitimately collected. They took what they wanted and crushed anyone who stood in the way. Yang started towards them, his mind racing for what to say that would prevent a confrontation, but it was the headman who came to Liu Yuan's defence.

'There are no rebels here,' the headman insisted. 'Just our villagers. Brother Yuan, please step aside.'

Liu Yuan did so only after a long pause during which he and the leader of the soldiers locked gazes like two wolves circling one another. The other soldiers pushed past to search through the houses while the villagers could do nothing but remain silent and wait.

Several of the other men from the work crew had also risen to their feet, but the elders urged them back. Yang agreed with their guidance. It didn't escape him that these were the sort of men he commonly recruited to the rebellion. Men who had been forced to stand by while enduring a wrong committed against them.

But this wasn't the time. The soldiers were armed; the villagers unorganised. And there were women and children about, close enough to be harmed. Once the soldiers struck down the first dissenters, the rest would waver. Some would flee. The wives and daughters of the fallen would wail.

Bite your tongue, Yang willed silently. *Bite your tongue for now. Just for now.* He thought his mantra was for Liu Yuan and the villagers, but Yang suddenly realised that it was meant for himself. His own fists were clenched tight at his sides.

The soldiers had returned empty-handed, which only made their leader angrier. 'All this junk and only a few coins to show for it?'

He picked up a porcelain bowl and hurled it to the ground. A startled cry rose up from the crowd as it shattered into pieces.

'You're holding out on us, old man.' The leader advanced on the headman, who held up his hands defensively.

'There's nothing more!' he insisted. 'We don't have any more money.'

The leader unsheathed his sword and smashed through a vase. His reaction seemed to encourage the other soldiers as they began grabbing and breaking pottery, anything they could get their hands on. Each crash was like a clap of thunder until they blended together into a deafening, discordant cadence.

Yang looked to Liu Yuan. Instead of becoming more enraged, a deadly calm had settled over him, as if he was absorbing the violence around him and using it to feed something inside. Yang shook his head sharply at his companion, but Liu Yuan did nothing to acknowledge the gesture.

Then a feminine cry rang out. Across the common, a soldier shoved Shifen out of the way before upending the table in her work area, sending all of the pieces she'd been toiling over to the ground. Jin-mei rushed forward to go to her friend when one of the solders grabbed her arm.

Before he heard her scream, Yang was already moving. Out of the corner of his eye, he saw Liu Yuan also in motion.

Yang grabbed on to the soldier's wrist, twisting his arm and allowing Jin-mei to pull free. In the next moment, Yang closed his arm around her protectively, angling her behind him. He faced off against the soldier with his hand raised, palm out, warding him away. It was a gesture of surrender, urging peace, but it also wasn't.

'She's my wife,' Yang said clearly, calmly. 'She's my wife, do you understand?'

He took in the man in front of him, his youth, his brashness. Saw the inexperience in his eyes. He was just following orders.

As the soldier stepped back, Yang nodded at him. As if in approval. The gesture didn't mean anything, shouldn't have meant anything in this situation to a thug with a sword against a peasant and his trembling wife, but it did and the soldier stood down. For the others who hadn't seen the exchange, all they knew was that the destructive mood was somehow broken.

'Let's go,' the leader commanded, sheathing his sword and spitting on the ground. 'There's nothing else here.'

The soldiers regrouped and walked out of the village with the same carelessness with which they had come.

The children started crying and their mothers tried to soothe them as they ushered the little ones away into the safety of their homes.

Yang turned to Jin-mei and pulled her against him, holding her tight. 'Are you hurt?'

Her answer was muffled against his neck as her arms wrapped around him, but she shook her head to let him know she was unharmed.

'Don't be frightened. It's over.' He rested a hand against her hair and surveyed the rest of the village. The sight of the broken pottery sickened him. More so the expressions on the villagers' faces. They were similarly broken, confused and angry.

'These soldiers have come by here before,' the headman was saying behind him. 'We're lucky if they only want money. A year ago, it was to conscript our men into the general's army.'

The man sounded weary, as if the confrontation had taken everything out of him. It was exhausting to hold one's tongue. Given the circumstances, the village elder had handled himself admirably. No one was hurt. Pottery was replaceable.

Then Yang's gaze came round to Shifen. The young woman stood over the remnants of her workshop. There were tears in her eyes as she stared at the shattered pieces. She was standing alone.

She was alone.

Yang broke away and ran from the common, out towards Liu Yuan's hut. Jin-mei trailed after him.

'Yang, what is it? What's wrong?' she asked, breathless.

There was no time to answer. When they reached the hut, it was empty, but a patch of dirt out front had been disturbed. Jin-mei caught up to him and stared down at the shallow hole in the ground. A dirty rag lay open beside it.

'What was in there?'

A sinking feeling settled in his gut. He knew exactly what it was that Liu Yuan had come here to retrieve.

'Knives,' he replied gravely. 'He needed his knives.'

Chapter Twenty

Yang ran through the woods in the direction the soldiers had gone. Two of the men from the work crew flanked him on either side. They had volunteered to accompany him and Yang hoped their familiarity with the surrounding area would allow them to catch up with Liu Yuan. Even though his muscles throbbed from that morning's exertions, Yang pushed himself forward.

'There's someone ahead,' one of them called out.

He saw them. A figure appeared to be kneeling on the forest floor. He didn't move as the three of them neared. Yang drew his knife before breaking through the tree line into the clearing. He'd been prepared for a fight, but what he saw stopped him cold.

The kneeling man was hunched over with his throat cut. The deed was done so quickly that he'd simply collapsed from his feet to his knees with no time to defend himself. There were other bodies strewn beside him. It was the soldiers who had raided their village. The satchel of coins lay on the ground between them, still tied shut.

'Stay close,' Yang told the others.

Even though he knew who had done this, instinct told him where there was this much death, there was danger.

One of the workmen edged closer, holding his club protectively in front of him as he stared at the carnage. The second man simply bowled over and vomited.

Yang barely held on to his own stomach. Liu Yuan hadn't merely defeated the soldiers. He'd *slaughtered* them. They had fought side by side before, but Yang had never witnessed this level of brutality from him.

But he'd always suspected Liu Yuan was capable of it, hadn't he? Wasn't that why he'd come here to enlist the outlaw's aid?

'Take the money back to the village,' he told the workmen.

'We can't leave you out here alone.'

He surveyed the clearing again. There were four bodies and only two of them had managed to draw their swords. The blades were stained with blood. For all the two villagers knew, the soldiers had turned on themselves or they'd been attacked by another group of bandits. They couldn't imagine this had been done by one of their own. Or someone they had considered one of their own.

'I'll be fine,' he assured. 'Go back and tell the others it's over.'

Before they could argue, he ventured deeper into the forest. His tracking skills in the wilderness were minimal: broken branches, grass that appeared to have been trampled. Then a bloodstain on the pale bark of a silver birch told him he was heading in the right direction. He found Liu Yuan shortly after, leaning against a tree trunk.

'It's Bao Yang,' he announced, slowing his step. Yang didn't want to risk the other man lashing out at him out of reflex. Especially when Liu Yuan seemed to aim unerringly for the throat.

'I know it's you.' His breathing sounded laboured. He straightened, but didn't turn around. 'One of them got away. He'll report what happened and they'll send others, won't they?'

Yang stopped more than fifteen paces away, deciding it was best to keep some distance between them. 'They might or they might not.'

'Even if I hunted the remaining soldier down now and killed him, it wouldn't end things.'

There was blood running down Liu Yuan's arm. Yang hadn't detected it at first, but he could see how it dripped from his fingers like drops of ink. It was likely Liu Yuan hadn't even realised he was hurt until the first rush of battle had subsided.

'You're not going anywhere,' Yang told him. 'I'm taking you back.'

He shook his head. 'I can't go back. Not any more.'

Liu Yuan's voice was tight with pain, barely able to find breath. Yang approached him as he would a wild animal, very slowly and with great care.

'You're injured and I'm not leaving you out here to bleed to death.' When Liu Yuan didn't respond, Yang was forced to use his sharpest weapon. 'Shifen is worried about you.'

Liu Yuan lifted his head slowly, as if it were a lead weight. 'She can't see me like this.'

'Then we'll clean you up.' Yang was certain Liu Yuan didn't mean the blood or his injuries. He had transformed into someone—or something else.

Yang took Liu Yuan's arm and propped it over his shoulder before starting back towards the village. Liu Yuan leaned his weight against him, but managed to move forward on his own feet.

'You shouldn't have gone off on your own, friend,' Yang said quietly. 'It was only money.'

'I never cared who I robbed when I was a bandit. I had to go and set things right.'

But by Liu Yuan's own admission, he had only made things harder for village. Even though he was trying to atone for acts the villagers had no knowledge of, the consequences of those actions had soaked through his skin to taint his blood. One could never escape his past.

Jin-mei was going mad with worry. Yang had left an hour ago after telling her to remain behind. The sky was getting dark now and she'd lit an oil lamp, placing it in the middle of the barren floor to make the hut seem less foreboding. Unfortunately, the flame beckoned in more shadows that danced long and black over the four walls. There was nothing to do but fret while her mind made up stories. The problem was she knew too many stories of lawlessness and criminal behaviour.

It was like her wedding night all over again—Yang running off into the unknown while she was left to wait.

There was a tap on the door, and she ran to open it.

Shifen stood there with her own lantern in hand. 'Has he returned?'

'Not yet.'

Only after Jin-mei had answered did she realise Shifen was likely referring to Liu Yuan and not Yang. It didn't matter. For the moment, they were two women sharing the same worries. She went to sit with Shifen on the bench outside so they could at least fret together. The interior of the hut was starting to feel suffocating.

'Brother Li and Brother Yun returned with the stolen money just now. They said that your husband went to find Liu Yuan.' Shifen's mouth pressed tight and a tiny crease formed over her brow.

'What is it?'

'They also said that the soldiers who came to rob us were dead.'

Bandits and murderers at every turn. Was this what the world was really like?

'I can't help but think—' Jin-mei halted. Perhaps she was about to reveal too much, but it was weighing heavily on her chest since watching the soldiers ravage the village. 'I can't help but think we somehow brought this upon you.'

The village had been peaceful—the lake, the waterfall, each person with their own task within the commune. The inhabitants welcomed all visitors. Even the brutes who'd come to rob them had been fed and treated with respect first before they'd turned on their hosts.

'We're outsiders,' Jin-mei said. 'Maybe those soldiers followed us here.'

'You're not outsiders any more,' Shifen replied firmly. 'And there are bad as well as good men in this world. Why would you think you had anything to do with those soldiers?'

'I must be feeling anxious, that's all.'

Shifen reached out to squeeze her arm reassuringly. A moment later, Yang and Liu Yuan emerged from the surrounding darkness. Jin-mei shot to her feet to go to them and immediately she could see something was wrong. Liu Yuan had a hand pressed to his ribs.

'He's hurt,' she said, staring at Liu Yuan. 'Yang, are you—?'

'I'm fine. Help me get him inside.'

She moved forward, but Liu Yuan remained rooted where he was. He was looking over her head.

'How bad is it?' Shifen asked from behind her.

Liu Yuan raised a hand as if to shield himself from attack. 'Please go,' he said roughly.

He started to turn around, but Jin-mei caught up with him. 'Stubborn man, she's been waiting for you.'

Jin-mei didn't know whether it was pride or some lovers' quarrel that made Liu Yuan want to avoid Shifen, but Jin-mei was sick with worry and her patience was spent.

'Get inside,' she ordered. When she tried to take hold of his arm, he shook it free. He did, however, start moving for the door. She turned to Shifen next. 'Do you have a physician?'

'There's no physician.'

Both Liu Yuan and Shifen both spoke at once, both halting afterwards as if they'd committed some awful impropriety. Shifen continued alone. 'The nearest physician is in a village a day away by boat. Is it that bad?'

She was looking over Jin-mei's shoulder to Liu Yuan. Their gazes held for so long that Jin-mei was tempted to duck away so the two of them could say whatever it was they so obviously needed to say to each other.

'It's not bad,' he replied finally.

Even from where Jin-mei was standing, she could see his sleeve was soaked and the hand pressed to his ribs was similarly stained with blood. Liu Yuan was also acting even more withdrawn than usual. What had happened out there?

It was Yang who took charge. 'Bring bandages and a sewing needle and thread,' he said to Shifen.

She hurried away, her lantern becoming a floating light in the distance. Jin-mei moved to Yang's side as he ushered the injured Liu Yuan inside. Once there, Liu Yuan sat with his back propped against the far wall.

Yang knelt and pulled away Liu Yuan's tunic to inspect the wound.

'How bad is the bleeding?' Jin-mei edged in closer, but Yang stopped her.

'Do you faint at the sight of blood?'

'I...I don't think so.'

Yang moved aside so she had a full view of the gash in Liu Yuan's side. Immediately her stomach churned and a thick fog clouded her head. She squeezed her eyes shut and turned away just before a wave of dizziness swept over her.

'It's actually not too bad,' Yang assured from behind her, as if he were inspecting a side of pork at the market. 'There's nothing vital there.'

'Isn't it *all* vital?' She couldn't get the sight of open flesh and blood out of her head.

'Bao *Furen*, if you could get...'

Liu Yuan's polite address seemed grossly out of place given the circumstances. With a deep breath, Jin-mei turned around to face the two men.

'...the wine please?' Liu Yuan gestured towards the corner.

She retrieved the jug and uncorked it for him. He thanked her before taking it with his good arm, and Jin-mei shuffled immediately out of the circle of lamp light.

'Are you going to be all right?' Yang asked from behind her.

'Just take care of him,' she said, feeling a bit of madness set in.

She brought boiled water so Yang could clean the wound. By then the two men were speaking as if it were nothing but a scuffle.

'Knives?' Yang chided. 'Against swords?'

'But you could tell half of them had never had to draw their weapons before,' Liu Yuan insisted.

'You can tell that?' she asked incredulous.

The two men regarded her. Yang's expression was indulgent while Liu Yuan's was tortured.

'She'll think I'm a monster,' Liu Yuan said as Jin-mei went outside to wait for Shifen. For the first time that evening, he sounded as if he were actually in pain.

'She won't think that.'

'She must already.'

'Stop being so dramatic…'

Chapter Twenty-One

'Who is Liu Yuan? Who is he really?'

Jin-mei asked the question of Yang the moment he emerged from the hut. Shifen had arrived with the requested implements and remained inside to tend to Liu Yuan.

'Tell me everything, Yang.' She didn't raise her voice or even make it sound like a demand. 'If we're to continue on as you and I, I need to know.'

'Continue on?' Frowning, he settled on to the bench beside her, his shoulder brushing hers. 'Jin-mei.'

He sounded hurt. He also sounded earnest, but there was always something about Yang that made her trust him. From the first moment when he'd beckoned her beneath the bridge. She was his partner, his co-conspirator. His one.

'How did you do that today?' she asked him. 'The soldier grabbed me and then all of the sudden you were there between us.'

'You're my wife. I had to protect you.'

His words filled her with warmth, but when he reached for her she held him off. 'I was so afraid for you, but you didn't show a hint of fear. You knew you could stop him with just a few words.'

'I don't understand, Jin-mei—'

'The person who taught me all my life how important it was to seek the truth turned out to be a liar.' Her voice faltered. The pain still felt too raw. 'You could convince me of anything, Yang, if I allow myself to believe. But I can't live a lifetime with my eyes willingly closed.'

Yang's arms did close around her then. Jin-mei sighed as he held her, wanting to cling to him and simply accept. Only now could she admit why she'd run so far, so fast. It didn't matter where she went as long as she didn't have to face her father. She couldn't look at Father's face, knowing how he'd lied to her. Because she still loved him. She didn't want to hate him as well.

'I never meant to deceive you, Jin-mei. When I allowed you to believe I was dead, I thought your father's twisted logic made some sense. You would be free of a marriage that was an accident. But since then, I've told you everything there is to know about me.' She felt his lips against her hair. 'I wanted someone to know the truth, even the parts that were less than honourable.'

'Then who is Liu Yuan?'

When he hesitated, Jin-mei realised Yang's rationale. He was willing to divulge his own secrets to her, but when it came to others, he held back. But didn't he realise everything was connected and intertwined?

'For nearly a year, your father tried to eradicate the outlaws hiding in the forest surrounding Minzhou,' he explained. 'Liu Yuan was the man leading that gang of outlaws.'

'He was a bandit, then.'

Jin-mei expected Yang to justify his friend's actions, but Yang's answer took her by surprise. 'He's worse than that. Liu Yuan cut a man's throat open while he stood on a crowded street. He did it for revenge.'

Revenge. Again that word.

'But he's reformed now?' she asked shakily.

Yang answered her question with one of his own. 'Can an outlaw ever truly be reformed? When those soldiers took the villagers' money, Liu Yuan remembered all the anger that had driven him for so many years. He became a killer once more.'

'What happened to the soldiers?'

'He killed them all.' Yang's voice broke. 'Jin-mei, I'm so grateful you didn't see it.'

A shiver ran down her spine. She had had misgivings about Liu Yuan from the moment she'd seen him, but she hadn't imagined this. Yet Shifen cared for him and Yang called him his friend. Even Jin-mei was beginning to see another side of Liu Yuan. He killed to protect or to right a wrong—it wasn't far from her interpretation of justice, but Liu Yuan didn't act without reason.

'You don't truly believe he's a killer at heart, do you?' she asked.

'Jin-mei.' Yang fell silent and his arms grew stiff around her. 'I came here to look for a killer. I needed someone who was ruthless, to help me complete what I started.'

'Oh, Yang—'

Something broke inside her. It seemed that right and wrong, good and bad—those were nothing more than words. She didn't know their meaning any more. No one was pure at heart. No one was untainted, even her.

Even if it wasn't yet time to go, they couldn't stay in the village any longer. Yang gathered what few belongings they'd brought and begged for supplies to make their journey back to the main artery of the river.

'Consider it a fair trade,' Shifen insisted. 'For the labour you and Jin-mei have provided.'

She appeared sad as she spoke. Yang didn't understand fully why until Liu Yuan approached the dock. He had a pack slung around his shoulder.

'Will your vessel carry a third passenger?' he asked.

An odd sensation tightened Yang's chest. This was what he'd planned, wasn't it? Through some twist of fate, he'd got his way. Before he could answer, Jin-mei came out from the shelter.

'You're just going to run away?' she challenged. 'You won't even tell Shifen farewell?'

'We've said all there is to say.'

After more than an hour stitching his wounds the night before, Shifen had brewed a dose of opium tea for his pain and then quietly left. She said nothing of what had occurred between them while they were alone. It was between the two of them and the heavens.

'I wouldn't deny you passage, friend, but I must defer to my wife.' Yang looked to Jin-mei. She hadn't told him whether her opinion of Liu Yuan had changed now that she knew the truth about him. Her opinion of Liu Yuan apparently wasn't too high to begin with.

'There's no use stranding you here if you're intent on leaving,' she said, not unkindly. 'I just wish you realised that there is someone who cares whether you stay or go.'

'I do realise.' Liu Yuan didn't look back as he climbed on board.

When they set out, Shifen appeared near the shore to watch their departure. Liu Yuan didn't wave to her, but he watched her as the boat drifted away, until she was nothing but a blue dot in the distance.

* * *

For Yang, the return trip was far from the idyllic journey into the valley, when he'd had Jin-mei to himself. Now she seemed distant, even at night when he held her in his arms beneath the shelter of the boat. Especially at night.

'I've caused a rift between you and your wife,' Liu Yuan told him in an almost-apology.

Even though Jin-mei was nowhere in sight, the conversation was far from private. She'd retreated out of the sun where she spent most of the day now while he and Liu Yuan sat in the bow of the fishing boat as it glided through the water, dense woods passing by on either side. It was the type of setting that left one plenty of time alone with one's thoughts.

'It isn't you,' Yang insisted.

He couldn't blame Liu Yuan alone. He was just the embodiment of larger events that were soon to come; other associates, allies and comrades Yang would join with to make a stand against General Wang. He wanted to tell Jin-mei that when this was over, then the hiding and scheming would be behind them. They would start their new lives then.

But Jin-mei was too astute to be assuaged so easily. And he didn't want to make a promise he couldn't keep.

They had arrived early at the appointed meeting place and were forced to camp for two days on the shore as they awaited word from the merchant Shen. During that time even Jin-mei appreciated Liu Yuan's company. Yang and Jin-mei were city dwellers at heart, while Liu Yuan was skilled at survival in the wilderness, able to trap fish and even a rabbit for their meals.

The easiest bounty in the area was snake.

'Don't tell Jin-mei,' Yang had said while he watched Liu Yuan skinning one of the creatures.

'I can hear you.' Her voice had rung clear from their camp on the other side of the brush. 'And I've eaten snake before.'

That evening Yang had seen Jin-mei and Liu Yuan speaking to one another near the water's edge. From afar, the conversation had appeared civil.

'What did you ask him?' Yang asked her that night when they were finally alone.

At night, he and Jin-mei continued to sleep on the boat while Liu Yuan opted to make his bed on the shore. Jin-mei turned in the crook of his arm to face him and his chest felt as if it would burst.

'I asked him why he turned to banditry. How many people had he killed? Did he feel sorry for all the people he'd wronged?'

'Did he answer to your satisfaction?'

She paused. 'I wasn't expecting any particular answers. I just wanted to know.'

'You don't hate him?'

Her hair tickled against his neck when she shook her head. 'I think I might trust him more now than I did before.'

Yang didn't kiss her, though he wanted to very badly. He didn't make love to her, either, and he wanted that so much he ached with it. His urge to join with her then had nothing to do with physical passion or desire; though he was certain those could be stirred up with only a little encouragement.

It would be for contact, for comfort. And for his own reassurance. He'd revealed more of himself to Jin-mei than anyone else and he wanted deeply for her to know all he'd done and yet still accept him inside of her. There were no boundaries between them when they joined together, flesh to flesh. It took away all his artfulness.

Yang knew it was impossible for Jin-mei to condone all of his actions, just as he knew it was impossible for him to apologise for them. So here they were. He contented himself with at least having her warm in his arms and listening to her soft breath as the sway of the water lulled them both to sleep. Even this small slice of time to themselves would soon be gone.

Chapter Twenty-Two

At the appointed time, the merchant Shen arrived himself to give the report. 'This is too important a matter to leave to underlings,' he told Yang.

And the news wasn't good.

'Wang Shizhen has seized all your property and holdings in the north. Anything he couldn't immediately profit from, he burned to the ground.'

Yang took a deep breath as he absorbed the information. It wasn't unexpected. He and the corrupt general were at war and Wang Shizhen publicly held all the power.

Liu Yuan and Jin-mei stood by silently. They'd heard the same news.

'This is actually good,' Yang said with a bitter laugh. 'Break the kettles and burn the boats, as they say.'

There was nowhere for him to hide any longer and there was no turning back.

Shen relinquished his wagon to them, unhitching one of the horses for his own return. 'Don't even consider paying me for any of this. Your father was like a brother to me.'

But it was clear this would be the last of their association—unless Yang prevailed.

They loaded their supplies from the boat on to the wagon in silence while the elderly merchant bid them farewell. Before he left, Shen handed Yang one final message folded in paper. 'Be careful,' he warned. 'They're looking for you.'

'You must have a plan,' Liu Yuan said once they were settled in the wagon. He turned to Jin-mei. 'Bao Yang always has a plan.'

It was hard for Yang to look at either of them at the moment. Up in the driver's seat, he took hold of the reins and started the wagon down the road. 'We had a secondary meeting place selected in case the first one was compromised. We'll go there now and see if anyone else shows up. If no one does, then Wang Shizhen has frightened everyone off and our rebellion is dead.'

Jin-mei had seen the note that the merchant had passed to Yang. He had to have known she'd seen it, yet he said nothing over the next days. She had to trust that if it was important, he would tell her. In the meantime, suspicion gnawed away at her insides. Almost a week had passed since they'd left the river to travel on land and still Yang hadn't said anything. They were in the heart of General Wang's domain now, which meant they were also close to Yang's home town as well as all of his familiar trade routes and operations.

'We have to stay clear of everything connected to the Bao name,' Yang warned. 'It all belongs to Wang now.'

They kept to wayward dirt roads and routes that appeared abandoned, but the isolation didn't make her feel any safer. At any moment, she expected a horde of men in black masks to come charging out of the forest.

'Black masks?' Liu Yuan raised his eyebrows at her. 'What do bandits care if you see their faces?'

She eyed their new companion. 'So you can't identify them to the local magistrate.'

'I think most people would find it quite difficult to identify a bandit.' He made a motion across his throat as he spoke.

A week earlier, the gesture might have made her blood run cold, but the day was extraordinarily hot and she had spent too much time with Liu Yuan. She was actually grateful for his presence now. Three was safer than two and who better to defend against outlaws than one who had been one?

'A seasoned thief can tell who will give him trouble,' Liu Yuan told her once after she had spent the morning whipping around at every sound. 'It isn't always the strongest or most well-armed. There's a look in the eye, the way one conducts oneself. He selects his victims accordingly.'

'Are you saying I would be a choice victim?' she asked, eyes narrowed.

'Not at all. You have the look of a magistrate's daughter. Too many questions, nothing but trouble.'

Yang had hid his grin behind his arm.

That was early in their trip. Yang had grown more quiet with each passing day, but other than the sombreness of the atmosphere, nothing had impeded their process.

'We should be there by nightfall,' Yang said, pointing into the distance.

'In the mountains?'

It had been two days since the last village and the terrain had become decidedly more untamed. No established roads marked their way and they were forced to slow down as the wagon moved over uneven ground.

'This is one of the few enclaves in the region that

General Wang hasn't usurped,' Yang explained. 'Mainly because there's nothing out here to extort or plunder.'

Indeed the ground seemed too rocky for farmland and the region was outside the reach of the many rivers that spanned the province. Jin-mei stared at the grey peaks in the distance and felt an uneasy quiver in her stomach. To her, the open country and the mountains had always been a wild place where rebels and bandits dwelled. Jin-mei supposed she was one of those outlaws now. Plotting rebellion was the worst of the ten abominations.

'The mountains appear to be impassable with a thick canopy of growth over the rock. The formations are also very steep and impossible to scale, but I discovered a pass that leads into them.'

'How did you do that?' Jin-mei looked around them. The surrounding area looked to be uninhabited.

'I was with my younger brother.' A wistful look passed over Yang's face. 'We had finished delivering a shipment and were returning home. We were young and adventurous. Tien wanted to explore so we strayed from our route and headed towards these mountains. On the way, we spotted a fox with a tail that looked larger than she was. It was a sleek creature with a startlingly red pelt. I joked with Tien, telling him that his future wife was there in the form of a fox spirit to spy on him. We ended up hunting it to the foot of the mountains where it disappeared.'

'Maybe she was a fox spirit,' she mused.

'Perhaps she was. We never found her, at least not in fox form.'

Yang grinned at her, and she could feel her insides warming. Outside of dodging Yang's enemies and his quest for revenge, they had travelled through the province together, sharing in adventures and absorbing the sights. There were times, like this one, when she felt the world was at her fingertips and it was Yang who had given it to her, like a gift.

'By some fortunate accident, the fox had led us to a hidden passageway into the mountains. What I saw when we emerged on the other side has never left me. Great stone towers that seemed to grow out of the ground to reach towards the sky. Once I took over the family business, I would use these mountains to hide away shipments of salt and other goods.'

He grew quiet again. Was he thinking about his estrangement from his brother? Or how this enclave in the mountains was the only place he had left now that his homes and holdings had been seized? She reached out to touch him, just a simple touch on his arm, so he could know that he wasn't alone.

By nightfall, they had reached the foot of the mountains as Yang had predicted, but they set up camp at the base rather than attempting to find the passage in the dark.

'Navigating the stone formations can be dangerous,' Yang warned. 'We'll go in early tomorrow morning.'

As usual, Liu Yuan spent the night outside the wagon to afford them some privacy. Usually he and Yang would trade off taking watch if they felt there was any danger, but that night they both deemed it safe enough to leave the fire burning and catch some sleep.

When Yang came up to lie down beside her, she turned into the crook of his arm. The gesture had become routine for them, one of the few they were allowed as they moved from place to place.

'Jin-mei.'

She was nearly asleep when she heard her name spoken in a low, quiet voice. She came fully awake. 'Yang?'

'Everything is fine. We're safe.' Yang kept his voice in a whisper as he pulled the wool blanket over her shoulders. 'But there's something I need to tell you.'

He sounded so grave. Jin-mei wished he hadn't waited until the middle of the night when she was groggy with sleep and couldn't see his face to read his emotions. All she had was the warmth of him beside her and his voice floating to her in the darkness.

'What is it?'

'I don't know how many of my old allies will be there. Or if there will be anyone at all to continue the fight. They know that I failed to kill Wang.'

She could hear the worry in his voice. 'What if there is no one there?' she asked. 'Would you stop then?'

He was silent for a long time. 'I can't.'

Jin-mei finally understood how deep he was entrenched in the rebellion. It wasn't only for revenge. There were others who relied on Yang and it was their cause too.

'They'll be there,' she assured him. 'People trust you. I've seen how you bring them over to your side.'

'When I had wealth and influence,' he argued.

'You're wrong. It's you. They trust you to lead them.'

It was his contacts, his knowledge of commerce in the province. How he was able reach out across the roads and rivers to connect others together. The knowledge of who Yang was and what he was capable of sank deep into her; it filled her with pride but sadness as well.

'You can use me,' she suggested, her voice tight.

'What?'

Jin-mei's heart was racing. Even though she was lying still, she had the sense that the earth had disappeared beneath her and she was falling, dizzy. She had already decided to stand by Yang and there was no turning back. He had to succeed if they were to have a future together.

'Use me to get close to the warlord,' she blurted out, all in one breath. If she paused to think, she would lose her courage. 'My father is a magistrate and Wang Shizhen has always wanted to spread his influence to Minzhou prefecture. Father has a warrant and search parties out looking for me. News will have reached this area by now.'

Her plan was a thin one—she had just started formulating it at this moment. But Yang could take it and weave it into something more, she was sure of it. 'Use that to get close to the general and then…then do what you have to do.'

'No. A hundred times, no.'

'But—'

'I want you as far away from danger as possible, not in the mouth of it.'

The anger in his tone shut her down immediately. They fell into a tense silence.

'I only wanted to help,' she said after a long pause.

She sounded so small, almost plaintive as if she'd wanted nothing more than his approval, but that wasn't it at all. Jin-mei didn't know why, but tears came to her eyes. Yang was going to put himself in harm's way once again and there was nothing she could do. She couldn't stop him, she couldn't stand beside him. All she could do was wait and pray.

'This all started because of my pride, Jin-mei,' he said quietly. 'Because I knew what was best and because my sister loved and trusted me to the ends of the earth.'

It became clear to her then. Yang wasn't worried that no one would show up, he was afraid that they *would* come.

She reached for his hand beneath the blanket, and his strong fingers curved around hers. For a while they did nothing but stare at the sky, large above them.

'There is a reason you are who you are, Bao Yang. You'll know what to do when the time comes.'

He let out a slow breath. 'The time is already here.'

Each one of her heartbeats rang out loud in her ears while she waited for him to continue.

'The merchant Shen had news for me, gathered by one of his informants at a relay station near Wang Shizen's headquarters. Since our last attempt, the general has been hiding behind his guards. It's rare that he will come out of his stronghold, but I've learned that he plans to meet with one of his associates. A bureaucrat of some influence who is apparently as suspicious as he is. The meeting place is in a hidden location, but we've discovered it and if we can get inside, he'll be vulnerable.'

'There will be guards posted everywhere.' She felt inept speaking of tactics, but something didn't sound right about this scenario.

'It will be a challenge,' he agreed. 'But this is our chance. Whether I have one man behind me or a hundred, I need to find a way in.'

This was what he'd been holding inside: that he was already planning his next and perhaps final strike. She could rail against him and beg him not to go, but Yang had chosen his path. Instead she turned her body into his, pressing her face into the crook of his neck.

She couldn't change the course of events. All she could do was hold on to him for as long as she could.

Chapter Twenty-Three

The passageway into the mountains was hidden behind a maze of rock and a canopy of dense growth, but it was wide enough for their wagon to fit through. Once they broke through the veil, the shadowy corridor opened to a lush valley flooded with sunlight.

Jin-mei gasped beside him. 'It does look like a forest made of stone.'

Yang was reminded of his first sight of the hideaway with his younger brother at his side. They had pushed open a tangled curtain of vines and branches to reveal another world. The surrounding peaks formed a natural protective barrier around the area. Down in the basin, large stone formations jutted up from the earth like long fingers. At that time, the land had been untouched and unseen and the awe of discovery had filled him with a sense of wonder and power.

But this morning, a substantial camp had been set up in the bottom of the valley. He scanned the collection of tents and shelters. Cook fires smouldered from within the camp.

They had come.

And now they expected him to lead them.

He directed the wagon down the slope into the valley, moving steadily towards the settlement. As they neared the perimeter, a small, lithe figure ran out towards them. He recognised Nan from Lady Daiyu's crew.

The girl paused before the wagon. 'Mister Bao! We thought you were dead.'

'Nothing can kill that man.'

Lady Daiyu approached with her bodyguard Kenji close by her side. Behind her, Yang saw the others. His comrades who had fled Minzhou after the attack. Long-time partners and associates. Yang dismounted and continued towards the heart of the camp while the news of his arrival spread. Within minutes, the entire camp had gathered around him.

These people weren't soldiers. These were merchants and labourers. The people he had walked among and spoken to. Each with their own grievances against Wang's rule. The ones who had come were leaders, the sort of men who took action and inspired loyalty in others. There were thirty people gathered here who perhaps represented a hundred more. Nothing more than a small pinprick against an entire army, but they wouldn't be alone. He had other allies waiting for the signal.

Yang wouldn't talk about past failure or how difficult their task would be. He would focus only on success. If he believed it, they would believe him and it would happen.

'There is an opportunity,' he began, 'but we have to strike now. We'll be facing armed soldiers and there will be bloodshed, so it's time to decide. If the price is too high, leave now.'

'We're here with you.' Yang recognised Guozhi, a long-time friend who had come from Sanming. 'Tell us what to do.'

Agreement rippled throughout the crowd. No one here was an innocent who had been beguiled. They had come here with a common purpose and he could sense the anticipation building among them. They were ready to act.

In the back of the crowd, Yang noticed a face. One that stuck out to him clearer than any of the others; a face as familiar as his own. His concentration broke as their eyes met—Tien was here. His brother had left swearing they would never see each other again, yet he had come.

'Send one representative to me in an hour,' he told the group. 'We'll begin planning immediately.'

His younger brother approached him as the group disbanded.

'I can't allow you to be part of this attack,' Yang told him before Tien had a chance to open his mouth. 'This is not your fight.'

Tien's lips quirked. 'Still trying to decide for everyone else, Elder Brother?'

Yang glared at him. 'It's too dangerous, Tien. After what happened to An-yu, I can't risk anyone else from our family.'

His brother held up a hand to stop him. 'This was always our secret hideaway. It was the first place I thought of when you told me my family was in danger. No one knew of it but the two of us. To my surprise, immediately after my family settled in here, other people arrived into the valley. I learned quickly they had come here because of you.'

This place had been their last hideaway. Now Yang had betrayed his brother's trust, along with every other wrong he'd inflicted upon him. 'I had no other choice. Wang Shizhen has taken or destroyed everything else.'

'Not everything,' Tien replied, his eyes serious. 'Yang, I stayed because I had to be certain you were still alive. I didn't want to leave things as they were; with you thinking I hated you.'

'I would deserve it if you did.'

'You're my brother. I know why you have to do this. Not just for An-yu, but to finish what you started. We all need to make peace with our actions and their consequences,' Tien said, sounding as if he were the older sibling.

Beneath his younger brother's serious expression, Yang could see signs of the adventurous youth he'd once been. Yang saw a remnant of himself there as well, reflected in their similarities. Family was a reminder of oneself, a mirror. One that he'd broken through his own carelessness.

'How did you make peace with all that's happened?' Yang asked.

'By blaming you,' he admitted. 'I thought that would alleviate my own guilt, but it didn't. I was second son so I left all the burdens to you. Neither of us is without fault, but we've both suffered. Whatever happens, I want you to know that you're my brother. My children will call you uncle.'

Yang's chest squeezed tight. 'Thank you, Tien.'

Tien reached out and put an arm around him in a brotherly gesture. As Yang stepped back from the embrace, he finally made sense of what Tien had just said.

'Your children?' Yang repeated.

Tien smiled, ducking his head shyly. 'My wife is with child again.'

For the first time in years, they were both smiling together.

'Send my regards to your wife. And best wishes to you for a boy.'

His brother nodded. 'Survive this, Elder Brother, so you can meet him when he arrives.'

Chapter Twenty-Four

Jin-mei had never realised a place like the stone forest existed. Towering rock formations rose out of the earth, looming like tiered pavilions. Smaller structures dotted the ground. Here, she passed by a great tortoise formed out of stone. There, the figure of a fisherman bent over a pond.

If the natural sculptures that inhabited the basin weren't wondrous enough, Yang led her to the foot of the mountains where the rock opened up into a wide cavern below.

'There are underground caverns throughout the entire area,' he told her. 'But be careful, some of them are quite deep and it's completely dark inside. It's very easy to get lost.'

So that was where he'd hidden his secret stash—inside a maze of caverns. This one, however, had been converted to a small living space. A slant of sunlight came in through the entranceway, revealing a humble collection of furnishings and implements. There was a wooden stool and a sleeping pallet woven from strips of bamboo. A layer of dust covered everything.

'I haven't used this hideaway in a while.' Yang took

two steps towards the cavern, looking around as if he too were seeing it for the first time.

Jin-mei laid her hand upon the shredded pallet. 'Did you enjoy living this way? Hiding in caves, skulking along secret routes?'

'The salt trade yielded a substantial amount of wealth over the years,' he replied, a bit defensive. 'Enough for our family to live in luxury.'

Until it all fell apart. She didn't need to remind him—he was already drowning in regret.

'In the beginning, it was a great adventure,' he confessed. 'It was a challenge to expand the routes my father had established. And then the money poured in like a river. There was nothing I couldn't do, but those days are done. You know they're finished, Jin-mei.'

After this one final act to pay his debt.

'You've done all you could for your family.' She knew she might as well have been talking to one of the stone figurines. Yang was trapped inside a prison he'd built himself. 'Your brother forgives you.'

Forgive yourself, she wanted to tell him. This debt didn't need to be paid with blood and certainly not his.

But to argue with him now would only weaken his resolve. Yang had to believe he would succeed. She had to believe it as well.

'The others are waiting for you,' she said.

'I should go,' he agreed.

He didn't. Instead Yang remained where he was, his gaze piercing deep into her as if he wanted to say something, but couldn't find the words.

'I'll be here when you return,' she said gently. She even managed a smile. 'I'll even be a good wife and clear out some of this dust.'

He nodded, not returning her smile. 'I love you, Jin-mei.'

The words fell like heavy stones down a dark well. They slipped away before she could grasp them. Her reply was still lodged in her throat when he turned to go, climbing out through the crevice that led to the outside.

His serious expression haunted her. She wanted the charming Bao Yang back. The one who was self-assured and invincible and incapable of failure.

You have my heart, she should have replied. *You are my soul.*

She couldn't say those things, all the things crying to get out from inside her, without also begging him to stay. It was a choice she couldn't force him to make, because she would lose.

She spent the rest of the day tidying up the cavern and then going to pay a visit to Tien's wife and their daughter. Little Ling seemed to have some memory of Jin-mei, calling her 'Auntie' while ducking shyly behind her mother.

'I've heard your happy news,' Jin-mei said.

'Yes, Elder Sister.' Shou-yun touched a hand to her belly which was still flat. 'Tien is very happy. We have hopes for a son this time.'

The two of them spoke as if there wasn't an uprising being planned all around them. Shou-yun and Tien would be leaving once the plan was set in motion and the rebels were on their way, she told Jin-mei, but for now they would stay so Tien could be with his brother.

For possibly the last time.

Jin-mei needed to stop having these thoughts! There was so much tongue-biting, so much swallowing of bitterness. More words were held back unspoken than spoken and it made her want to break things.

She thanked her sister-in-law and then embraced her, bestowing every blessing she could think of. Little Ling allowed Jin-mei to hug her as well and she held on longer than she should have, her cheek resting against the child's silky hair. This was her new family. If something happened to Yang, they would be her only remaining family.

Stop. She needed to stop.

Liu Yuan came to check on her once she was back in her cavern domicile.

'What's happening?' she asked him. 'Have they decided anything?'

'You don't truly want to know,' he answered curtly. 'What would you do with the knowledge anyway?'

She glared at him, but he was right. There was no reason for her to know the details when it would only feed her fears.

'Do you have any quarrel with General Wang?' she asked him.

'Not in particular. I don't even care that he's a cruel tyrant.'

'Then why are you here?'

Liu Yuan sat down on the sleeping area beside her, and she became aware of how oddly close they'd become over the past week.

'I became involved when I stood by Yang's side with a knife in my hand. I went that day to get my revenge and Yang went to get his,' he answered.

'You're here for honour, then.'

'I'm as much a wanted man as Yang is, but his name is well known where mine is not. When we stood together, a bond was created between us, whether we wanted it or not. There is something unfinished between all of us—Yang, the general, myself. I couldn't escape this fate; the relentless cycle of karma created by my actions.'

For some reason, Liu Yuan's explanation made more sense to her than any rationale she had tried to come up with. Yang had made promises to the people who had gathered here to follow him. He'd made a promise to Wang Shizhen when he'd looked him in the eyes and plunged a knife into the warlord's chest. If he tried to walk away now, this debt would follow him.

Liu Yuan left to return to what she had started considering the war council. More hours flowed by with her waiting alone. Eventually the sky grew dark, and Jin-mei laid down upon the sleeping pallet, pulling the woollen blanket up around her.

Yang had still not returned so she drifted off into sleep. She was awoken some time later by the sound of someone striking a tinder pouch.

'It's me,' Yang said. There was a small orb of light surrounding him from his oil lamp.

She rubbed her eyes. 'What are you doing?'

'Lighting the brazier.'

'But the air is warm—'

'It gets cold in the caves at night.'

How senseless for them to be having this conversation right now, arguing about conserving coal. 'Come here,' she implored.

Yang gave the smouldering coals a stir before coming to her. She was already reaching for him when he extinguished the oil lamp, leaving them stranded in the inky darkness with only a faint glow from the brazier.

Yang was a formless shadow beside her, but she felt his presence acutely in the scent of his skin and the sound of voice. She didn't need to see him.

'I've missed you terribly,' she complained without meaning to complain.

She only meant to draw him closer, but his mouth descended, touching first against her chin before correcting in a gentle path to her lips. He kissed her fully then, focusing on nothing but the kiss until she was breathless beneath him. Her fingers curled into his hair to hold him in place. She could stay like that for ever.

'Tomorrow,' he whispered.

The heaviness of his tone said it all. 'That soon?'

'We must. There's not much time.'

He could have been talking about the two of them and not the rebellion. They hadn't had enough time to themselves.

Using touch alone to guide him, Yang ran his hands along her waist and worked her sash loose. 'I'm going to seduce you, Wife.'

Her chest swelled with emotion. 'You can't seduce me any longer. We're married.'

'Wrong.' He pressed a kiss to her throat. Another to her shoulder as he slipped her tunic away. 'I'll keep on seducing you for the rest of my life. And you'll let me.'

They were silly words, lovers' words which only made sense like this. She laughed, wishing with all her heart that her amusement wasn't tinged with sadness.

'I love you too,' she blurted out and was unable to stop the tears from falling down her cheeks. She tried to wipe them away without Yang noticing, but failed.

He hushed her and bent down to kiss her cheek, then licked softly at the trail of salt with the tip of his tongue. 'Don't hide. Whatever you feel tonight, you don't need to hide it from me.'

His lips found hers unerringly this time. The rest of their clothing was removed with no more fumbling or searching and he fitted his hips against hers. Yang knew exactly where she was now.

He made love to her slowly while she listened to the rhythm of their breathing; his deep and heavy, hers lighter and becoming more rapid and shallow as his body moved inside her. There was nothing else in this world but this: flesh, skin, breath, darkness.

They clung to each other as they shuddered and climaxed, Yang slightly before her, but still together.

Then, when they were able, they started again.

She fell asleep with Yang still inside her. By then, her body was overwhelmed with sensation, drugged by pleasure. She was no longer seeking release, just closeness and warmth and the feel of Yang surrounding her.

When she next opened her eyes, the grey morning was upon them and she wished she'd been able to stay awake after all.

She was wrapped in the wool blanket, and Yang was no longer beside her. He was sitting at the edge of the stone bed, and she could make out the strong lines of his back in the dim light. His spine stiffened with awareness as she sat up.

'There could be a child,' he said, still looking away from her.

'I know.'

They had been together for nearly a month. She didn't know for certain yet, but she would know soon. By then, Yang would be gone and her long wait would have started.

'If it… If he's a son—' He frowned and then looked away again. 'If we have a son, teach him well so he knows right from wrong, Jin-mei. Not like…not like me.'

Yang was usually so self-assured and confident to a fault. She'd never seen him look so grave, and a small crack formed in her heart for him. 'What if she's a daughter?'

Finally he did smile a little. 'Then she'll be like you.'

She wanted to insist that they would have sons and daughters and live a long, happy life together, as if by declaring it she could banish whatever fateful mood he'd woken up to that morning.

'If we have a son, we'll both teach him.'

Yang grew serious once again. 'I think you'd be better at it than me.'

She had to bite her lip to keep from crying. Why were they only having this conversation now? In parting as a farewell? They should have started their marriage like this, speaking of the children they would have, but with a sense of joy, not sorrow.

Yang looked like he wanted to confess something to her then, but was struggling to get the words out. 'Forgive me,' he said finally.

Jin-mei shook her head. 'There's nothing to forgive. Just come back to me.'

They kissed once more and then held on to each other, saying very little. Words would have only distracted them from what needed to be conveyed.

Chapter Twenty-Five

'I must ask a favour of you.'

Yang stopped Liu Yuan as he was preparing to load the wagon. The former outlaw turned to him, and Yang was struck with the twisted humour of the situation. A thief and murderer had become the man he trusted above all others.

'I need you to stay behind,' Yang said.

Liu Yuan raised an eyebrow at him. 'This is unexpected.'

'There are enough people taking part in the raid. I need someone to keep Jin-mei and my brother's family safe. And if I fail…' He faltered. It was dangerous to think of failure, but he couldn't leave Jin-mei unprotected. 'If I fail, Jin-mei will have no one left.'

The stone forest was hidden enough, but they couldn't stay there for ever. They would have to leave and find a place where Wang couldn't reach them.

'You think this band here is enough to face the general and his armed garrison?' He indicated the handful of merchants and labourers Yang had gathered.

How much could he reveal? 'There are others. We're acting as only one arm of the attack.'

'I see,' Liu Yuan murmured. 'I'm not surprised there's more to this plan of yours, but you still need me regardless.'

His strategy wasn't all that masterful. There was the plan and then there was the plan if that one failed. After that, the only option was for everyone to flee for their lives.

'You buried your knives,' Yang pointed out. 'You were trying to make a new life for yourself when I dragged you back in.'

'So you're asking me to stay behind to spare me?'

'You didn't want to be a killer any more. I don't wish to make you into one.'

Liu Yuan shook his head. 'Don't get sentimental, Bao. It will get you killed.'

He needed to take his own advice. Liu Yuan had never been wronged by the warlord and didn't stand to profit from his death. He had come out of loyalty or, perhaps remotely, even friendship.

Or maybe out of sheer habit. Liu Yuan had never liked authority.

'Maybe I'm asking you to stay behind because you're bad luck,' Yang taunted. 'I missed Wang's heart last time.'

The former bandit shrugged. 'You missed because your aim is bad. Are you certain you don't want my knives beside you?'

It had to be friendship. Liu Yuan was a complicated man, but one thing about him was easy to see. He protected the people he came to accept as his own.

'Just keep my wife safe for me.'

He told Liu Yuan where the last of his money was stashed and the passages out of the stone forest in case they were ambushed there. Once everything was arranged, Yang had to push his concerns to the back of his mind and think of nothing but what needed to be done. And then he would come back to Jin-mei, even if only his spirit remained to make the journey.

Jin-mei stood beside Tien and his wife as they watched the last of the insurgents leave. The parties had spaced out their departures and, once on the roads, they would separate further to mask their movements, reconverging for their final strike. She didn't know when the attack would happen or when to expect Yang's return. Within days, was all he told her.

The stone forest was left empty and desolated in the aftermath, inhabited by silent stone figurines. Jin-mei passed by one formation that looked like a fox with its ears raised and a sleek tail. She couldn't help but smile a little, thinking of the story of how Yang had discovered this place. Maybe it was a good omen.

Maybe she was searching too hard for reassurance.

She returned to the cavern and lay down to rest. Neither she nor Yang had wanted to waste any of their precious time together the night before so there had been little sleep. Exhaustion took over now as she closed her eyes.

Formless dreams plagued her, and when Jin-mei came awake again, she didn't know how much time had passed. A glimpse outside showed that the sun was starting to set. Perhaps she should gather the others together for the evening meal. There was no one left but Tien's family and Liu Yuan and both sides were strangers to each other.

As she passed by the iron brazier, Jin-mei remembered Yang telling her that the cavern became cold at night. She didn't remember a chill the night before, but she had spent the night his arms. A layer of grey ash lay over top of the container. Using a bamboo stick, she stirred through the ashes to see how much coal remained. A scrap of paper turned up in the coal and an impression in vibrant red ink showed through the soot.

Picking up the scrap, she shook it clean and her throat constricted, choking back her cry. The rest of the paper had burned away with only part of the personal seal remaining. She could see only half of the impression, but it was familiar enough to her that she recognised it immediately. Her father had stamped his chop on to countless documents while she sat beside him, fascinated.

She climbed out of the cavern with the burnt paper in her hand, yelling for Liu Yuan. He must have been nearby because he appeared immediately.

'My father.' She held up the paper, her hands shaking. 'General Wang is meeting with my father, isn't he?'

Liu Yuan stared at the red seal, not comprehending. Yang hadn't told him. Maybe he hadn't told anyone.

'I can't let this happen. I have to stop it.'

'You can't.'

'He's my father,' she snapped. 'My *father*.'

Her voice rose to a shrill pitch. This wasn't her. This was some madwoman who'd taken over her body. She forced herself to calm down. 'You at least know where they're going, don't you?'

He exhaled sharply, scrubbing his knuckles over his jaw.

'Do you know where they're going?' she insisted, louder this time.

'Yes.'

'Then take me there.'

'What would you do, stop the attack?'

Jin-mei shook her head, confused. Scared. 'I don't know, but I have to do something.'

Her father wasn't the best of men, but he was still her father. The events of the last days fell into place. Yang only giving her the barest of information about what was in the message. All the times he had looked as though he wanted to confess something to her. How he'd asked for her forgiveness.

'Was it not your father's death that you moved heaven and earth to avenge?' Jin-mei could see Liu Yuan wavering. 'Yang just left today. The others too. We can still catch them. Please.'

A look of pain crossed Liu Yuan's face. 'Bao Yang can't stop the attack, you have to realise this.'

'Just let me speak to him. Yang wants vengeance against the general, so let him have it.'

She would beg Yang to spare her father. Yang wasn't cruel by nature and he would have to do it for her sake. She was ready to fall on her knees before him if she had to.

'I'll take you,' Liu Yuan relented, scowling. 'But anything you do might put one or both of them in more danger. Your father or your husband, Bao *Furen*. You will be forced to choose.'

Chapter Twenty-Six

Yang had done unscrupulous things in the past and he'd confessed the worst of them to Jin-mei. She knew how he'd used his own family, how he'd bartered away his very soul to gain wealth and power. She even knew he had morally questionable things still to do, yet she'd accepted him into her body as well as her heart. She'd asked for one thing only from him—that he be honest with her.

There had been no way to be honest about this. Yang had no choice but to face General Wang Shizhen, and her father was caught in the middle. One day, Jin-mei would understand. Maybe one day, much later, she would even forgive him.

Once Yang left the protection of the stone forest, he joined Lady Daiyu's faction on her ship.

'I'm honoured to have been chosen by our illustrious leader,' Daiyu said with a smile.

Yang stood beside her at the prow of the ship, watching as the vessel sliced through the water. 'It's faster this way. And more pleasant company.'

'Enough with your sweet talk, Mister Bao. You're married now.'

He glanced at the woman beside him, one of the many bandits and lovers he'd made connections with throughout the years. 'Thank you for coming to my aid.'

She tilted her head at him. 'Thank me when we win. And with a hefty reward. That bastard Wang Shizhen took half my cargo on the last run.'

Bandits weren't sentimental people. Yang turned his attention back to the rivers which served as the arteries and veins of the province.

No matter how tightly the general tried to control the province, the water belonged to the merchant fleets, to traders and fishermen, smugglers and pirates. They would be able to navigate close to the meeting point without being detected, but the last leg of the advance would have to be in small groups travelling on land.

'If the current and the winds are favourable, we'll arrive in two days,' she told him. 'Will that be fast enough?'

'I hope so.'

The fateful meeting place was in supposedly neutral territory near a river port. Both Wang and the magistrate had agreed to bring a limited number of bodyguards to a hidden location.

The southern perimeter would be the weak point. Magistrate Tan was no soldier and his guard detail would have to travel from afar and assemble in unfamiliar territory. The bureaucrat had chosen this location for his ability to avoid ambush and make a fast retreat to the nearby county seat.

The rebel forces would come in from the south, but the initial attack wouldn't originate there. It would come from inside.

Yang's plan depended on arriving before the northern and southern perimeters had been set up. That initial strike force would smuggle themselves close to the meeting point and lie in wait.

All things considered, it was a better plan than the last time he'd assaulted General Wang. That time, he'd doubted he would make it out alive. This time they were in neutral territory and in an open location. Yang also had more hands on his side, as long as everyone did as they'd promised.

He turned once more to Lady Daiyu. 'I need some advice. Can you love a man who's lied to you?'

She shrugged. 'They all lie to me.'

'What if the lie was for your own good, to keep you safe?'

'Oh, Yang. You're in trouble,' she replied with a snort. 'Those are the worst kind.'

Jin-mei would be forced to choose between her husband and her father. The question hung over her with every step, and she still didn't know her answer. Yang was a lying, scheming, smooth-talking bastard whom she'd fallen in love with. Her father was a sneaking, corrupt and duplicitous fiend who she also loved dearly.

Though the other parties had set out only half a day before them, their trail had dissipated like smoke. There was no sign of them outside of the mountains.

'It doesn't matter,' Liu Yuan told her. 'They've all scattered to take different routes. We must head for the meeting point.'

They travelled by horse, resting only when they had to. By the end of the second day she was ragged with exhaustion. They couldn't stop. An hour could be the difference between keeping Yang and her father from killing one another.

'Why didn't he tell me?' she demanded, more to the heavens than to her companion.

'There was a time when revenge meant everything to me,' Liu Yuan told her. 'More than my own life and even the lives of those I loved.'

It was more than he'd ever revealed to her.

'Was it worth it in the end?' she asked.

'I never avenged my father. His killer took his own life.'

'Violence begets violence,' she murmured. A shudder went down her spine. It was taboo to speak of death and tragedy so openly.

They continued on over rivers and mountains.

'Did you find peace once it was all over?' she asked Liu Yuan much later. He hadn't found satisfaction, but had he at least been able to restore the balance of the universe, a sense that things were right once more?

He had no answer for that.

As they neared the river port, they had to move by foot. Liu Yuan took her up into the hills and she had to use her walking staff as the way became steep.

'There will be guards everywhere.' He scanned the incline before continuing up. 'But with the rocky terrain, it's impossible for them to create a secure border. There will be lookouts and patrols, but there are always ways to get in.'

Minzhou had been surrounded on three sides by rugged mountains. Liu Yuan had been able to hide there despite her father's efforts to hunt him down. If anyone could help her now, it would be him.

They started up a crag of rock with Liu Yuan in the lead. Her foot slipped as she tried to find a handhold and for a moment, her stomach plummeted. Liu Yuan closed a rough hand around her wrist to haul her up.

With her heart racing, she settled on to the ledge and tried to catch her breath. 'Thank you—'

He raised his hand to cut off her reply. 'We're here,' he whispered.

Liu Yuan was staring over the peak, and her heart pounded even harder. He beckoned her closer and she came up beside him, very carefully peering over the other side. Down below, she could see an open pavilion with a wooden rooftop. There were soldiers assembled around the structure. She assumed the general was already situated beneath it, hidden from view.

An entourage was approaching the pavilion wearing official state robes. She recognised the man at the front immediately. It was her father.

Her blood ran cold. The meeting had already started.

'I have to get down there.'

At the edge of the pavilion, her father stopped abruptly. She saw him stagger on his feet and a cry went up among the retainers. With a gasp, Jin-mei rose and stared down from the rock, not believing what she was seeing.

Her father was bent over with a hand clutched to his chest. The hilt of a knife protruded from his fingers. A knife. Even from where she was hiding, she could see the blood.

'Assassin,' Liu Yuan hissed.

Jin-mei screamed.

Chapter Twenty-Seven

From the sudden cry at the pavilion, Yang knew the knife had hit its target.

'Now,' he commanded.

Guozhi lit his hand cannon and fired it into the sky above the trees. The explosion shattered the air, signalling all the factions it was time to move. He waved his cohort forward, and they surged out from the brush and from the rocks with weapons drawn. Meanwhile, other forces would be attacking from outside. They had to break Wang's inner circle before he had a chance to regroup.

As he rushed out into the clearing, Magistrate Tan's entourage was crowded around him. General Wang's guard had started to form a protective barrier as well. Movement on one of the surrounding peaks caught his attention. He expected it was the warlord's lookout, armed with crossbows, but instead a lone figure started sliding down the hillside.

'Is that one of ours?' Lady Daiyu asked beside him. She'd drawn her sword.

On his grave. 'It's Jin-mei,' he muttered.

She cried out for her father and ran for him, right into

the heart of the raging battle. Yang broke into a run, his pulse pounding.

How was this possible? Out of the corner of his eye, Yang saw Liu Yuan bounding down from the same peak to chase after Jin-mei. She had nearly reached her father.

'Focus!' Lady Daiyu shouted beside him. Their slim opening was closing rapidly.

Soldiers bore down on them, and Yang took his knife in hand, very much wishing he was able to wield something larger and more fearsome. Daiyu's bodyguard Kenji took position in front of her as the first wave hit them.

They pushed forward with weapons flashing, staying close as they had planned. Every second counted, but Yang was torn. Did he rush towards Jin-mei or continue the charge towards General Wang? Soldiers were swarming the entire area now and there was no more time to think.

Two of her father's retainers tried to stop her, but Jin-mei pushed past them to kneel at the grass beside her father's motionless body. The front of his robe was soaked with blood and his eyes were closed.

'Father. Oh, Father.' She wept, reaching for his hand which was still warm. The only thing she could think of was that he would die thinking she'd abandoned him.

'I don't hate you,' she blurted out, barely able to see through her tears. 'You're my father. You'll always be my father.'

He opened one eye, which latched on to her. His expression twisted, not in pain or agony, but in fury. 'That worthless dog! What are you doing here?'

Jin-mei stopped mid-sob. 'Father?'

He sat up, his hand closing around the hilt of the knife.

Frantically, Jin-mei tried to stop him as he started to pull it out. 'Don't! You'll bleed to death.'

The blade was embedded into his heart. At least, that's where she thought his heart would be. But Father didn't act as though his life's blood was draining away. Quickly, he surveyed his surroundings.

'You might want to stay down a little bit longer,' a deep voice warned from above them.

The retainers had shed their outer robes. Jin-mei recognised one of them as Constable Han and the other— was that the constable's wife?

'We don't have time to explain.' Li Feng was turned towards the pavilion, surveying the cluster of soldiers. She had a sword in her grasp, holding on to it as if she'd been born to it. 'Bao Yang will never make it through.'

'Stay with Lady Tan,' Constable Han told her.

But the swordswoman was already gone, fighting towards the centre of the fray. The constable cursed as he turned to address Father again. 'Stay down, sir.'

Obediently, her father fell back down to the ground while Jin-mei stared, speechless. This was madness.

Father reached out to take hold of her hand while he looked up at her from the ground, his eyes dark with emotion. 'I'm unharmed. And I'm very happy to see you again, Daughter.'

She choked back a sob even as relief flooded through her. Her father and Yang had obviously co-ordinated some fiendish scheme that she still didn't quite comprehend. 'All this blood—?'

'Chicken blood.' Father beamed proudly, but then thought better of it when she scowled at him. He reached up to touch her cheek. 'Don't cry, Jin-mei.'

'Did you two plan this right from the start?' she demanded in disbelief.

The sounds of swords clashing nearby interrupted her. Father sat up to put a protective arm around her as the ring of armed guards formed a barrier around them.

They were still in the heart of danger, but she needed answers. 'Have you been conspiring together ever since the wedding?'

'Oh, no! I really wanted Bao Yang dead. Filthy bandit scum, putting his hands all over my daughter.'

She didn't know whether to hit him or hug him. 'You're a dishonest, scheming, unscrupulous—'

'Yes,' he agreed, holding her tighter. 'Yes, all those things.'

A daughter should never say such things to her father, but it was too much. The raging battle, seeing her father struck down, and then Yang's duplicity. He'd hidden everything from her when he could have just told her the truth. He was twice the scoundrel her father was. She couldn't stop her tears from falling.

A shadow fell over them. 'Jin-mei, we need to go.'

She looked up to see Liu Yuan had reached her. He and Constable Han stood over them, Liu Yuan with his knives in hand and the constable with his sword.

Constable Han nodded. 'Let's get them to safety.'

Chapter Twenty-Eight

Yang spun around, not knowing whether the person advancing on him was friend or foe. Luckily she was a friend.

'Jin-mei is safe,' Li Feng reported. Her sword flashed as she surveyed the field, assessing the threat.

He had to take her word for it. The battle was thick around them with Lady Daiyu's crew fighting to his right. His own comrades from Taining remained close. Li Feng had once been one of their number.

She grabbed on to the front of his robe to drag him forward. 'Follow me.'

Yang let her take the lead as she wove through the fight. Li Feng was a sword dancer, an acrobat. She could move faster than anyone he'd ever seen and she did so now, finding openings and darting through them with startling efficiency. No soldier even engaged her in combat until she was within General Wang's inner circle. One of his guards raised his sword against Li Feng, but never made contact before her thin blade slipped into the seam of his armour, piercing through his ribs.

Yang's faction had broken through the personal guard, Wang's final line of defence. Li Feng engaged the captain, leaving one final man for Yang.

Wang Shizhen's eyes narrowed as they focused on Yang. Though he was a general, he didn't wear a sword or any battle armour any longer. He'd become a bloated and corrupt official, complacent and expecting his men to fight his battles for him.

'Bao Yang,' he sneered. 'The salt merchant.'

Yang didn't slow his advance. The beat of his heart had become a battle drum and his blood ran hot through him. 'You're going to die today,' he told his enemy. 'For my sister.'

He hadn't expected to say anything to the man. He'd planned to charge in like he'd done before and plunge his knife into the general's chest. But this time Yang would stand over him until he knew Wang was dead.

'Then do it,' the general spat and stood his ground. He might have grown complacent, but he was still a warrior at heart.

Yang rushed forward, knife raised. Wang Shizhen rose to his full height, appearing to double in size. Opening his arms, he pounded a fist over his chest. A taunt. *You tried before and couldn't kill me then.*

With a snarl, Yang crashed into him, throwing all of his weight and more against the general. Wang staggered, but didn't fall. He was larger than Yang was and unquestionably stronger. Yang drove his blade towards the general's heart, but a large hand clamped over his wrist and turned it aside. A fist connected against his jaw, snapping his head back and blackening his vision. There was no time to recover before he was thrown to the ground.

The taste of blood filled his mouth. A new streak of pain shot through him as Wang's boot connected with his ribs. Summoning all his strength, Yang rolled away enough to take the next hit against his shoulder.

'You're nothing,' the general bellowed.

Yang struggled to his feet only to be shoved once more to the ground. Wang Shizhen was throwing him around like a wooden puppet. His vision swam as his heart pounded with fear. Vaguely, he acknowledged that it was pride once again that had brought him here. He'd wanted Wang Shizhen to die by his hand to assuage his own anger, his own guilt.

The next blow didn't come. Someone else was fighting the general. Yang dragged in a breath and uncurled his fists, only then realising he no longer held his weapon.

He wasn't a warrior. Yang had always been too physically weak to fight the general alone. He'd relied on the help of others to face his enemy. But long before that, he'd sacrificed his own sister in an arranged marriage to the general, knowing he couldn't stand up to Wang Shizhen himself.

His vision finally cleared enough for him to focus on Wang. The general was once more headed towards him, a look of pure hatred on his face. The rest of the battle receded as Yang focused on the man he'd vowed to kill. The pain in his body faded, replaced with a coldness he'd never yet experienced. Wang appeared to be moving slowly, as if through water.

Yang's mind became quiet. Even his anger had stopped cold as he reached into his belt. His hand closed around the dagger he always kept there and in one motion, he pulled it out and let it fly.

The blade struck his enemy in the throat. Wang's eyes widened. He reached his hand up listlessly as he fell to his knees. And then the fearsome general crumbled into the dirt.

Yang rose to his feet, his body crying with pain. He retrieved his other knife from the dirt before slowly approaching the general. For a second, he stood over

Wang's still form, just staring at it. The man's face was to the ground, and Yang wedged his boot beneath a shoulder to flip him over. The throwing dagger remained lodged beneath his chin. He'd died with his eyes open.

There was no sense of triumph or elation. Yang only knew that he longer hated this man. And he no longer hated himself either.

He turned and walked away from the body, not bothering to close its eyes.

Chapter Twenty-Nine

There was little celebration in the aftermath of the attack. With Wang Shizhen dead, the rest of his soldiers were easily overcome. Several of the general's high-ranking officers took the attack as an opportunity to stage a coup, though Yang didn't learn of it until his fight was won. The question of who would take over the warlord's forces now lay in the hands of the remaining leadership as well as Magistrate Tan. Yang wouldn't have been surprised if that wily official had a hand in the coup as well.

All Yang knew was that his part was finally done. Everything had gone according to plan except for one thing: he no longer had anyone to return to.

He saw Jin-mei once after the battle. She was alive and safe, and he thanked the heavens for that, but she had also been huddled beneath her father's arm. When she looked at Yang, her gaze merely slid past him. His heart had threatened to beat out of his chest.

Jin-mei was in shock, he'd told himself. She needed time to recover and compose herself. He'd have a chance to speak to her once things had calmed down and then he would explain and grovel and throw himself at her feet if that's what she required. He would convince her.

But that was the last Yang had seen of her. Wherever Tan was keeping her, it was under an ironclad watch.

Over the next week, the merchants and labourers who had joined beneath his command quietly disbanded to return to their affairs. The official report was that General Wang had been killed in a power struggle between his officers, a story which suited Yang just fine.

In the end, only Lady Daiyu and her crew remained and it was only as a favour to him. Soon she would have to raise anchor as well. Yang resorted to sending letters into Tan's camp which were summarily ignored. Apparently the magistrate had got everything he needed out of Yang and their association was over.

A single glimmer of hope came one afternoon when Yang heard Li Feng's voice on the shore. She was speaking with her brother who had a satchel slung over his arm.

The sword dancer was married to Tan's head constable. She had to know where Jin-mei was being kept.

Yang wanted to jump directly down from the deck on to the bank, he was so eager. Instead he managed to keep his composure long enough to descend the gangplank without running.

'It's too late. She knows what I am,' Liu Yuan was saying as Yang neared.

'It's never too late,' Li Feng replied.

She was nearly as tall as her brother. The two of them were similarly long-limbed, with a graceful strength in their movements.

It was as good a time as any to interrupt. 'Are you going back to Lintai village?' Yang asked.

'No,' Liu Yuan replied.

'Yes,' Li Feng answered for him.

They exchanged a contentious glance in the hidden language of siblings.

'That's good news,' Yang said by rote. 'Where is Jin-mei?'

Another knowing glance passed back and forth between the siblings.

'You should have gone to her immediately,' Li Feng chided. 'You've put her through a lot of heartache.'

Yang scowled. 'I've been trying to reach her, but her father won't allow it. He's been intercepting all my letters.'

'Actually, Jin-mei has been receiving them. She's just extremely angry with you.'

His heart sank. Jin-mei could hold a grudge for a long time. He'd seen it with his own eyes.

'You know where she is, then,' he countered. 'If I could just see her, I can explain everything.'

'I remember exactly how good you are with words,' Li Feng remarked drily. 'Do you know she made herself ill, pushing herself beyond exhaustion rushing to save her father? Then she found out it was all a ruse.'

'Tan could have at least admitted it was mostly his idea,' Yang muttered. 'Do you know he was the one who decided he would put a pouch of chicken blood in his robe and stab it himself when no one was looking? I had no knowledge of that part of the plan.'

Li Feng crossed her arms over her chest, her fingers tapping impatiently while his explanation continued. They too had been lovers at one time, a brief affair that he knew had been ill fated from the start, but still he'd been unable to resist. Those days were long gone now. There was only one woman in the world for him.

'She's my wife,' he said simply. 'My one and only. Give me a chance to fix this.'

Li Feng fixed a steely-eyed look on him that was sharp enough to pierce armour, but he didn't waver. It wasn't a particularly charming or persuasive argument, but it was the truth and all he had left. It was his very last gambit and, fortunately, it paid off.

'The magistrate has commandeered the local inn,' Li Feng relented. 'Jin-mei's room is on the second floor, but the entire building is under constant watch. If Tan Li Kuo sees you now, he'd be only too happy to have you killed for good this time.'

That didn't bother him. The only thing that concerned Yang was what he could possibly say to convince his wife to continue being his wife.

'Aren't the two of you able to break through any defence?' he asked.

Li Feng looked to her brother who looked back at her. For the first time in quite a while, he saw the two of them smile.

They had to wait until night-time, and Li Feng insisted he had to wear black. Then there was rope and a grappling hook and Liu Yuan to stand on lookout and get him out should anything go awfully wrong. The three of them moved along the river in complete darkness and crossed into the nearby town. The inn in question was close to the river with a good view of the water.

'Slowly count to one hundred and then go,' Li Feng instructed before starting towards the building.

'Wait, why aren't you wearing black?' Yang asked.

She paused to glance coyly back at him over her shoulder. 'I'm married to the head constable now. I'll just distract him.'

Li Feng sauntered off, leaving Liu Yuan and him behind to count out the seconds.

'Jin-mei was trying to save you as well,' Liu Yuan said in the darkness.

Yang forgot what number he'd reached. 'What do you mean?'

'She wanted to save you as well as her father. If anything had happened to either of you, she would have lost you both.'

Because if he'd caused her father's death, then there was nothing that could be done to keep them together. The two of them were alike in that respect: they loved and hated with equal passion.

'Let's go,' Yang said, not caring if it was time or not. He couldn't wait for another moment to see Jin-mei.

In the end, the approach was an easy one. Liu Yuan managed to attach the grappling hook on the first try and then remained below as Yang made the climb. The window of the room was open, and he climbed through, already preparing his first words to Jin-mei.

The moment the curtain parted, he found Jin-mei dressed in her sleeping clothes, staring at him with her eyes wide in panic.

'Please.' He held out his hand to appeal for peace as she opened her mouth. 'Don't scream. I just had to see you again. I needed to see you again. You look…you look pretty.'

His tongue was tied in knots, and she did look pretty, which only made his heart pound even harder.

'Jin-mei,' he began again, feeling her name echoing in his heart.

There were a hundred things he thought of saying to her at that moment. He'd stayed up every night since, pondering how to make things right. His original plan had been to somehow talk his way back into Jin-mei's heart, but that was no longer his intention. He just had to tell her how he felt.

Yang looked awful. Frighteningly so. The entire half of his face looked like one big bruise, mottled and black and purple in places. On the right side, his jaw was still swollen. She was so shaken after the battle she hadn't taken note of much more than that he was alive—and that she was angry enough to strangle him. That anger came back in a flood as he stood there, still trying to charm his way back into her heart.

'That was a cruel trick you played,' she said coldly.

'You were never meant to see any of that.'

A fire sparked inside her. 'Was I supposed to just wait obediently for you? Then if your rebellion failed, I would suddenly discover that I'd lost not only my husband, but my father as well. All I asked of you was honesty.'

Her chest hitched. Honesty was apparently the one thing Yang couldn't promise her.

'I was so scared. I was frightened for you and then when I found out you were going against my father, I couldn't think of anything else.'

Yang remained quiet for once, looking both vulnerable and earnest with his wounds. 'It's over now,' he said finally. 'No more plotting. No more schemes.'

'Until the next harmless lie you decide to tell me. I can't trust you!' Tears of frustration came to her eyes, and she wiped them away impatiently. Yang didn't deserve her crying over him. 'I can never trust you again,' she said brokenly.

'Your father was the one who insisted you remain as far away as possible.'

'My father may be a scoundrel,' she snapped, 'but he

lies to fight corrupt officials or...or to protect me from the worst scoundrel of all. Which is *you*.'

He was taken aback. 'But one of the reasons I did this was for your sake.'

'Like you only smuggled for your family's sake? When would you have had enough money?' she demanded. 'When would I no longer need your lies to protect me?'

His brother had been right. Everything Bao Yang had done was for his own selfish needs. Jin-mei wrapped her arms around herself, feeling the chill of her decision seeping into her skin. 'We're a poor match,' she choked out. 'We have been from the start.'

Yang came forward and for a moment she thought he would put his arms around her, but he stopped himself. He was completely at a loss, which only gave her a cold, flat sort of satisfaction because she was lost as well. For a little while, she had actually believed they could be together; balance one another as husband and wife should.

'I know I can't convince you,' Yang said in a voice so heavy it weighed on her soul. 'You were mine and now I've lost you.'

She turned away from him. It was the only way she could say the next part. 'One can have only one father. I can't choose my father, but I can choose my husband.'

They were both silent for a long time. Jin-mei didn't know how to end things, now that they were over. Did she just say farewell and let him walk away for ever?

'As far as anyone knows, the man you married is dead,' Yang said quietly. 'You can return home as a respectable widow. I will disappear and one day you—' His voice caught and it was a moment before he could recover it. 'One day you can even marry again. To someone worthy.'

The urge to turn around and throw herself into his arms nearly overtook her. She had wanted so much for him to be that someone. She wanted the life they had planned together in the few moments between fleeing and plotting, but it had all been a fantasy.

'Please go now,' Jin-mei pleaded, hoping Yang couldn't tell how her face was covered in tears. The tears didn't change anything, but she had fallen in love with him and still loved him. She might always love him.

'I was selfish,' he admitted. 'In every negotiation, I made sure I had the advantage.'

She could hear him coming closer and, with each footstep, her heart beat faster.

'And I had a talent for always getting what I wanted, no matter whom I sacrificed to do it. I kept on coming out ahead, but always losing. Bit by bit, I lost the things that were important to me. And yet I never learned my lesson. That changed the moment I met you. Please turn around and look at me…one last time.'

Jin-mei felt his hand on her shoulder, heating her skin through the silk of her robe. The breath rushed out of her and it took all her will not to turn around. If she looked at Yang, she would falter. She would be charmed all over again, simply because it was easy to believe in things she wanted to be true.

She shook her head. Yang exhaled slowly, as if it hurt to breathe. 'Then let me say this to you so you know. You are everything, Jin-mei. You are the world to me. I finally possessed something that wasn't worth gambling away, but I didn't realise it until too late.'

For a long, endless moment she could sense Yang's presence behind her. So close, yet there were mountains between them. But then he was gone. When she dared to turn around, there was nothing but the breeze sifting through the curtains at the window and the black night beyond.

The tap that came on her door a little later wasn't Yang. Jin-mei should have known it before she answered, but her heart was still full of foolish hope.

Li Feng stood in the doorway, holding out a handkerchief. Jin-mei took it gratefully, swiping at her eyes and nose and thoroughly frustrated when the tears just came back anew once she was done.

'He's gone.' Jin-mei pressed her lips together to keep from sobbing.

She knew she was a miserable sight with her swollen eyes and running nose, but Li Feng only nodded sympathetically and came in to sit beside her on the bed. The constable's wife even patted her hand out of sympathy, though the gesture felt awkward for the other woman.

'Your husband looked heartbroken when he left, if that makes you feel any better. I've never seen him so heartbroken. He usually acts as if nothing can touch him.'

'You knew him, didn't you?' Jin-mei asked. 'You were…friends?'

Li Feng looked uncomfortable. 'Bao Yang has a lot of "friends".'

She most certainly knew him.

Jin-mei hadn't quite sorted out all the details, but the bandit Liu Yuan and Li Feng were brother and sister and they had all been involved in a plot with Bao Yang as the mastermind. And apparently her father had a hand in it too. And perhaps Constable Han as well. It was enough to make Jin-mei dizzy and she already had a headache from crying.

'I did the right thing,' she insisted to no one in particular.

Li Feng looked sceptically at her, but didn't disagree. At least not until a minute had passed. 'What does your heart say?' she asked mildly.

'My heart says I love him and also that he's a lying, cheating scoundrel.'

'Your heart isn't wrong on either point.'

She didn't know if the constable's wife had come there to comfort her or convince her to go back to Yang, but in either case, she was far from settled and doubting her decision all over again.

'Yang isn't a good man,' Jin-mei said stubbornly.

Li Feng's response was immediate. 'No, he's not.' But then, a heartbeat later. 'Yang isn't a bad man either. He's just a man.'

'But if he had done the same to you—'

'I would have gutted him,' Li Feng replied sweetly.

How could she be so casual about it? Jin-mei had been raised with a very strict sense of justice and social code and a fear for those who operated outside the confines of society. But the man who'd taught her all that had been the worst of liars himself.

'But then I'm not in love with him,' Li Feng continued. 'And he's not in love with me. I believe that Bao Yang truly loves deeply, but he doesn't know what to do with that emotion. All he knows is how to plan and plot and try to control the world around him.'

'I told him everything he's done has been for selfish reasons,' Jin-mei said. It had been one of the harshest things she'd ever said, but she'd believed it to be true at the time. Now she tried to see Yang's actions stripped down to what they were. The barest essentials.

He'd acted out of pride, but he also acted out of honour and, she could see it now, out of love. He wanted to provide for his family, he'd wanted the best for his sister. And he'd do anything in his power to protect Jin-mei as well, to the ends of the earth.

'You've stopped crying,' Li Feng said gently, encouragingly.

She still felt miserable and probably still looked it, but at last Jin-mei was able to finally compose herself. 'What's the most senseless thing you've ever done for love?'

Li Feng laughed at that. 'I tried to kill Han.'

Jin-mei smiled. She could see the two of them becoming good friends if she was to return to Minzhou.

'It was an earnest effort,' the constable's wife elaborated. 'A duel to the death with swords out and blood drawn.'

Jin-mei wasn't smiling any more. 'The most senseless thing I did was run into the middle of a raging battle.'

To keep the two men she loved most from killing one another. And after that, the most foolish thing she'd done was to try to punish them both for it.

She regarded Li Feng, who had appeared to make peace with a world where men were not entirely good, but not entirely bad either. That was the world as it existed when Jin-mei was no longer in the shelter of her childhood home. She had just had to learn the lesson very quickly.

'Your brother tells me you can escape out of anywhere,' Jin-mei ventured.

Li Feng raised an eyebrow, and her eyes brightened. 'Are you afraid of heights? What about water?'

Jin-mei was afraid of many things. Mostly she was afraid of what she was about to do. She was about to commit another irrational act for love.

Chapter Thirty

There was no use staying any longer. Yang could stay at this port for ever, pining away for Jin-mei, but it wouldn't do anything to endear him to her. She wouldn't be charmed by him. The more he tried, the more she would distrust him.

'That's why I need her,' he protested.

Lady Daiyu had just given the order to lift anchor. She'd stayed behind for an additional day, but she had wages to pay and a ship to run.

He watched the shore gradually drift away. 'Without Jin-mei, who will keep me in my place? I'll be insufferable,' he reasoned.

'Just because I'm a woman, doesn't mean I want to listen to your troubles,' Daiyu told him pointedly.

Her man Kenji was no help either. 'You're already insufferable.'

Yang sighed and turned away from the bow. 'Is there any strong wine down in the cargo hold?'

Jin-mei needed more time. He had no choice but to wait and be wretched while time passed. Then he'd try again to win her back. He'd convince Jin-mei of his honourable intentions and how they were fated to be together. Maybe he'd just beg.

'Well, your bad luck has plagued us again, Bao,' Kenji said drily. 'We're under attack.'

He looked back to see both Daiyu and her burly body-guard staring at the water. Daiyu was smiling.

A sampan drifted towards them from the other side of the river, the boatman guiding it across the gentle current. Inside the vessel stood a single passenger, wearing a robe the colour of the sunshine. Jin-mei. His wife.

Yang had never grinned so wide for so long. If he could have leapt into the water to go to her, he would have.

As her boat neared, the crew threw down a loop of rope and raised her up on to the deck. Yang took hold of the very last section, pulling her up and into his arms.

'I'm undeserving. I am the unworthiest of men,' he admitted to her, his grovelling punctuated by laughter. 'May the heavens strike me down if I am ever false to you again—'

'Stop. Now you're just doing this for show.'

She swatted at him and he grinned even harder as he drew her into the shelter of the deckhouse, away from the sun and the amused stares of the crew outside. Then he held her tight against his chest. Jin-mei was here and it was so good to have her in his arms. *So good.* He would never let go again.

'My wife,' he said warmly.

She braced a hand against his chest. 'I have some conditions.'

'Yes, of course.'

'Don't lie to me ever again,' she warned.

'Never,' he vowed.

'Because I can tell when you're being dishonest. I know your signs now.'

She looked beguiling with that fierce little frown line

over her brow. He kissed her forehead, the tip of her nose. 'What are my signs?'

'Your eye twitches,' she said, defiantly avoiding his mouth when he tried to kiss her.

'Really? Interesting.' His eye most certainly did not twitch.

'And you have that smile, just like *that*.'

He did kiss her then, still smiling. He kissed her again until she was smiling too. Then laughing. This was what their life together would be like.

With a sigh, he rested his forehead against hers, serious all of the sudden. 'I'll do everything I can to make you happy,' he promised. 'Today until the day we're both old and grey. And then until my last breath. Am I lying now?'

He felt her hand against his cheek. 'No.'

Finally she curled herself into him, resting her head against his shoulder.

'It can finally begin,' he said, stroking a hand over back. 'We can start our lives together as we should have from the beginning.'

'No more underhanded and illegal activities?' she asked.

'No more.'

No more revenge. All of his wealth was gone, except for a small amount of silver stashed in the caverns of the stone forest. His family home and their assets had all been confiscated, but none of that mattered. He didn't want them. It was all blood money and he wanted to start afresh. With Jin-mei beside him, he looked forward to the challenge.

'We'll find a peaceful place,' he began.

'And raise two sons and two daughters,' she reminded him.

Yang chuckled. 'We can start on that part right away.'

Their dreams of bliss were interrupted by a cry from outside the deckhouse.

'Bao Yang, get out here, you dog. We're under attack.'

It was Kenji. From his strident tone, he wasn't joking this time. Yang went back on to the deck with Jin-mei trailing behind him.

'We have trouble ahead,' Lady Daiyu told him, frowning deeply as she looked over the prow.

The crew stood by, tense as they waited for their next command. An armed regiment had assembled at the wooden bridge up ahead. Archers lined the entire span with bows drawn.

'Fire arrows?' Yang asked incredulous.

Torch bearers accompanied the archers and there were foot soldiers on both shores. Among the soldiers stood Jin-mei's father. Though he wore the robes of a bureaucrat, Tan looked as fierce as any general.

'There's a way out of this,' Yang muttered. He just hadn't thought of it yet.

The only person who didn't seem terrified was Jin-mei. She stepped forward as they neared the bridge and raised her arm to wave at her father. After the longest pause in the world, Tan lifted his hand to wave back stiffly. The lines of anger on his face relaxed. A moment later, the archers lowered their arrows.

'My father is just being over-protective,' Jin-mei said as the ship passed by unchallenged. 'I'm his treasure.'

Over-protective? Yang supposed he couldn't fault the man in the end. The two of them were alike in so many ways. They might have been scoundrels at heart, but family was everything.

The crafty magistrate managed a solemn nod in Yang's direction. It wasn't quite approval. Yang closed his hands around Jin-mei's shoulders and nodded back. She was his treasure now.

'I love you, Jin-mei.'

It was the truest thing he'd ever uttered.

She closed a hand gently over his. If ever a single touch could wash away his wrongs, it was this one. Jin-mei reaching out to him in acceptance despite all he'd done.

'Let us go now and find our home,' she said softly as the river's current carried them away from the swords and arrows towards a new beginning.

* * * * *

REQUEST YOUR FREE BOOKS!

HARLEQUIN®

HISTORICAL

Where love is timeless

2 FREE NOVELS PLUS 2 FREE GIFTS!

YES! Please send me 2 FREE Harlequin® Historical novels and my 2 FREE gifts (gifts are worth about $10). After receiving them, if I don't wish to receive any more books, I can return the shipping statement marked "cancel." If I don't cancel, I will receive 6 brand-new novels every month and be billed just $5.69 per book in the U.S. or $5.99 per book in Canada. That's a savings of at least 12% off the cover price! It's quite a bargain! Shipping and handling is just 50¢ per book in the U.S. and 75¢ per book in Canada.* I understand that accepting the 2 free books and gifts places me under no obligation to buy anything. I can always return a shipment and cancel at any time. Even if I never buy another book, the two free books and gifts are mine to keep forever.

246/349 HDN GH2Z

Name _____ (PLEASE PRINT) _____

Address _____ Apt. # _____

City _____ State/Prov. _____ Zip/Postal Code _____

Signature (if under 18, a parent or guardian must sign)

Mail to the **Reader Service:**
IN U.S.A.: P.O. Box 1867, Buffalo, NY 14240-1867
IN CANADA: P.O. Box 609, Fort Erie, Ontario L2A 5X3

Want to try two free books from another line?
Call 1-800-873-8635 or visit www.ReaderService.com.

* Terms and prices subject to change without notice. Prices do not include applicable taxes. Sales tax applicable in N.Y. Canadian residents will be charged applicable taxes. Offer not valid in Quebec. This offer is limited to one order per household. Not valid for current subscribers to Harlequin Historical books. All orders subject to credit approval. Credit or debit balances in a customer's account(s) may be offset by any other outstanding balance owed by or to the customer. Please allow 4 to 6 weeks for delivery. Offer available while quantities last.

Your Privacy—The Reader Service is committed to protecting your privacy. Our Privacy Policy is available online at www.ReaderService.com or upon request from the Reader Service.

We make a portion of our mailing list available to reputable third parties that offer products we believe may interest you. If you prefer that we not exchange your name with third parties, or if you wish to clarify or modify your communication preferences, please visit us at www.ReaderService.com/consumerchoice or write to us at Reader Service Preference Service, P.O. Box 9062, Buffalo, NY 14240-9062. Include your complete name and address.

HH15

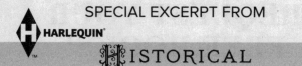
It was darker now. There were fewer lanterns and even
fewer guests in this remote corner of the garden. Her pulse
began to leap. They'd reached their destination—somewhere
private.

"It seems we have reached the perimeter of the garden,"
North commented, his eyes full of mischief. "What do you
suppose we do now?"

Alyssandra wet her lips and turned toward him so they
were no longer side by side but face-to-face. "I've talked
for far too long. You could tell me about yourself. What
brings you to Paris?" She stepped closer, drawing a long line
down the white linen of his chest with her fan. She would
genuinely like to know. She'd spent the past three weeks
making up stories in her mind about what he was doing in
France.

But she'd not come out to the garden to acquire a thorough history of the Viscount Amersham. That would come in time, as those layers came off. Tonight was about making first impressions, ones that would eventually lead to…more. Even so, she rather doubted her brother had expected "more" to involve stealing away to the dark corners of Madame Aguillard's garden with somewhat illicit intentions.

"I *could* tell you my life story," he drawled, his eyes darkening to a deep sapphire. "Or perhaps we might do something more interesting." Those sapphire eyes dropped to her mouth, signaling his definition of *interesting*, and her breath caught. *Something more interesting, please.*

It was hard to say who kissed whom. *His* head had angled toward her in initiation, but *she* had stepped into him, welcoming the advance of his mouth on hers, the meeting of their bodies; gentian blue skirts pressed against black-clad thighs, corseted breasts met the muscled firmness of his chest beneath white linen.

Her mouth opened for him, letting his tongue tangle with hers in a sensual duel. She met his boldness with boldness of her own, tasting the fruity sweetness of champagne where it lingered on his tongue. Life pulsed through her as she nipped his lip and he growled low in his throat, his arm pressing her to the hard contours of him. She moved against his hips, challenging him, knowing full well this bordered on madness; desire was rising between them, hot and heady.

Don't miss
RAKE MOST LIKELY TO REBEL
by Bronwyn Scott
available June 2015 wherever
Harlequin® Historical books and ebooks are sold.

www.Harlequin.com

HHEXP0515

HARLEQUIN®

A Romance FOR EVERY MOOD™

Love the Harlequin book you just read?

Your opinion matters.

Review this book on your favorite
book site, review site, blog or your own
social media properties and share
your opinion with other readers!

Be sure to connect with us at:
Harlequin.com/Newsletters
Facebook.com/HarlequinBooks
Twitter.com/HarlequinBooks

JUST CAN'T GET ENOUGH?

Join our social communities
and talk to us online.

You will have access to the latest
news on upcoming titles and special
promotions, but most importantly,
you can talk to other fans about your
favorite Harlequin reads.

Harlequin.com/Community

 Facebook.com/HarlequinBooks

 Twitter.com/HarlequinBooks

Pinterest.com/HarlequinBooks

THE WORLD IS BETTER WITH

Romance

Harlequin has everything from contemporary, passionate and heartwarming to suspenseful and inspirational stories.

Whatever your mood, we have a romance just for you!